MW00951597

Praise

WRIGHT COUSIN ADVENTURES SERIES

"We love these books!"

"Good Stories! I have a kid who can't read enough and a kid who can't find anything she likes to read. They both loved this book. My girls are 10."

"Highly Recommend! Great Story for kids! My kids give it a quadruple thumbs up!"

"Awesome read! Our children, ages 15, 13, and 8, love hearing books by this author. These books are hard to put down and have been great for our family! I recommended our local library purchase his books him."

"These books are full of tasty little tidbits of true information including some historical references and accurate STEM information. I loved these for my kids."

"[The Treasure of the Lost Mine] is a well-written adventure story which the children in my class enjoyed very much. I read it to them over two weeks and they enjoyed all the thrills and spills...reminded me of a classic adventure book from Enid Blyton...Good fun."

"The characters in these books are great role models. Keep up the great writing Mr. Smith!!! Your readers appreciate your humor, and all the awesome tech in your books. When are you going to make a theme park or movies for these books?!!!"

"My pre-teen grandson received the entire set from me for Christmas. Decent fun stories for children. Highly recommend!"

Wright Cousin Adventures
Trilogy 4

"Adventures in Gütenberg"

Includes Books 10-12

The Sword of Sutherlee
The Secret of Trifid Castle
The Clue in the Missing Plane

Gregory O. Smith

For information go to:

www.GregoryOSmith.com

Cover design by Greg & Lisa Smith
Book formatting by Greg Smith
ISBN E-book:

First Edition: November 2023

This book is dedicated to my patient and supportive wife and
family, and to my 3 persevering editors—Lisa Smith, Anne
Smith, and Dorothy Smith—without whom these books would
not have been as legible or nearly as much fun!

Contents

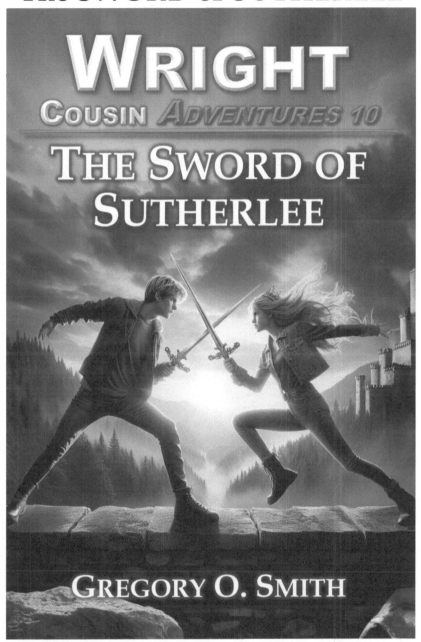

WRIGHT

COUSIN ADVENTURES 10

THE SWORD OF
SUTHERLEE

GREGORY O. SMITH

"Right," said Kimberly, "now where could Tim *possibly* slip in a spy guy picture on this book cover... We've got this one totally covered."

THE SWORD OF SUTHERLEE

GREGORY O. SMITH

Dedication

To those who build, protect, and strengthen the good in families, wherever and whoever you may be. You are the *real* heroes.

And to my wonderful editors, Lisa, Anne, and Dorothy Smith.

Author's Note

In this book, you will meet Maria, the youngest of the Straunsee girls. She had been hinted at in the previous books, but her character took me totally by surprise during the writing of this book. *She is so much fun!*

So get ready for challenging swordfights, mysterious dungeons, Smorganvue gleep-thorns, and more lively fun as the Wright cousins dive into the *Sword of Sutherlee!*

~ Gregory O. Smith

CHAPTER 1

The Flying Sword

It was a small law, a silly law, really. It was an old law, centuries old. It had been written in a different time—a time of knights and kings, princesses and queens—when the sword was the ultimate weapon. And yet, there it was.

It would have stayed in the dusty old law books in the legislative library, but a clerk accidentally knocked an old, leather-bound book off an ancient oak shelf. When she picked it back up off the floor, there, on page 234 was the law:

"He who bears the silver sword, bears the kingdom of Gütenberg."

"Look at this," said the clerk. "I've never seen this law before." She wrote a small memo about "old Gütenbergian laws" that needed to be updated and mentioned the missive in passing. But the law stayed. Mr. Kreppen made sure of that.

After their flight into space, the five Wright cousins—Jonathan (age 18), Kimberly (17), Tim (14) and twin cousins, Robert and Lindy (17)—were visiting their royal friends, the Straunsees, in the country of Gütenberg. His Majesty, Alexander Straunsee was king of Gütenberg. He and his four daughters, Allesandra (age 21), identical twins Sarina and Katrina (17), and Maria (13), lived in the Straunsee Castle. King Straunsee's wife had died several years before.

The Wright cousins had been staying in the guest rooms of the Straunsee castle. Princess Sarina Straunsee was teaching Jonathan Wright how to fence. They were practicing their sword fighting on an outer wall parapet walk of Straunsee Castle. The early morning sky was overcast and the cold nip of Fall was in the air.

"I don't know how you do it," said Jonathan. "You make it look so easy."

"You are doing well, Jonathan," said Sarina with a smile. Sarina had watched many classic American movies growing up and she could speak American English without an accent. "Just hold your sword a little higher," she added in her sweet and pleasant voice. "Now, try thrusting, and see how I parry, or defend myself, by deflecting your blade."

The rest of the Wright cousins watched with interest as Jonathan and Sarina sallied back and forth, one moment on the defensive, the next on the offense.

"Come on, Jonathan, hurry up and win," called out Tim Wright from the sidelines.

"That's easy for you to say," Jonathan replied with a smile. "Sarina's had years of training. I'm just glad she's taking it easy on me."

Sarina grinned and said, "Do not worry, Jonathan, my friend, I would never hurt you on purpose." They practiced several minutes more and Sarina said, "Let's stop for a moment to catch our breath."

"Good call," said Jonathan, wiping the sweat from his brow. "Thank you."

Sarina and Jonathan set their swords down on the top of the wall and slipped off their fencing helmets. The rest of the Wright cousins soon joined them as they looked over the castle parapet at the green valley and river far below.

Sarina Straunsee had first met the Wright cousins when they rescued her from kidnappers in *The Case of the Missing Princess*. Since then, they—particularly Jonathan and Sarina—had become good, steadfast friends.

"Well, Sarina, how did Jonathan do today?" asked Kimberly.

"He is definitely improving but it shall take many, many more lessons. Years, I am afraid," said Sarina with a grin. "We will have to practice much."

"Definitely," said Jonathan with a smile.

"You guys and your mushy-mush," said Tim.

"Oh, Sarina, it's so pretty here, just like you," said Jonathan, acting mushier to tease Tim back. "I can see why you love it so."

"You should see it in the snow," Sarina replied, joining in and smiling. "Everything is so pristine and sparkly. We could build a smooshy-smooshy snowman together."

"That would be fun," said Jonathan.

"Ugh, I think I'm going to die!" said Tim, spinning around. "My brother's gone mushy!"

Sarina and Jonathan burst into laughter.

Tim shook his head from side-to-side. As he did so, he saw something out of the corner of his eye. "Hey, what's that down there?" he said, reaching to point out a moving object down in the valley below. Tim's hand accidentally bumped the hilt of Sarina's sword and sent it rolling. Seeing the danger, Jonathan and Tim both tried to stop the sword but it rolled over the outside edge of the wall.

Scrambling to see where it went, the five Wright cousins and Sarina leaned over the wall to see the sword plunge seventy-five feet, bounce off a small tree on the cliff face, and go sailing again through the air. It hit a bush, started a small avalanche of rocks and dirt, and went tumbling down the mountainside out of sight.

"I'm sorry, Sarina," said Tim. "I didn't mean to." He thought for a moment and said, "Tell you what, from now on, you guys can be mushy all you want."

"Thanks, Tim," said Sarina, her face growing serious. "We need to find that sword. It was from the castle armory."

"Let's go get it," said Jonathan. "Are there any trails that go down there?"

"There is an old path," Sarina replied. "But I haven't been on it for many years."

"It looks steep down there. We'd better take some rope in case we need to do some rappelling," said Jonathan.

"And some food and water," said Lindy.

"And a grappling hook," added Tim.

"We should have one of those somewhere," said Sarina. "But really, we do not all have to go."

"And who's going to stop us?" said Jonathan with an encouraging grin. "Especially since you have no sword."

"Then an expedition it is!" said Sarina gratefully.

Within fifteen minutes, Sarina and the cousins had rounded up supplies and started out of the castle.

"My friends and I are going for a walk," Sarina informed the guards at the castle gateway.

"Would you like one of us guards to go with you?" asked the main guard.

"No thank you," replied Sarina. "We will be quite fine."

"Thank you, Princess Straunsee," replied the guard. "Enjoy the mountains, but remember, there is rain in the forecast."

Sarina, ever glad to be away from the formalities of the court, took in a deep breath of freedom and let it go. "Come," she said to the Wright cousins. "Let us find that sword."

Sarina quickly led the Wright cousins down into the canyon below the castle. "Be careful," she called out as they walked. "This is an old trail and it is not well kept."

The trail soon narrowed so they had to go single file.

"The last time I was down here," said Sarina, "my sisters Katrina, Allesandra, and myself were playing hide and seek. I ran down this trail. They never did find me."

"Then how come you're here?" asked Tim.

"I found myself," Sarina replied.

"Oh," said Tim. "I guess that works."

"Be careful on this part," instructed Sarina. "There is a slippery slide area."

The cousins continued following the princess. The trail wound its way in and out of trees. They soon came to an area that had evidence of a recent landslide. They glanced up to see their position in relation to the Straunsee Castle. "This could be the area," said Sarina.

Jonathan eyed the hillside below them and said, "If we're going to try to go down where this slide goes, we'll need to use a rope to help us."

"That's for sure," said Kimberly. "I don't know why I let Tim come on this hike."

"Because it's a fun adventure," said Tim. "Besides, I'm the one that lost the sword, remember? So, I'm going to help find it."

Jonathan secured their rope to a large tree and the group

started carefully picking their way down the steep side of the mountain. They went down next to the slide area, but not in the slide itself as that would be too dangerous. As it was, they had to be careful to avoid knocking rocks loose so the lower climbers wouldn't be hit.

"Look out below," called out Robert when he accidentally started some rocks rolling. Sarina and Jonathan stepped to the side to avoid being hit by the rocks. Once they were clear, they continued down the mountain. They soon arrived at a narrow, leveled-off area that proved to be an even older trail.

"I have never seen this path before," said Sarina, glancing in both directions. "But I am grateful it is here."

Sarina and Jonathan led the way. In some ways, it was a more substantial trail than the one they had just left. It was not quite wide enough for two people side-by-side, but it was a comfortable, sturdy trail. Parts were buried in rubble, but in key places, the trail had been built with long-lasting rock retaining walls above and below the path. Brush and moss covered much of the rocks. They were well-made walls, not hastily fitted.

The trail switchbacked and wound back below itself. The group soon arrived at a leveled-off spot. There was evidence of a recent landslide, so the cousins and Sarina fanned out to look around for the sword. They were about to move on when Lindy spied something metallic in the rocks several feet below the trail. "That might be it," she said. She carefully slipped down to investigate it more closely. After clearing away some of the debris, she exposed a dusty sword handle.

"Here it is," Lindy said jubilantly. She gripped the handle and gave it a firm tug. At first the sword wouldn't budge, so she cleared more dirt and rock away from it. She tugged again and the sword came loose. As she withdrew it, the blade looked old and rusty. In fact, only half the blade was still there.

"Boy, things sure rust quickly around here," said Tim.

"Sorry, guys," said Lindy. "False alarm."

"Perhaps mine was not the only sword that has fallen from the castle," said Sarina.

The group studied the sword for several moments. Lindy slipped it into her backpack and Sarina and the cousins continued looking for Sarina's sword. If one had landed there before, it was a good possibility Sarina's sword might be there as well.

Jonathan followed the pathway some twenty feet more. It ended near some large boulders. Not boulders, exactly, but more an outcropping of large rocks still in place in the mountain. He saw some squared-off rocks about shoulder-height and started to clear the rubble away from them. As he did so, he found it to be the top part of an archway, including the keystone. "Sarina, hey you guys, come here, I've found something!" he called out.

By the time Sarina and the rest of the cousins arrived, Jonathan had uncovered the top two feet of the arch and some of the space underneath it. "It looks like an old tunnel entrance," he said excitedly."

"Where do you think it goes?" said Sarina, quickly joining Jonathan in the digging.

Robert, Kimberly, Tim and Lindy also joined in. As the group dug out the rubble, they discovered that the passageway had been purposefully walled off to hide the tunnel, for the rubble soon turned out to be the remains of a crumbling wall.

"Who do you think might have built this?" asked Kimberly.

"I don't know," Sarina replied. "My country is an ancient one. There have been many kings."

After clearing out a three-foot-tall opening, Jonathan and Robert checked the tunnel for soundness. "It looks solid," said Jonathan.

"Good," said Sarina. She smiled at Jonathan and eagerly switched on her phone light. "Let's see where it goes."

With the rest of the cousins looking on, Jonathan and Sarina slipped down into the tunnel. After several feet, it was tall enough for them to stand.

Fifteen feet in, they came to a door. The door was made of thick, wooden planks. It had three large strap iron hinges and a stout iron handle. A latch held the door closed. The lock was gone but it was evident it had been removed forcefully as there were several dents in the door from a sledgehammer or some other blunt instrument.

Jonathan and Sarina glanced at each other with eager anticipation and Jonathan unlatched the door and pulled it open. It creaked as if it hadn't been opened for a very, very long time.

Sarina shined her light into the opening. They saw a passageway about seven feet tall and four feet wide. After making sure it was safe, they stepped over the threshold and walked some ten paces.

The tunnel opened into a large room about fifteen feet wide and twenty-five feet long. There were thick wooden shelves lining three walls. It was evident it had been used as a storage room at one time but the shelves were now empty. Two of the sets of shelving had been tipped over.

"What happened here?" asked Robert as he, Lindy, Tim, and Kimberly caught up with Sarina and Jonathan in the tunnel.

"Good question," said Jonathan. "It looks like it's been ransacked."

The cousins searched the room for many minutes. Finding nothing, they were about to leave when Lindy spied some papers behind one of the sets of shelves. They looked old and yellowed, so she retrieved them very carefully. There appeared to be writing on them. A leather lace bound the papers together on the left side. Sarina and the others gathered around Lindy to look at them.

"It doesn't look like English," said Robert.

"No," said Sarina, shining her light and studying the text. "It looks like the old language."

"What's that?" asked Tim.

"Our language and the writing of it has changed over the centuries," Sarina replied. "This is an older, script form of handwriting. I recognize a few of the letters. That's a 't', that one over there is an 's', and that's an 'a'. My twin sister, Katrina, knows it better than I do."

The cousins and Sarina searched the room for additional artifacts but found nothing else. They left the room, re-latched the door, and crawled back up out of the tunnel. Lindy, document in hand, followed them.

"Lindy, what do you think it says?" asked Tim.

"I don't know," Lindy replied, "Maybe it leads to a treasure!"

CHAPTER 2

The Record

Sarina and the cousins sat down to eat a morning snack outside the tunnel. Tim and Robert finished early, so they resumed their search for Sarina's missing sword.

"I hope we find it," said Tim, "I don't want it to be lost on my account."

"It was an accident," said Robert. "It could have happened to anyone."

"Yeah, but still—." Tim stopped mid-sentence. "Hey, look at that guy up there," he said, pointing to a person hiding behind some rocks above the tunnel they had just found.

"Act like you didn't see him," said Robert.

"But I did see him," said Tim.

"Yeah, but stop pointing at him. You'll scare him away."

"Oh," said Tim, puzzled, but compliant. "Well, there's a tree over there. That's kind of cool."

"Good," said Robert. "Keep it up."

"Hey Kimberly," said Tim. "Look at that tree over there."

"Okay," Kimberly replied. "What about it?"

"It's green," said Tim.

"Green is good when you're a tree," Kimberly said.

Robert, meanwhile, had slipped over to Jonathan near the mouth of the tunnel and told him about the spy. They decided to come up on each side of the person and surprise him. Staying close to the side of the mountain, each snuck up to where Tim had seen the spy. Robert was the first to get there. "Hi," he said, stepping out from behind a rock, "can I help you?"

The person turned around, surprised, and said, "Hi Robert."

"Oh, hi, Katrina?" said Robert. "I'm glad it's you. I thought you were somebody spying on us."

"Spying on you?" Katrina said, a hint of chuckle in her sweet and pleasant voice. "No, I'm trying to find Sarina. My father wishes to talk to her about a sword."

Robert winced and said, "Yes, she's right down there. Follow me."

Robert led Katrina down to where the others were. On the way, he told her what they had just found. Jonathan caught up with them.

"Hi Katrina, how did you find us?" asked her sister, Sarina.

"One of the castle guards has been watching you from the wall," said Katrina. "What's this about a document?"

"Here it is," Lindy replied, "I hope you can make more sense out of it than I've been able to."

"Well," said Katrina, looking it over, "it is definitely the old script."

"Yes," said Sarina. "I understand many of the letters. Can you figure out what it says?"

"We've got some books on it in our library," said Katrina. "Let's examine it more there. Father is asking about the sword you borrowed from the castle armory."

"I lost it," said Sarina, crestfallen. "It fell off the castle wall and slid down here somewhere."

"I'll help you look for it," Katrina said. "We'll have to hurry, though, we're supposed to be back up at the castle in about forty-five minutes."

The group renewed their search for the missing sword, looking above and below the trails. After twenty-five minutes and no sword, they reluctantly gave up their search and headed for the castle. It was starting to lightly rain.

When they got to the castle, they met King Straunsee. Sarina told him about the sword and the king sent some of the castle staff out to look for it using metal detectors. King Straunsee was then called away for government matters, so princesses Sarina and Katrina led the Wright cousins into the family library. It was a large, beautiful library with a deep, rich carpet. The walls were lined with dark walnut wood shelves. Natural light flooded in from north-facing windows. There were several research computers and thousands of old books.

Katrina retrieved several books from a "languages" shelf and the group all sat down to study the old papers Lindy had found. Sarina, of course, sat down next to Jonathan.

"Okay," said Katrina, "Sarina, I will read the letters off to you. Please write them down and we will see if we can figure out what this is about." Katrina then began. Once they had figured out the words in their old language, they could work on translating the writing into English. It took about one-and-a-half hours.

Robert and Tim, in the meantime, had asked permission from the Straunsee girls to try out the computer flight simulator at the far side of the room. "That would be fine," said Sarina.

Sarina unlocked the console and logged in. The boys soon found out the flight simulator wasn't for a small civilian plane. It was for a sleek, supersonic aircraft, somewhat similar to the one the boys had seen in the desert long before.

"All right," said Tim and Robert as they settled into their seats. "*Desert Jeepers*, here we come!"

At first, the boys used computer assist to help them get

started. Robert was playing pilot, Tim his copilot. They went through flight check-offs and taxied out onto the tarmac. Robert turned the nose into the landing strip, ran the engines up, released the brakes, and swoosh, they were off! Moments later, they smashed into a building at the far end of the airport.

"Robert," said Tim, "you wrecked us good. How am I supposed to be copilot if you smashed our plane to bits?"

"Give me a break. We'll try it again," said Robert, resetting the simulator take-off scenario. "This thing is kind of tough."

Once again, they were at the simulated airport runway. Robert released the brakes and they started moving down the landing strip at an ever-increasing speed. Side buildings swept by. Robert pulled back on the stick and the plane started lifting off the ground. He pulled back harder and the plane shot skyward with a roar.

"This is more like it," said Tim. They had screens to the front, sides, back, and overhead. The G-forces seemed to strain their vision. Robert leveled off at 20,000 feet and lit the afterburners. The plane shot through the air.

"Where are we?" asked Tim.

"Beats me," Robert replied. "I've just been trying to figure out how to fly this thing. You're the navigator."

"Oh, right," said Tim, looking down at the earth's surface far below. "I'd say we're somewhere between...Tokyo, Japan, and Rochester, New York. Wait, that's either Florida or Canada down there."

"That's Hawaii," said Robert. "I think we're in big trouble."

"Trouble?" said Tim a moment later. "Have you seen our fuel supply?"

"I guess we should have filled up before liftoff," said Robert. The plane began to sputter and was soon falling toward earth like a lead balloon. *SMASH!*

"Ouch!" said Tim.

"A good crash is one you can walk away from," said Robert.

"That's a good *landing*," Tim corrected.

"Oh, yeah, that's right," said Robert, "*landing*. No wonder I keep getting it wrong."

After ten more crashes, Robert and Tim walked over to see how the translating process was going.

"Are you done yet?" asked Tim.

"No," answered Sarina. "This is pretty challenging. It seems to be some kind of ancient myth or story."

"They're using some old words we don't know the meaning of," added Katrina. "But we've translated some of it."

"What have you gotten so far?" asked Robert.

"This part," said Sarina, pointing at the ancient document, "talks about a *sword of power*."

"The king's sword," added Katrina. "Something about where it is. We haven't been able to decipher the name of the place, yet."

"The sword seems to be powerful," Sarina said. "We don't understand this part here. It is a very old name for something."

"A powerful sword?" said Tim. "That sounds cool. Maybe it's like a laser sword or something. Let's go find it!"

"It's probably just a fairy tale," said Kimberly. "We've got to finish doing our homework working on this writing, first."

"Homework?" said Tim, "Um, I think Robert and I better get back to the old flight simulator. We've just about got it solved."

"Yeah, thirteen crashes in a row. We're doing great!" said Robert with a grin.

"You're welcome to help us with this writing if you'd like," said Katrina with a smile.

"No, we've got our piloting stuff to do," Tim replied quickly.

"Thanks anyways."

Tim grabbed Robert's arm and tugged him toward the simulator.

"What are you doing?" asked Robert. "Maybe they needed our help or something."

"Our help?" said Tim. "You and I don't know their language. How could we help them? No, Robert, trust me, we'd better just let the pros get back to work. We have a plane to fly!"

There was a knock at the Straunsee library door. Sarina arose to answer. "Yes, thank you," the cousins overheard her say at the door. "Thank you very much." Sarina talked for a moment. When she returned to the others, she was bearing the sword that had been lost. "One of the guards found it," she said. "It was tangled in a pine tree above the upper trail."

"No wonder we didn't find it," said Kimberly, "We were looking too low on the mountain."

Sarina and Jonathan took the sword to the castle maintenance shop where they cleaned it up and burnished it. Aside from a few scratches and nicks, it was none the worse for wear.

"These things are built to withstand a lot," said Jonathan.

"Thank goodness for that," Sarina said with a smile. "Let's return it to the armory before anything else happens to it."

The youths quickly returned the sword to the armory. The rack it had been on before was taken by another sword, so Sarina set it on a new rack. She phoned her father to tell him the good news and she and Jonathan returned to the library greatly relieved.

"How is it going?" asked Sarina when they got to the table where the other youths were translating the papers.

"We are kind of stuck," said Katrina. "I'm going to have to do some more research."

Sarina grinned. "Father says they've received a lot of new snow up in the mountains. Why don't we go skiing?"

"Sounds fun," said Katrina. "We could use a break."

Lindy and Kimberly agreed.

There was a loud groan from across the room at the flight simulator.

"What's wrong?" called out Kimberly.

"We just crashed again. Number thirty-two," said Robert.

"Yeah, and that's not counting the other six times we drove off into the ditch," added Tim.

"Those don't count," Robert replied. "How was I supposed to know a cow was going to be walking across the runway. That's the copilot's job."

"Copilot's job?" said Tim.

"You guys want to go skiing?" asked Lindy.

"Sure," Tim replied, glancing at Robert, "as long as we don't have to fly in any airplanes."

It was a three-hour drive to the mountain ski resort, so Sarina arranged for them all to fly in the Straunsee helicopter instead and made it there in thirty minutes.

The cousins and the Straunsee girls had a fun afternoon of skiing. The snow was fine and powdery and the runs were fast. On their last ride up the mountain on the ski lift, Sarina and Jonathan sat behind two talkative women.

"So, what do you think about that sword thing?" they heard one of the women say.

"What sword thing?" replied the second woman.

"Didn't you hear? You know, about the kingdom belonging to the person who has the sword," said the first woman.

"You're just making it up," said the second woman.

"No, I overheard two law clerks talking about it in the office this morning. There's some old law on the books that says the king must have the right sword or they can't be king. It's hundreds of years old."

"Did anybody tell King Straunsee about it?" asked the second woman.

"Oh," said the first woman, "of course, he has the sword. Otherwise, he wouldn't be king. Right?"

"I certainly hope so for his case. He's put a lifetime of work into improving our country," said the second woman.

"Some of the people in the legislature are organizing a group to determine the validity of the sword. It's the law, you know,"

"I wouldn't mind having the sword myself," said the second woman. "That way I could eat chocolate anytime I wanted."

"And that castle they live in," agreed the first woman. "I'd love to live there."

Jonathan and Sarina looked at each other in alarm. "I need to talk to my father," Sarina said quietly.

"Yes," Jonathan replied. "And we'd better be sure the sword is locked up in a safe. Boy, if someone should steal it, there could be all kinds of trouble!"

CHAPTER 3

Search for the Sword

When Sarina and Jonathan got off the lift at the top of the run, they signaled for Katrina and the others to wait while Sarina and Jonathan found a private place to phone King Straunsee.

"Greetings, Sarina," answered King Straunsee, "how is the skiing?"

"It's wonderful, Father," began Sarina, "I wish you could have joined us. Father, Jonathan and I overheard some women on the ski tramway. One of the women said you have to have a certain sword to be king of Gütenberg. Do we have that sword?"

"Sword?" said King Straunsee.

"Well, we heard some women say there's a law on the books that says you have to have a special sword that makes you king of Gütenberg. It's the sword of Smorgleburger or something-or-other."

King Straunsee chuckled. "Somebody is just having fun with them," he said. "I have never heard of such a law."

"I don't know, father, they seemed awfully serious," Sarina said.

"Believe me," said King Straunsee. "I would have known about it if there were such a law. Someone is just pulling your elbow."

"Please have it looked into, father," said Sarina. "I don't want anything to threaten our ability to help the people of Gütenberg."

"Okay, for your sake, I will," King Straunsee replied with a smile. "You just keep having a wonderful time with your friends. They will have to return to America soon, you know."

"Don't remind me," said Sarina, glancing at Jonathan with a wavering smile. "Please check on it, father."

"I will do that. See you all at dinner, Sarina," King Straunsee said.

"What's wrong?" asked Jonathan when Sarina had gotten off the phone.

"My father is going to have the law researched," Sarina said, "but he also reminded me that you guys are all going to have to go back to America soon. Jonathan, I don't want you to go. Not yet. I have so much I want to tell you, so many people to introduce you to, so many beautiful places for us to visit."

Jonathan looked her in the eyes and smiled. "You're not getting rid of me that easy," he said. "Come on, let's go ski." Sarina smiled and they met the others and headed down the slopes.

It was a fun time, swooshing back-and-forth across the runs as they skied down the mountain. Even Tim made it down without falling, and that's saying something!

When they arrived back to Straunsee Castle, they were greeted with a flurry of activity. Katrina and the Wright cousins headed to their rooms to get changed. Sarina first wished to speak with her father.

"What's going on, Father?" asked Sarina when she located him in the great hall.

"It seems you were right. The sword law is a real law," King Straunsee replied. "Sarina, we have over a thousand swords in this castle."

"A thousand and one," said an aide. "The maid just found one in the broom closet."

"Oh, that one's mine," said Sarina. "The broom handle was a little too long and I wanted to shorten it."

"A thousand and one," said King Straunsee.

"Make that a thousand and three," said another aide. "We forgot the ones over the mantel."

"Hey, what's with the dented shovel on the wall in the family room?" asked an aide from another room.

"Oh, don't count that one," Sarina called back. "That's Allesandra's shovel from space."

"A space shovel?" asked the aide. "What will you girls think of next!"

"Father, what does the king-law sword look like?" asked Sarina.

"We do not know yet," replied King Straunsee. "That is being looked into right now."

Sarina walked over close to her father and whispered, "Father, if someone else does come up with the sword, would they take over the kingdom of Gütenberg?"

"Perhaps," King Straunsee whispered back matter-of-factly.

"If they do," whispered Sarina with a mischievous grin, "could we go live in America, in the Wright's hometown?"

"Daughters!" replied King Straunsee with a smile. "Sarina, do not worry, we will find that sword even if we have to turn this castle upside-down."

Sarina grinned. "I wonder," she said, turning on her heel and going off in search of Jonathan.

While Jonathan called the Wright cousins together, Sarina also located Katrina and included her, too. They held a quick huddle to decide their next plan of action.

"What do you guys think?" asked Jonathan.

"Father is busy with the castle swords," Sarina said. "I think we should look into Lindy's document. If it is more than just a fairy tale, then we can tell father about it."

"I agree, and we could use some help on the translating part," said Katrina. "Let's take it to Mr. Gervar."

Mr. Gervar lived in the castle and was the document keeper for the castle archives. The youths contacted him and he told them he would be happy to look at the document. As the youths crossed the large castle courtyard, the rain outside was turning to snow.

"It is the old script," the octogenarian, Mr. Gervar, stated, adjusting his glasses. "I have not seen this particular dialect form for many years. It is the language of the kings."

"Is that good?" asked Sarina.

"It is not bad," said the old man. "There is a riddle here. As far as I can tell, it is made to appear a fairy tale, but at second glance, I am inclined to believe...I do believe it is a true account. Where did you find it?"

"Our friend here, Lindy Wright, found it in a tunnel below the castle," Sarina replied. "The tunnel was empty save for this and some shelves. There was a beautiful stone archway at the entrance."

"Then it may be of some importance," said Mr. Gervar. "I will study it tonight. Please stop by in the morning."

The cousins spent a fitful night trying to sleep, everyone except Tim, and he slept soundly. When Sarina, Katrina, and the cousins visited Mr. Gervar in the morning, he led them over to the documents spread out on his table.

"It is old, as I suspected," said Mr. Gervar. "Very old. It refers to Karlruhnfeld and the sword of power, the sword of the king."

"Where is Karlruhnfeld?" asked Katrina.

"That is an ancient name for Rhunfeld castle. The document says that once, the kingly sword, the sword of power, was kept there. It was moved to a safer place. The path to it begins with the door of the fireplace. Please note, it may be only a fairy tale, but if it is indeed the sword your father seeks, I wish you Godspeed."

"Then Rhunfeld Castle it is," said Sarina. "Thank you, Mr. Gervar. If you find anything else, please let us know."

"You can contact me," said Katrina. "I will be staying at the castle today."

"Katrina?" said Sarina.

"I want to stay here to help Father," Katrina replied. "You guys go and follow this new clue. I will continue to do research here."

"Thank you, Princesses," said Mr. Gervar with a smile. "For your father's sake, I hope that this is not a wild chase for the geese."

After thanking the kind man again, Sarina, Katrina, and the cousins quickly left for their quarters. It was still snowing. They didn't know whether they would be traveling through the snow on foot or searching indoors, so they prepared for both. Backpacks filled with food and supplies and cross-country skis loaded aboard, they traveled to Rhunfeld Castle by helicopter.

Rhunfeld Castle was a large fortification in its day. It was built to block invaders coming up the Trymyllt Valley from Wassern. The walls were tall and strong, but much of the castle had been destroyed during the siege battle of Trymyllt-Feldspar in 1462 AD. It had never been fully rebuilt. The largest remains of the castle were the keep, or fortified tower, usually lived in by the family of the castle master. The "keep" had been turned into a museum and was well visited.

When the Straunsee helicopter touched down at Rhunfeld

Castle, it was snowing again. The wind was blowing from the west and it had a bitter tinge to it. The youths zipped up their parkas tightly and disembarked.

"We will be about one hour," Sarina told the pilot. "Please remain for us."

"Yes, princess," said the pilot.

As the youths approached the castle keep tower, Tim got his first on-the-ground look at it. It looked strangely familiar. They rushed through the falling snow up to the front of the building and were quickly ushered in.

"Welcome, Princess Sarina," said a woman at the front desk with a big smile. Her nametag said "Eva Gelb." "It is a pleasure to have you here. But what brings you out on this chilly day?"

"Our friends from America have not seen your castle yet," said Sarina. "May we have a tour, please?"

"Certainly," said Miss Eva Gelb. She had another worker replace her at the desk and then she set out to share the amazing castle experience with them. Miss Gelb told them of its history, of the battles fought, showed them a model of what the castle used to look like, and information about the families who had lived there. They walked through four levels of the tower. "We don't usually let our guests see this part of the tower," said Eva Gelb, "but since you are guests of the Straunsees, you may see it."

"Watch it be a large room with a big fireplace with crisscrossed swords over the mantel," Tim whispered to Robert.

Miss Eva Gelb led them to the third level, opened a large door and swung it wide. The room was large and well-furnished. There was a massive rock fireplace with coats-of-arms and crisscrossed swords mounted above the mantel.

"This is where the castle-head family spent much of their time," explained Miss Gelb. "It was the safest place during a siege and was very comfortable, as you may discern."

Tim elbowed Robert. "I told you," he whispered.

"Lucky guess," said Robert.

"No," Tim whispered. "I feel like I've been in this room before."

"Tim," Robert replied, "this is the first time we've ever been to Gütenberg."

"I know," said Tim, "that's what so weird about it."

Eva Gelb's phone rang. She answered it and, a moment later, said to Sarina, "If you will excuse me, I must help one of our patrons on the first floor. It seems they have locked themselves in the broom closet. Please, take your time to enjoy your visit. When you are ready, let yourselves out by the way we came in."

"Thank you," said Sarina. "You are most kind."

The woman bowed and left.

When the door closed after her, Tim spoke up suddenly. "We've been here before, guys," he said. "I don't exactly remember when, but we've been here. There's a door to the right of the fireplace, remember? We used the secret key."

"Secret key?" said Kimberly.

"Yes, I remember this room perfectly," Tim replied. "Hey, do you think I'm getting a photographic memory like Lindy?"

Lindy shook her head. "It doesn't work that way," she said. "I have to *see* it before I can remember it."

"Okay," said Tim. "But you *should* remember this. The key is behind that stone in the wall over there. It opens that door to the right of the fireplace. We've used it several times before."

"Tim, there is no door beside the fireplace," Kimberly said matter-of-factly.

"Yes, there is," said Tim. "It's right there, can't you see it?"

"Tim, stop it. We have never been here before," said Kimberly.

"There is so a door and a key to it," said Tim adamantly. "I'll show you."

With that, Tim walked up to the rock wall, tapped on a stone twice, and the rock slid open. Tim reached inside, took out a large brass key and held it up for Kimberly and all to view. "You see?" he said exultantly, "I know what I'm talking about."

"Okay," said Kimberly, "good guess. Now let's see the door."

Tim confidently led the others over to the far side of the large castle fireplace, studied the wall, and said, "There it is." He stuck the key into a hidden slot, turned it one full revolution, and a large stone section swung inward.

"There, you see?!!" said Tim, "I told you I'm not cuckoo."

Tim glanced into the dark, spider-webby passage and stepped backwards away from the wall. "Now," he continued, "who wants to be the guinea pig, I mean, go first into this nice, creepy, scary, awful passage?"

"Where does it go?" asked Robert.

"You know, it's the tunnel of Smorlig," Tim replied. "It goes through the wall to a staircase."

By now, Sarina and the rest of the cousins were doubly baffled.

"Cool," said Jonathan, looking into the tunnel. "Let's check it out." He dug out his phone and switched on its light.

Sarina glanced around the room for a defensive weapon. She eyed the crisscrossed swords over the mantle but they were mounted too securely. She instead retrieved a fireplace poker and ducked into the dark tunnel after Jonathan.

"We're coming, too," said Robert as he, Lindy, and Kimberly turned on their lights and entered the passageway.

"Well, aren't you coming, Tim?" asked Kimberly when she saw him hesitating. "You don't want us to leave you behind, do you?"

"Oh, I'll just stay right here," said Tim with a serious grin. "I'm too young to die!"

"Come on, Tim," said Kimberly, grabbing his arm and pulling him into the tunnel after her. "You found it, you get to explore it."

The heavy door swung closed after them. Tim tried to pull it back open but the door wouldn't budge. They were trapped!

CHAPTER 4

In the Dark

"I—I don't remember it being so dark," Tim said a little timidly. "I'm going to have to be more careful about what I find."

"We'll have to find another way out," said Jonathan.

Jonathan brushed away webs as he led the group. The tunnel seemed to go right through the middle of the wall. Every now and then, the cousins could see into other rooms of the castle through narrow, well-hidden slits. As they progressed, they saw the dining room, the kitchen, the great room, and the old library from the secret passage.

"Tim, where does this lead to?" whispered Kimberly.

"That's what I've been trying to remember," Tim replied. "I don't think it was a very nice place, though."

"Tim," called back Jonathan, "we've come to a fork in the passage. Which one do we take?"

"The left one," Tim replied. "The one to the right leads to the dungeon. There's a trap door in the floor. I almost died there twice."

"Tim!" said Kimberly, "would you stop it with the dying stuff. You're scaring me to death! I...didn't mean that...I meant you're really scaring me...a lot."

"How do you think I feel?" said Tim.

Jonathan turned to the right for just a second and came running back. "Tim, you were right, there is a trap door in the floor. It almost got me."

Re-taking Sarina's hand, Jonathan led the group to the left. The passage narrowed and then widened again. "Another fork," he called back. "Which one do we take?"

Tim thought for a moment. "Take the left fork again. No, wait. That one leads to the waterfall and the trolls. Take the one to the right. The trolls like to jump up and get you. I already got...never mind. Just take the one on the right."

Jonathan led them down the passage to the right. By now, it felt like they were halfway into the mountain. "Tim, maybe you should lead us," Jonathan called back. "You seem to know where we're going."

"You're doing fine," Tim called forward. "I don't mind being last. At least not until the bat monster tries to get us."

"Bat monster?" said Kimberly.

"Yeah, that's the part where we all have to duck. It comes out of the wall at shoulder height."

"Um," said Robert, "maybe it's time to crawl for a little ways."

"I agree," Tim replied. "The bat monsters are really bad. They're almost as bad as the gleep-thorns."

"Gleep-thorns?" said Kimberly with a timid voice.

"Yeah," said Tim. "The gleep-thorns jump up from the floor and steal your shoelaces. They don't tie them or anything. Great Aunt Opal would love them."

"Hey, guys," said Kimberly. "What do you say we go back and let Sarina's guard dudes check this place out."

"We can't," said Tim, "we've already committed ourselves. Once we entered the tunnel, the Shinkbrauns closed the door and trapped us in here. There's only one way out. The way of the flaming torch!"

"Oh boy," said Jonathan. "Okay, Tim, just tell us when to crawl and when to stand."

The group continued to follow the passage. "Get down!" warned Tim. Everybody leaned down. Seconds later, a black shape came out of the wall at shoulder's height. It flew across the tunnel and disappeared. Robert started to straighten up a bit.

"Stay down," said Tim. "There are two more of them." Two more dark shapes soon flew by. "Okay, it's clear," he said. "Now for the gleep-thorns. When you see a small light on the floor, jump over it. Otherwise, they'll get your shoelaces and sometimes even your shoes. We'll need our shoes for the field of thorns."

Four hops and a skip later, Sarina and the cousins arrived at an unlit torch. They looked it over.

"It's supposed to be lit," said Tim. "Maybe it's the wrong torch."

The youths shined their lights around the small room. There were two other torches, both unlit.

"Well, I'm not sure about this," said Tim. "One of them has to be lit."

"Maybe we're supposed to light them," said Robert. "Does anybody have a flint and steel?"

Sarina shined her light; the middle torch seemed to glow.

"That's it," said Tim. "I remember now, it was the middle one. Twist the torch to the right and the wall will open."

Jonathan twisted the torch and a panel in the wall opened outward. Light poured in and they stepped out into a beautiful greenhouse garden. As they looked around, the panel closed behind them.

"Welcome to *The Sword of Smorganvue*," said Tim. "It's a great video game. But I didn't know it was for real. This is awesome!"

"The Sword of Smorganvue?" said Kimberly.

"Yeah, if you beat Level 3," Tim explained, "you get the powerful sword of Smorganvue. It gives you your own castle and kingdom? Hey, what's going on? Your dad, the sword, Princess Sarina, it's just like in the game."

Tim and everyone else looked at Sarina.

"I don't know," Sarina said. "I've never been on this part of the tour before."

"Tim, do you remember where the sword was?" asked Jonathan.

"Well, first we have to go through the garden. It's level 2," said Tim. "We've got to watch out for the Burlaps."

As the cousins headed into the garden area, the tour guide woman, Miss Eva Gelb was watching by security camera. She tapped a phone number and lifted her phone to her ear. "Hello," she said. "Yes, the Straunsee group have just left by the passage."

"That is good," said a man's voice. "Did they mention anything about the sword?"

"Yes," replied Miss Gelb. 'I listened to them through the microphones in the secret passage. You were right, the youngest young man, Timothy Wright, seemed to know much about the *Sword of Smorganvue*. He will be very useful."

"Follow them. Let me know what they look at. Everything. I want to hear every word they say. They have the documents."

"I have already activated the special security cameras," said Eva Gelb. "I will download the files to your computer as we discussed. You had better give me that royal position you promised me in the new government."

"You will get it, do not worry. Just keep me informed. Good-bye."

Tim led them through the garden in Level 2 and clear through the end of Level 3, including the "Valley of the Dwarves" rock garden and the "Spoon of Thyme" outside the castle. It was just as it was in the game, except that it was *real*, actual walls, gardens, and things you could touch. Their trail ended on the top of a rocky, forested ridge one hundred yards above the castle.

"Where do we go from here?" asked Robert.

"I don't know," Tim replied. "We should see the sword. The game stopped here. Boom, it was done. I almost got the sword and then it disappeared. No more levels, no more challenges."

"That's kind of a weird game," said Robert. "Maybe they were wanting to sell you the sequel or something."

"Right at the end," said Tim, "they asked for volunteers to help them find the Royal Sword of Smorganvue and they gave a link."

The Wright cousins and Sarina looked around at their surroundings. It was lightly snowing. The castle museum, gardens, and valley were below to the west. In the far distance, they could see the beautiful mountains of Straunsee Castle. It was an amazing scene.

Sarina's eyes locked on a distant rock formation. The light snow seemed to shroud it, falling ever so lightly. Suddenly, a gust of wind cleared her view. Sarina gasped and ran over to it. Jonathan and the other cousins followed her. She nearly slipped several times but kept on going. When she got to it, she studied it intensely. She reached out to touch the large rock and felt grooves on its surface.

"It looks like a crown," said Robert, stepping back a few paces.

"And it's been carved out of the stone very carefully," said Jonathan.

Lindy took one look at the rock—her photographic memory kicking in—and said, "It's like the one at the tunnel passage where we found the manuscript."

"You are right, it is the same," said Sarina.

"What do you think it means?" asked Kimberly.

Sarina looked at Jonathan. There was fear in her eyes as she took his hand. "We must go. I think I understand now. Jonathan, everyone, we must hurry or the kingdom will be lost!"

CHAPTER 5

Swift Flight

Sarina and the Wright cousins scrambled back down the mountainside and through the snow toward Rhunfeld castle. Sarina called the helicopter pilot to have him warm up the engine. As they passed the castle keep, they found it locked and the museum closed.

"That's strange," said Sarina. "Closing time isn't for another 6 hours."

"Maybe it's because of the new snowstorm coming in," said Lindy.

"Maybe," said Sarina, "maybe not. Let's get back to the helicopter."

The helicopter's rotors were turning slowly as Sarina and the cousins boarded. Sarina took the front bucket seat beside the pilot. "Take us home," she said, "and please hurry!"

"Yes, princess," said the pilot.

When all were strapped in, the helicopter lifted off the ground and headed for Straunsee Castle. As they flew, Sarina phoned her sister. "Katrina, we're on our way back," she called out over the noise of the helicopter. Tell father the thing is in the tunnel we discovered. Hurry! And get some of the guards down there. It will be harder to navigate with all the snow, but we can't wait. Tell father!"

"I will," said Katrina. "I hope you're right. Father has been going crazy trying to find that thing. Be safe!"

"You too, twin sister," Sarina replied.

The helicopter pilot flew over the valley, trying to avoid the downdrafts along the face of the mountains. Five minutes out from Straunsee Castle, the pilot turned toward the mountains.

"What are you doing?" asked Sarina. "The castle is farther."

"I'm taking a short cut, princess," said the pilot with a smile and heading toward a canyon.

"This is no shortcut," said Sarina. "I demand you take us to the castle, now!"

"Don't worry, princess, I just want to show you something and then we will be on our way again."

The pilot headed straight up a rugged, snow-filled canyon. He came to a rocky knoll and stopped the helicopter, hovering in mid-air.

"What are you doing?" demanded Sarina.

The pilot reached into his parka and drew out a pistol, pointing it at Sarina. "I am showing you and your friends the beautiful mountains of our homeland," he said. "Now, open that door and jump."

"What?" said Sarina. "Have you lost your mind?"

"I give you ten seconds to be out," threatened the pilot. "Now move! I will no longer be babysitter to the royal family. I am to be the new Counselor of State."

"What has gotten into everybody's heads?" said Sarina. "I feel like I'm living in another world."

"You will be soon," said the pilot with a smirk on his face. "Now you and your friends, jump!"

"You will be charged with murder," said Jonathan.

"I know the new soon-to-be judge," said the pilot, aiming his pistol at Sarina's heart. "I will get off the charges on a technicality. Now jump!"

Jonathan quickly put on his backpack and motioned for the others to do the same. He'd been caught totally off-guard. He grabbed Sarina's backpack, too, and stood up and opened the door. The heavily falling snow pelted him. He noticed the helicopter was drifting nearer to the ground. If they tried to take over the pilot, they would crash and burn. There was only one way out.

"Sarina, let's go," said Jonathan. Sarina got up and met Jonathan at the side doorway. The pilot suspiciously kept his pistol pointed at her. Sarina glanced fearfully outside into the storm and the white earth below. Jonathan reached for her hand. Sarina looked into his eyes and took his hand, squeezing it so hard their knuckles turned white. Then they jumped. Robert, Lindy, and Kimberly soon followed, with Kimberly screaming all the way down.

Tim was about to jump but the pilot grabbed his arm. "Hold on, Timothy Wright," said the pilot. "We're not done with you. Now strap yourself into the front seat or I'll let you have it!"

Tim sat down and looked below, trying to see what had become of the others. The pilot quickly turned the helicopter and flew back out over the valley.

"Wait till my mom hears about this," said Tim, shouting above the roar of the copter. "You'll be in big trouble, mister!"

"Those are tough words for a little kid," said the pilot. "Now no funny business."

The pilot switched on his headset and radioed out, "I've got the pawn and discarded the others. Where do you want me to meet you?"

"Straunsee Castle," a man's voice replied. "Land in your usual place. We will meet you there."

"Roger," the pilot replied, keeping an eye on Tim.

Five minutes later, the pilot brought the helicopter up the canyon toward Straunsee Castle. Tim could see the large castle, all lit up, several hundred feet below. The heliport was in a section of the castle on the far side away from the Straunsee residence. The pilot brought in the helicopter and landed smoothly, its rotors whipping up snow as it landed. As the blades came to a stop, two men and the woman from the museum, Miss Eva Gelb, rushed out to the helicopter. They forcefully ushered Tim away into a part of the castle he had never been to before: the dungeon. They pushed Tim into a dimly-lit cell and slammed the door closed, locking it after him.

"Let me out of here," shouted Tim, jumping up to look out the small, barred window in the door. "You can't do this to me, I'm an American citizen. I demand to see the U.S. ambassador!"

"We are looking for a sword," replied Eva Gelb in the hallway just outside the door. "You seem to know much about it. You will tell me all you know."

"I'll never tell you," said Tim. "You'd just use the sword to kick out the Straunsees and take over the kingdom. You guys are crazy if you think I'd ever help you! I won't, I won't, I won't!"

"Then we will keep you in there and give you a chance to think about it. Oh, and don't worry, nobody can hear you down here; you're three levels underground. I should know, I used to be a tour guide here while I was going to college."

"Let me out of here!" said Tim.

"Not until you tell me where the sword is," replied Miss Gelb.

"But I don't know where it is," said Tim. "I was just playing a video game."

"Very well," said Miss Gelb. "Have it your way. Stay down here until you starve to death, I don't care. The ghosts and the rats will get you, anyway."

"Not the ghosts and rats," said Tim. "They're not nice!"

"Then tell me, you little bratwurst American," said Eva Gelb.

"You mean *brat*, Miss Gelb," said Tim. "And flattery will get you nowhere."

Eva Gelb switched off the light for Tim's cell and stomped away, turning off the hall lights as she went.

Tim held up his hand to his face. It was so dark in his cell he couldn't see his hand. "Help!" he called out. His call was met only with echoes.

CHAPTER 6

In the Blizzard

Jonathan and the others lay still until the helicopter had flown out of sight. "Is everybody okay?" Jonathan finally called out. There were four replies from "ouch" to "groan."

Robert sat up, rubbing his shoulder, and said, "Jonathan, I don't think jumping out of that helicopter was the best idea you've ever had."

"At least we're still alive," said Jonathan. "That guy was going to kill us."

"Crumazoid pilot," said Sarina, brushing off her parka and trying to shake the snow and twigs out of her long, blond hair.

"I'm just glad we landed in deep snow-covered bushes rather than those rocks over there," said Lindy, getting to her feet.

"Where's Tim?" called out Kimberly as they gathered in a small clearing.

"I didn't see him jump," Robert said. "He must still be on the helicopter."

"He better not be," said Kimberly, "we Wright cousins have got to stick together."

"I'll call the castle and get help," said Sarina.

Sarina dug into her parka pocket, found her phone, and made a quick call to her father. She couldn't get through, so she called her sister, Katrina.

"The helicopter pilot did what?" said Katrina. "Yes, of course, we'll get the police on him." Katrina screamed and her phone went dead.

"Katrina, Katrina, are you okay?" called out Sarina. There was no answer.

Sarina tried calling again but her phone only made a humming, clicking sound. The others checked their phones and got the same effect.

"Either our phones aren't rated for a twenty-foot jump out of a helicopter or they're being jammed," said Robert.

The youths spent the next five minutes trying to get their phones to work but finally had to give up.

"We're going to have to hoof it," said Jonathan. "Sarina, how far are we from your castle?"

Sarina thought for a moment. "If this is the ridge I think it is, my guess is about 9.6 kilometers or 6 miles as the eagle flies," she said.

"What's the best way to get there?" asked Jonathan.

"If we go over the next ridge, it will cut off a lot of time," Sarina replied. "We should be about the same altitude as the castle."

"Well," said Jonathan, looking around at the others, "let's get going before it gets dark."

Jonathan and Sarina set out in the lead, followed by Kimberly, Lindy, and Robert. The snow was falling heavier now. It was up to their knees in places. They hiked as quickly as they could. After about half a mile of rugged going, Kimberly asked that they stop for a minute because her left knee was bothering her. "I must have landed on it wrong when we jumped," she said.

"Do you think you should wrap it?" asked Lindy.

"No, I just need to rest it for a minute," Kimberly replied.

The group took a five-minute rest and started out again. As they neared the top of a snow-covered ridge, Robert noticed Kimberly was limping.

"Let me carry your backpack for you," said Robert.

At first, Kimberly refused by saying that Robert was already carrying one, but he insisted and she finally turned it over to him. "Thanks," said Kimberly.

Ten minutes later they stopped again. This time, Lindy helped Kimberly wrap her knee, over her trousers, with an ace bandage left over from their skiing trip the day before.

"Good thing you have on flexible trousers," said Lindy.

They set out again. As they hiked down into the next canyon to reach the distant ridge, there was a strong wind pushing the falling snow into their faces.

"Sarina, I'm sure glad these parkas you loaned us have good hoods," Lindy said with a grateful smile.

"Me also," Sarina replied, tightening the draw string on her hood. "Though I did not expect we'd need to use them like this."

The sky was growing darker as they neared the next ridge. "We should be at the castle soon," Sarina said optimistically. "It should be over in the next canyon."

The group pushed hard up the side of the next ridge. When they got to the top of the ridge, they eagerly looked into the next canyon but found no castle.

"Somebody must have stolen it," said Robert, readjusting the two backpacks he was carrying.

"Tim," said Kimberly, looking directly at Robert, "it's not nice to joke about the kingdom being lost right now,"

"Tim?" said Robert with concern. "Kimberly, are you okay?"

"I'm just kind of cold, Tim, I mean, Robert," Kimberly said tiredly, "but I can keep going."

Robert glanced at Jonathan, Lindy, and Sarina with a look of concern.

"We'd better get you warmed up, little sister," said Jonathan. "We don't have any stoves with us, but maybe we can find some wood to make a fire. For now, keep moving your arms and legs to get your blood circulating better."

Sarina led the group down into the next canyon, blazing a trail through the snow and looking for anything familiar as she went. She had the bad feeling they were off track. She pulled Jonathan aside for a second and whispered, "I didn't want to worry Kimberly, but Jonathan, we may be lost. We should have been able to see the castle by now."

"Let's find some shelter so we can get out of this storm," Jonathan replied. "I'm getting worried about Kimberly."

"Me too," said Sarina, the stress showing on her brow.

"You look tired, Sarina," said Jonathan. "I'll take the lead and break trail."

"Thanks," Sarina replied. "I'm sure glad you're here and we can face these challenges together."

Jonathan led the way. The snow was now over their knees. Sarina followed his path gratefully. Lindy was next, followed by Kimberly. Robert continued to be the caboose.

As they were climbing out of the new canyon toward the ridge, Jonathan spied a dark shadow in the large rock outcropping up ahead. He turned and headed for it. "You guys wait here," he called back. "That may be a cave up there. I'll go check it out."

The rest of the group, grateful for the chance to rest, waited in the falling snow. Jonathan disappeared from view at the base of the cliff and soon came sliding back down toward them. "It's a small cave," he said excitedly. "It should serve us well to get out of this storm. Follow me."

Snow was pelting their faces as Jonathan and Sarina helped the others up to the cave. Kimberly, particularly, had a tough time of it, but they were able to push and pull her along to get her up into it.

Immediately after entering the small cave, the youths were amazed at how good it felt to finally be out of the strong winds and driving snow.

"I've got a flashlight in my backpack," said Robert, looking into the darkness. He dug through the front pockets, retrieved one, and switched it on. It lit the cave.

"It's deeper than I thought," said Jonathan, digging for a light of his own.

"Do you think it's a bear's cave?" asked Kimberly.

"Of course not," said Robert. "Everybody knows bears don't like squared-off timbers."

"What are you talking about?" asked Kimberly, her lips shivering from the cold.

"That beam laying on the floor over there," said Robert, shining his light at a large timber near the back of the cave. There was another timber just below it. "Bears definitely did not put them there."

"What do you think they were used for?" asked Lindy.

"I don't know," said Robert, going over to investigate, "but they should make good, dry firewood if we can get them split up."

Robert climbed over to the timbers and tried to pull the top one loose. "It's stuck," he said. He started pulling the dirt back from them and found them to be longer than he first expected. When he was done, he had uncovered a five-foot timber. The one below it was even longer. Jonathan climbed over to help him while Sarina and Lindy tried to help Kimberly get warmed up.

Robert and Jonathan got the second timber pried up out of the dirt. It was old oak and had tool marks on it where someone had squared it up.

The boys quickly began whittling away on it with their pocketknives, making kindling ready for lighting a fire. They soon had a pile of shavings and finally succeeded in splitting one of the timbers into several pieces. That done, they built a small fire ring of rocks and laid their materials: kindling first, then a little bit larger wood, and finally larger on top. When they were done, it looked like a toy log cabin. The fire would start in the base and burn upward as it went.

"I hope somebody has some matches," said Robert after they were done.

"I do," said Sarina. "They're in a waterproof container."

Sarina quickly dug them out of her backpack and handed them to Robert. Robert struck a match and held it to the base of the kindling. A slight breeze promptly blew it out.

CHAPTER 7

The Fire

Sarina and Robert both lit matches. This time, they shielded the tiny flames with their cupped hands as they held the matches to the kindling. The kindling burned slowly at first, but after several agonizing minutes, a larger flame appeared and the wood began to burn. The flickering flames shone on the cave walls and ceiling.

Shivering Kimberly was given a front row seat. She and the other cousins slowly began to thaw as they sat and watched the growing fire. They could hear the howling winds of the continuing blizzard outside. Every once in a while, a flurry of snowflakes would blow into the mouth of the cave, where they would quickly melt. The youths were warmed physically and also cheered by the campfire. They retrieved food from their backpacks and ate hungrily. As the fire grew, the warming youths had to scoot back away from the increasing heat.

As the night darkened, the youths grew drowsy. For safety, they decided to post a guard and take turns sitting inside near the mouth of the cave. When Sarina's turn came early in the morning, Jonathan stayed up with her so they could visit. They talked about their first meeting at Fort Courage during *The Case of the Missing Princess* and their swordfight and adventures there.

"Sarina, what do you want to do when you grow up?" asked

Jonathan.

"I like helping people," Sarina said, "regular people. I want to teach them truths that they can live by. Truths, that if followed, they can improve their own lives and find greater happiness."

"You want to be a teacher?" said Jonathan.

"A teacher of good things," said Sarina, "like my mom was."

"Kind of like teaching hungry people how to fish, not just giving them a fish?" said Jonathan.

"Yes, kind of," Sarina replied. "But more than just teaching them how to fish or find food, but other things, too. There is so much more to life than just getting by, just being entertained, just looking out for oneself. Family—*real family*—is where it's at. When my mother died, life became hard. Not just because we had to do more chores, but when she died, we lost the queen of our home. My father lost his sweetheart and best friend; we lost mother's kind and loving ways. Her patience with us. Her guidance. When we came home from wherever we'd gone to, she wasn't there anymore to greet us and have us tell her about our day. She was awesome, Jonathan, I wish you could have met her."

"Me too," said Jonathan, patting her hand.

Sarina smiled and glanced up. "Jonathan, look at that!" she said.

Jonathan turned to see where she was pointing. A second fire had popped up at the back end of the cave.

"Where'd that come from?" said Jonathan, going over to investigate. The flames were coming up from another timber in the floor. "No wonder it's been so warm in here," he said. "There's more wood burning in this cave."

Bewildered, Jonathan studied the floor for a moment. He spied a crack in the floor he hadn't noticed before. Leaning over, he looked into it and saw that it looked deep. He stepped back and looked at the sleeping cousins around him. "Hey, you guys," he called out, "I think we'd better get out of here. Get your gear."

Robert and the others sat up, rubbing their eyes and reaching for their backpacks.

Sarina came over to look. The crack in the floor suddenly widened and the entire floor collapsed. Sarina and the cousins slid on twelve-foot-long timbers deeper down into the mountain. There was smoke, dust, and glowing coals all around them as they scrambled to get clear. The timbers, having dumped their load of dirt, now burst into flames. The "cave" they had been in was actually a caved-in zone on top of old shoring timbers set up to secure the ceiling of a tunnel eight feet below. The burning timbers cut off the youths' escape out of the mouth of the cave and into the snow, and more timbers were starting to burn.

Jonathan whipped out his light and shined it down the dark passageway going deeper into the mountain. He could feel a strong draft. "This way," he said. The others switched on their lights and followed him. They were grateful for their warm night's sleep.

The new passage, or tunnel, appeared to be an old metal mine, for there were brightly colored ore veins in the walls and ceiling. There was even a set of iron mine car tracks heading down the middle of the tunnel. The youths followed them, hoping it would lead them to another exit from the mountain.

The air in the tunnel was a cool fifty-five degrees Fahrenheit and currently free of smoke. The floor was also remarkably clear of rubble. The tunnel curved to the right, now following the vein.

As they walked, the youths came to several large rooms, some of them timbered to strengthen the ceilings. Each room was empty save for the tracks.

After a quick hike, they arrived at a large room, its ceiling forty feet tall and its breadth fifty feet. In the middle of the room sat three mine cars, their wooden sides well-worn from hauling rock. Beside the mine cars, set on the ground, were several large wooden boxes. Sarina and the cousins hurried over to see what they held. As they lifted the lid of the first box, they spied several cast iron cooking pans and pots. A second box enclosed more cooking utensils and household items.

The last box they examined was latched. As they undid the latch and lifted its lid, they saw a roll of red velvet fabric on top of other fabrics. The top roll held several jeweled, golden goblets. Below that was another roll of velvet. As Sarina reached in to touch it, something metallic clanked inside.

She carefully lifted the roll and as she did, a golden hilt and scabbard slipped out and hit the end of the box with a *THUNK!*

"A sword!" gasped Sarina, still holding the fabric.

Kimberly reached for the sword, but Jonathan held her hand back. "Let Sarina touch it first," said Jonathan. "It probably belonged to her ancestors."

Sarina carefully set down the velvet and retrieved the sword. She turned it over and over in her hands. It glistened in the light. She drew it from its scabbard. The blade was shiny, its hilt engraved with ancient writing. Sarina hefted it. "The balance is quite well," she said, showing it to the other youths.

"Do you think it's the king-sword?" asked Kimberly.

"I hope so," Sarina replied with an eager smile. "We will take it to my father."

Sarina carefully wrapped the sword back in its velvet covering and held it in her arms. "I can't wait to show it to Father. Let's go."

As they exited the room, they found several unlit torches; Jonathan and Robert each grabbed one.

"What are those for?" asked Kimberly.

"A backup for our lights," Jonathan replied. "If our batteries die, we don't want to be stuck in the dark."

The youths quickly headed down the tunnel. The increased pace caused Kimberly's knee to start hurting again so they had to slow down. Robert again started carrying her backpack to help her.

As the youths continued, one-by-one their lights began to dim. Jonathan and Robert lit their torches, giving a surreal appearance to the tunnel walls. They came to another room, this one empty again but the tracks and tunnel ended. They searched the room and found a wooden door. They unlatched it and tried to open it but it resisted their efforts. Pushing harder, they heard a scraping sound. They got it open enough to squeeze through and found themselves standing in the storage room where Lindy had earlier found the documents below Straunsee Castle. A wooden bookshelf had been covering the door. The passage had led them all the way through the ridge.

They quickly glanced around the room. Lindy reported that nothing had changed and they worked on opening the main door to the outside tunnel. All were eager to get the sword to King Straunsee.

Finding a latch lever on the inside of the door, they released it and were able to push the door open. At the portal of the tunnel, where it had been walled up with dirt and rubble, they now found a new wall. This time it was a wall of snow. Using pieces of wood, they began digging through the snow to get out of the tunnel. They had to pull snow back down into the tunnel to make progress and dig through five feet of snow. It was Robert's board that finally broke through. He widened the hole and stuck his head out. Everything was white!

Climbing up the mountain to Straunsee Castle was far different than it had been days before. The snow was deep and hid the trail they had used. It was exhausting work to climb through the snow. They pushed, packed, and stamped steps in the snow, trying to get through it. At places, the snow was waist high. Jonathan and Robert took turns breaking the way through the snow.

Their progress was slow but they finally reached a road to the castle and followed it. It had been plowed so the going was now much easier. As they approached the castle, a guard came out to greet them. He seemed rigid and glanced warily over his shoulder from time-to-time.

"Oh, Princess Sarina," he said, "I am grateful I am the first to greet you. Do not proceed any further toward the castle. Your father and sisters have been put under 'protective custody.'"

"Protective custody?" said Sarina.

"Yes, the President of the Legislature is worried—because of the leadership crisis—that your father will be mobbed."

"That's ridiculous," Sarina replied, "I see no protests nor protestors."

"Princess," said the guard in a low voice, "the only danger your father truly faces is from some of the legislators and lower judges. They have seized the castle. They seek position and power. Leave so they cannot take you as well."

The guard glanced toward the castle and called out loudly: "I am sorry but the castle is not open for tourists this day."

Shocked, Sarina and the others turned around and walked back the way they had come. The guard walked back to his post at the front gate.

"Who was that?" asked a fellow guard.

"Oh, just some tourists from America. I told them now

wasn't a good time to visit the castle," replied the first guard.

"Good job," said the fellow guard. "We don't need any more prying eyes. There is enough going on around here already."

CHAPTER 8

Landing

Without announcement, three large police vans and two helicopters had arrived earlier at Straunsee Castle. The police teams had immediately deployed to secure the facilities. The police commander found King Straunsee in the main courtyard.

"We've received anonymous threats that you and your family's lives are in danger," declared the police commander.

"I have received no such threats," said King Straunsee. "Why wasn't I told about this beforehand?"

"There was no time," explained the commander. "Mr. Kreppen, head of the legislature, ordered us out to protect you and your family. Please return to your residence."

King Straunsee, escorted by two of the capital police force, returned to his home. The policemen posted themselves just outside the front door as the king went inside. Katrina saw the concern on her father's face as he entered the living room.

"What's wrong, Father?" asked Katrina.

"We are being confined to our living quarters," King Straunsee replied. "Some reported danger or other. Katrina, go quickly to your room and throw some clothes into a backpack for yourself and Maria, and find Maria. We must leave quickly. I will meet you at the family room secret passage in five minutes. And be prepared for snow, we may be skiing cross-country. I fear this may be a coup!"

Katrina felt the urgency in her father's voice and immediately headed for her room to prepare to flee. She quickly grabbed up a backpack and rushed over to her dresser to fill it with clothes. Her sister, Sarina, called to warn her about the murderous helicopter pilot.

"The helicopter pilot did what?" said Katrina, opening her dresser drawer. "Yes, of course, we'll get the police on him."

A big black spider ran across Katrina's hand. She shrieked, shaking it off, accidentally throwing her phone to the floor. The spider got away. Katrina promptly picked up the phone and found the call had ended. She tried to redial but couldn't get through.

Bags in hand, Katrina and her father met in the family room and were heading toward the still-closed secret passage door there.

"Going somewhere?" called out a snide voice from behind them. The king and Katrina turned around to see Mr. Kreppen, flanked by several others, in the doorway. All were dressed in gray suits. "Really, now, Alexander," Mr. Kreppen said, "your security system was far too easy to overcome. I am concerned about your safety. You are far too valuable. We have received reports that your life is in danger."

"Mr. Kreppen, you are the president of our legislature. You surely know there have been many false calls through the years. Why, your life is surely just as much in danger as mine is," said King Straunsee.

"This is a very credible threat," said Mr. Kreppen. "I am sorry, King Straunsee, but we must confine you and your daughters to your quarters. There will be a capital police guard posted outside your bedrooms to make sure no one is able to harm you."

"And if we do not choose to go along with your plans?" said the king.

"Then we shall be forced to restrain you," replied Mr. Kreppen. "Though I do believe you will be most cooperative. Your daughter, Maria, is already in protective custody within the castle. For her safety, and yours, I cannot divulge her location. Oh, and I'll take your bags, please. Such important persons as yourselves should not be required to carry such items."

King Straunsee and Katrina set down their bags. As Katrina's touched the carpet, the big black spider skittered across the floor and raced up the outside of Mr. Kreppen's pant leg. Mr. Kreppen kicked and spun around madly, trying to shake it off. Seeing no sign of the spider, he stopped, composed himself, and said, "Return to your rooms!"

With Mr. Kreppen were two judges, a legal secretary, and an agitated reporter. A group of capital policemen backed them up.

"The legislature will make sure things are done right as the *missing* king-maker sword—I mean, king-sword—has set up a crisis situation in our country," Mr. Kreppen announced to his group. "We must protect the king at any cost. You can see the urgency of this 'protective custody.' No harm must be allowed to come to the king and his family as we sort the matter of the kingship out. As you will see, the legislature can fulfill a vital role at times like this. We will find the king-maker sword. In fact," he chuckled, "I wouldn't be surprised if someone from the legislature ended up governing our country in some future time."

The police escorted King Straunsee and Katrina off to their bedroom suites and guards were posted at their doors.

*   *   *

The dungeon cell Tim was in was very dark. He felt his way around and finally found a cot to lay down on. As he did so, he heard a scary noise. It was part scraping, part squeak, and then he heard a voice whisper something.

"Who's there?" called out Tim in alarm.

It was silent for a moment and then a high-pitched voice whispered, "I am your sister."

"Kimberly is that you?" said Tim.

"No, I am your other sister," came the voice again quietly.

"I only have one sister," Tim replied.

"I am your *twin* sister," the voice replied. "We were separated at birth."

"Oh yeah? Then how old are you?" asked Tim.

"Thirteen. How old are you?"

"Fourteen," said Tim. "See, there's no way we could be twins."

"You were born at one minute before midnight, I was born three minutes after midnight," said the girl's voice.

"Oh yeah? Then when's your birthday?" asked Tim.

"The day after yours," the girl replied.

"I guess that would work," said Tim. "So, if you're my twin sister, how come I've never heard of you before?"

"I was brought here to Gütenberg because I am a princess," said the girl's voice.

"If you're a princess and I'm your twin, what does that make me?" asked Tim.

"Fourteen," the girl replied.

"You're right," said Tim. "Gee, for a girl, you sure know a lot."

"Thank you. Now, are you ready to get out of here or are we going to keep talking? We've got a lot to do tonight."

"We do?" said Tim.

"Yes, my father needs my help. It is time for the ghosts of Castle Straunsee to return."

"Ghosts?" Tim asked, gulping. "Wait a minute, you're not one of them, are you?"

There was a long silence and then the voice replied, "I cannot answer that on the grounds that it may discriminate me."

"Oh," said Tim. "We're not supposed to discriminate. That would be unlawful and against the law. Besides, it just wouldn't be nice. Let's get out of here. How do we do it?"

"You need to boost me up to the opening in the wall over there. Did you bring a flashlight?"

"No," Tim replied.

"Don't you know that when you're going to be captured you always need to bring a flashlight?" asked the girl's voice.

"Nobody told me about that one," said Tim.

"Oh, I see that you've got a lot to learn," said the voice. "Well, please come over and help me up to the escape tunnel."

"Okay," said Tim, getting up and heading in the direction of the voice. He was halfway across the room when his knee hit something hard. "Ouch!" he said.

"Oh, yes, and watch out for the cot in the middle of the room," said the girl's voice.

"Thanks for telling me," said Tim, rubbing his knee. He felt his way around the cot and continued toward the far wall. Walking with his arms stretched out in front of him, he finally felt a cold stone wall. "Where are you?" asked Tim.

"Up here," replied the girl's voice. "Just push up on that shelf over your head so I can climb across it to the passage.

Tim raised his hands above his head, felt a shelf about six inches above him, and gripped it to steady it. "Okay," he said, "I'm ready."

Tim felt the shelf wiggle a little and get heavier, then he

heard a grating sound. The noise stopped and the shelf got lighter.

"Okay, now it's your turn," said the girl's voice. "I'll stabilize the shelf while you climb up."

"All right," said Tim, finding toeholds in the stone wall and pulling himself up.

"Okay," said the girl's voice. "Now, over this way a little. You'll find the opening about one meter above the shelf. Climb up into it after me."

"Where does it go?" asked Tim.

"It is part of the ventilation system father put in to remove the stale air from this musty old place," said the girl's voice.

Tim was soon inside the vent. To his surprise, it was made of sheet metal.

"We will need to be quiet," said the girl's voice, "otherwise that woman and her guards will hear us. Follow me quietly."

"Okay," said Tim.

The girl started crawling on her hands and knees. Tim followed her. He had to scrunch down lower as the duct pipe was a little tight for him. Even then, he bumped his head several times on the inside of the pipe. They had gone about thirty-five feet when Tim heard a spooky sound. It started out low and grew louder. It was kind of a "*whoooooooooooooo*" sound. All was silent, and then it went "*whoooooooooo*" again.

"Wh-what was that?" whispered Tim.

"The ghosts," replied the girl's voice. "They always show up about this part."

"Will they get us?" Tim asked.

"*Whoooooooooooooo*," went the sound again.

"I think we should get out of here," said Tim.

"Don't worry," whispered the girl's voice. "We *are* getting out of here."

They crawled several more feet and the "*whooooooooooo*" sounded again. It seemed to rumble through much of the lower castle.

"Did you hear that?" asked one of the guards with Eva Gelb.

"What?" she asked.

"That '*whoooooo-whoooooo*' sound," said the guard.

"Probably just the train down in the valley," said Miss Gelb.

"Oh," said the guard. "Maybe I just never heard it before."

"You've worked here how many years now and you've never heard it before?" asked Miss Gelb.

"Six months," the guard replied. "And no, I've never heard it before."

"*Whoooooooooooooooooooo*," went the sound again.

"That is definitely *not* a train," said the guard. "It sounds more like a ghost."

"Don't be silly," replied Miss Gelb. "I've worked a lot of years in castles and castles do not have–."

"*Whoooooooooooooooooo*."

"Ghosts," said Miss Gelb, completing her sentence and looking around. She and the guard heard a rustling, scraping sound in the next room and rushed in to investigate. The room was totally empty, except for a grey, steel duct that went across the ceiling. Miss Gelb and the guard looked at each other and scooted back out of the room.

"*Whoooooooooooooooo*," they heard again in an eerie, distant voice. "*You must leave this place or you will become a ghost!*"

"Don't look at me, Miss Gelb, I didn't say it," said the guard.

Eva studied the hallway they were in. There was another rustling sound. "It sounded like it came from that way," she said, pointing toward a room at the far end of the stone hall. "Let's go stop the joker that's doing it."

Eva Gelb and the guard rushed over to the room to

investigate. When they got there, the room was empty. She looked at the guard. "Whatever that is, stop it," she directed.

Tim and the girl were silent until they heard Miss Gelb and the guard leave the room. It was slow going in the conduit for Tim, with light shining through small holes only so often. There was a definite draft, though, and it helped immensely with its fresh air.

"Okay, let's go," whispered the girl's voice, and they started forward once more through the duct.

Up ahead, Tim saw an area of light shining into the duct. The girl he had been following had vanished!

CHAPTER 9

Getting Help

Tim looked behind him and forward again. "There weren't any side branches," he thought. "Where did she go? And how am I going to get out of this crazy place?"

Tim started crawling faster forward to try to catch up with the girl. He soon came to a fork in the ducting. "Which way, now?" he thought out loud. "Right or left?"

Tim turned to the right and headed down the duct. He saw some light ahead and hurried toward it. When he got there, it was just a small slit of light at another junction of ducting.

Tim paused, trying to figure out which way he should go this time. As he did, he heard some scuffling behind him. He turned to look behind him but could see no one. "Was the girl a ghost girl?" The thought made him want to move very fast, so he turned to the left. The sound behind him was getting closer and it made him crawl all the faster. He turned right again, and then left. The sound was still after him!

Down in the hallway, Eva Gelb and the guard heard scuffling sounds above them and looked toward the ceiling.

"It must be big rats or something," said the guard. "The kind that jump on you when you're not looking."

"You've got a gun," said Eva Gelb, "use it!"

The guard fumbled for his weapon. By the time he had

gotten it out of its holster, the noise was gone.

"Come on," said Miss Gelb, "let's go find out what that was."

The longer Tim stayed in the ductwork, the more spooked he became. He was now crawling in hyperdrive, scooting down the pipes as fast as he could. He came to another junction, turned right without even looking back, and saw a bunch of light ahead. He reached it in no time. It was a vent louver. All he had to do was knock it out of the way and he would be free! He pushed on it with his hand, but it wouldn't come loose, so he crawled a little farther and then tried to kick it out with his foot.

"It's up there!" Tim heard Miss Gelb shout below him. Tim lunged forward and kept on going.

"Whoooooooooooooooo," Tim heard echoing down the duct.

*   *   *

Sarina led Jonathan, Kimberly, Lindy, and Robert along the base of the castle wall through the snow. Jonathan was now carrying the newly found sword still wrapped in its fabric. Sarina was eager to help her dad and sisters, so she led the small group toward one of the castle's secret passages. It was a Straunsee family secret. Knowledge of it had been kept and passed down from father to child for centuries.

They followed the foot of the wall, to stay out of view, until they came to a large bluish-gray boulder. Fifteen feet below it was a natural rock outcropping. When approached from the correct angle, a narrow slit could be seen. Sarina glanced around to make sure nobody was watching, walked up to the rock, and disappeared. Jonathan and the others quickly followed her. Once inside, they switched on their lights and followed the passage. It led slightly uphill and was narrow, only about three feet wide, and twisted and turned. They soon came to a door.

Sarina knew where the secret latch was, pushed it, and pushed the door inward. Behind the door were stairs, some made of cemented rock and others hewn out of the natural rock.

Sarina quickly led the youths up the stairs. When Kimberly's knee started to bother her again, Robert and Lindy stayed with her while Sarina and Jonathan continued up toward the Straunsee family residence. They came to a fork in the passage and Sarina turned to the right. The stairs now started to spiral upward and they came to a small room, hewn out of the rock.

"How do we get out of here?" asked Jonathan as he looked around the room. There was no door to be seen.

"Right here," said Sarina with a smile. She pushed a well-hidden button and a stone door swung open. She quickly stepped through the doorway and Jonathan did the same.

"Sarina, this is awesome," said Jonathan. "I can't believe this."

"We used to play 'sardines' in here sometimes," Sarina said with a grin. "Come on, we're almost there."

They took another flight of stairs which ended at a narrow passageway. From the dark passage, they could see into the family room and, farther on, into the dining room. Sarina looked around in the family room and seeing no one there, carefully opened a secret door. Sarina and Jonathan quickly slipped through the opening and closed the door behind them. To Jonathan's surprise, it was the same wall that Allesandra's space shovel was mounted on, beside the large rock fireplace.

"We must get this sword to my father," whispered Sarina. She and Jonathan began to search the Straunsee home. As they rounded a corner, they spied an armed guard sitting on a chair outside King Straunsee's room and jumped back out of sight.

"What's that guard doing here?" whispered Sarina.

"I don't know," Jonathan whispered back. "How can we get

past that guard to get this to your dad?"

"Let's find Katrina," Sarina said. "She can tell us what's going on."

The two youths headed for Katrina's room and carefully scoped it out. It was being guarded as well.

"We'll have to use the panel in the living room," whispered Sarina.

Sarina led Jonathan back to the living room and walked over to a wood-paneled wall that was richly covered with beautiful relief carvings of forest animals and a waterfall. She quickly pressed on the nose of a deer and a four-foot by two-foot door opened before them. Leaning forward, they stepped inside and Sarina pressed a button to close the door after them. They again switched on their lights and Sarina led the way. When she got to Katrina's room, she very softly knocked four times on another wooden panel. She repeated the four knocks and waited. There were two soft taps in reply.

"Two means safe," Sarina explained. "If there was danger, she would have used four taps. Sarina twisted a knob and the panel before them opened. Katrina was standing on the other side of the door and was holding her finger to her lips for them to be quiet.

"We saw the guard," whispered Sarina. "What's going on?"

Katrina quickly told Sarina and Jonathan about the "house arrest" their family was under.

"We found a sword," said Sarina when Katrina had finished. "We think it might be the one father was looking for."

Jonathan momentarily showed Katrina the hilt of the sword and covered it again.

"I sure hope so," said Katrina. "We've got to get it to father and still keep it out of Mr. Kreppen's hands. He's trying to take over the country."

"I never have liked that man," said Sarina. "He's always reminded me of a slimy fish."

"Have you got any food?" Jonathan asked. "I'm starving."

"Follow the passage to the left down there," said Sarina, pointing farther into the wall. "It will take you to the kitchen. Get some food for me, too," she said with a smile. "There are some triple chocolate brownies on the counter beside the refrigerator."

"*Were* some triple chocolate brownies beside the fridge. Father and I finished them off yesterday," said Katrina.

Sarina leaned over and whispered into Jonathan's ear, "I put some extra ones in the cupboard just above that. They're just behind the cookbooks. Don't let anybody see you. It's my top secret chocolate hiding place."

Jonathan turned and headed down the passage.

"What?" said Katrina.

"Oh, nothing," said Sarina with a smile. "Now hurry, I've got a plan. Here's what we're going to do..."

When Jonathan returned, he found two Sarinas in Katrina's room. Both had on the same clothes, the same hairstyle, the same shoes, the same sweet smile.

"Hi, Jonathan," both girls whispered at the same time.

Jonathan glanced at the first Sarina, then at the second Sarina, and then back to the first. "No fair," he said, "you girls are identical twins."

"That's how we're going to fake them out," said Sarina 1.

"Right," said Sarina 2 with a grin.

Jonathan looked at them both again and reached out to take Sarina 1's hand. "You're the real Sarina," he said, giving her hand a soft squeeze. She smiled warmly.

"Katrina!" whispered Sarina 2.

Sarina 1 grinned and said, "Don't listen to her."

"Katrina," said Sarina 2. "I found him first."

Jonathan let go of Sarina 1's hand and said, "We'd better get going."

Sarina 1 and 2 glanced at each other. "Sisters!" they both said at the same time. Sarina 1 kept grinning.

*   *   *

Tim scrambled along the ducting. He didn't know where he was going, but he was going there fast. Before he realized it, he had reached the end of the ducting and was sailing through the air. He landed on a single mattress in a dimly-lit, rock room. Looking up, he could see bars in the window of the room's door.

"Rats," he said, getting back up to his feet. "Another dungeon cell. I must have taken a wrong turn somewhere."

Tim pulled himself back up to the duct pipe and started back out.

*   *   *

The two girls and Jonathan quietly snuck through the adjoining family room over to King Straunsee's bedroom suite. There was no guard on duty and the door was open. Sarina carefully peeked in and found her father was gone. "Katrina, where's father?" whispered Sarina 2.

"I don't know," said Katrina. "They confined him to his room just like me. Maybe they took him to the armory to find the king-sword."

"You're probably right," whispered Jonathan. "How do we get there?"

"Follow me," said Sarina.

Sarina and Katrina led Jonathan to the escape tunnel secret

passage. After opening the door at the shovel, they ducked in and closed the door after them. They then headed down the spiral stairs and reached the place where Robert, Lindy, and Kimberly were waiting for them. Sarina led them all to the left-hand passage toward the castle armory. They came to a new fork in the tunnel.

"That one goes to the Great Hall and the carriage house," said Sarina. "This one to the right will take us to the armory. We'll need to keep our voices down from now on."

Sarina led them down the tunnel to the right and they soon came to some stone stairs.

"Better wait here," said Sarina. "I'll go ahead and look around."

Sarina slipped noiselessly up the steps and peered through a slot in the wall looking into the armory. At the far end of the room, she saw several men and women studying the swords on the racks. Her father was standing there, under guard, with them. The walls were lined with hundreds of swords and old muskets from days past.

"Come on, King Straunsee, if you will just turn over the sword to us, you and your family may go free. You have my word on it," said Mr. Kreppen.

"You and I both know that if I turn the sword over to you, my family and I will never leave this castle alive," said King Straunsee.

"Alexander," replied Mr. Kreppen, "I am not out to get you. This is no personal vendetta. I only want the sword. It will enable me to help our country more efficiently."

"Efficiently?!" replied King Straunsee. "You've already taken our country for millions through your corrupt programs!"

"I *will* have that sword," said Mr. Kreppen with a sinister look on his face, "or you will *never* see your daughters again!"

Mr. Kreppen glanced at the guard and said, "Take him back to his room!" The guard nodded. With that, Mr. Kreppen turned and stomped off.

"There must be a thousand swords in this castle," complained one of Kreppen's sword searchers. "How are we supposed to find that king-maker sword. It's like looking in a haystack for a needle."

"A thousand and ten," said King Straunsee with a grin, "but who is counting."

"I am," said the man. "Wipe that smile off your face, King Straunsee, or I'll have you help me."

"Be glad to," said King Straunsee.

"No, no, I'd better not," said the man. "I've heard you are very good with the blade."

"Inflated gossip," King Straunsee assured the man. "I am, at best, a poor student of the art. I have heard your Mr. Kreppen is quite accomplished, though."

"Yes, I am sure he could teach you a few things," said the man. "He has won many a duel."

"Oh," said the king, "then I dare not meet him in a match."

"Perhaps, then, I could arrange one," said the man with a cruel grin.

"Enough idle talk," said the guard. "Come on, Straunsee, Mr. Kreppen wants you back in your room."

The guard led King Straunsee out of the armory. Sarina watched a few moments more and then returned to her sister and the cousins. "They've taken father back to his room," she said. "I still have not seen Maria. Any idea where she might be?"

CHAPTER 10

Prisoners

"No," said Katrina. "I've been stuck in my room, too. They've jammed all of our communications so we can't reach out to anybody."

"If we can find Maria and get father, we can leave the castle and get help," said Sarina. "We might have to ski for it."

"We've got to find Tim, too," added Kimberly.

"He might be in the dungeon," said Katrina. "I overheard the guards talking about him being brought here by helicopter."

"Robert," said Jonathan, "you go with Kimberly and Katrina to find Tim and Maria. Sarina, Lindy, and I will go try to spring King Straunsee. We'll take the sword. Meet us back at the passage where we met you a few minutes ago, in half an hour."

Robert and the others nodded.

Katrina led the way toward the dungeon area. "This passage doesn't go directly to the dungeon," she explained. "That's in an isolated area. We'll have to go through the carriage room and cut across the courtyard to the dungeon stairway."

"Okay," said Robert, "Katrina, this is so cool! I've always wanted to build a secret passage at our house."

Katrina grinned.

Sarina led her group back to the Straunsee's home living quarters. They arrived after King Straunsee. Through a narrow slit near the family room, they could see two guards now standing watch at King Straunsee's room. The door was closed.

"We'll have to go by way of the window balcony," said Sarina. She led them into Katrina's room, where they exited out onto the balcony. Katrina's and their father's balconies didn't connect, so they climbed up onto a narrow ledge and started working their way along it.

"Be careful of ice," said Sarina.

"And don't look down either," added Lindy. "It's only about three hundred feet down there.

"Thanks, Lindy," said Jonathan, hanging onto the side of the castle with one hand and holding the wrapped king-sword in the other.

"About another twenty meters and we'll be there," said Sarina.

One near-fall and three strong icy wind gusts later, they made it onto the king's balcony. Sarina softly did four taps on the glass door there, waited, and tapped again. A moment later, King Straunsee appeared and let them in. He led them to a side room.

"Father, it's so good to see you," whispered Sarina, hugging her father tightly for a moment and then letting go. "They have two guards posted at your door."

"I know," said the king. "They have also jammed our communications. I have been working on a way to fry their jammer. I have just about got it."

"Father, we found this in an old mine," said Sarina, motioning toward the bundle Jonathan was holding.

Jonathan carefully unwrapped the sword and handed it to the king.

"Do you think it is the king-sword?" asked Sarina.

King Straunsee studied the hilt and then unsheathed the blade. The blade glistened. "It is of very fine workmanship," he replied. "It may be. We'd best keep it—."

The king's door suddenly burst open and three men raced into the room. Two of them had pistols drawn. "I'll take the sword," said their leader, Mr. Kreppen.

"It is not yours to take," replied King Straunsee, brandishing the sword and motioning the youths to get behind him.

"I will happily fight you on another occasion, Straunsee," said Mr. Kreppen. "But right now, my legislature and citizens await word of the king-maker sword, and you appear to have found it. *Give* me the blade or you and your young friends will go for a jump off your balcony."

"He's bluffing," said Sarina. "Don't do it, Father, he'll just use the sword to crown himself king."

"I already am king," said Mr. Kreppen arrogantly. "There are just a few mere formalities that need to take place to complete the transition."

To the chagrin and bewilderment of the teenagers, King Straunsee lowered the sword and set it down on a small table with the scabbard.

"But father," said Sarina.

"He dare not kill us yet," whispered King Straunsee. "He still needs us."

"Wise choice," said Mr. Kreppen.

Mr. Kreppen retrieved the sword, looked it over, and sheathed it. "Yes," he said confidently, "this is the king-maker sword. Amazing to think of how powerful it truly is. It is time for the announcement." Kreppen turned and said, "Guards, I appreciate your surveillance camera arrangement, you will receive extra pay. We're going to have a news conference to announce my coronation. I am the new king. Bring along the Straunsees and their friends and see that they do *not* interrupt my coronation. I want them seen but not heard."

Mr. Kreppen's two guards ordered the king, Sarina, Lindy, and Jonathan to follow Mr. Kreppen to the armory. Once there, the youths were locked in a storage room.

"Alexander, I need you a little longer," said Mr. Kreppen with a sinister smile. "You will express your support for my coronation to ensure a smooth, non-violent power transition. Once you have done that, you will be free to leave Gütenberg. If you choose not to help me, you will never see your family again. The choice is yours."

*   *   *

The snow was only falling lightly now. The roads to Straunsee Castle had been plowed. Mr. Kreppen quickly brought in more of his personal capital police force to secure his grip on the castle. Once done, he invited dignitaries and the media to come to the "Royal Castle" to witness and report on his coronation. Gütenberg was about to receive its next king and "anybody who was anybody" would want to be there.

"We're here in the Great Room of the royal castle," announced a television reporter. "According to Gütenbergian law, the king of Gütenberg is the one who has the royal sword. Today, it has been revealed that King Alexander Straunsee has no such sword in his possession. A search has been made and it turns out that our own president of the legislature, Mr. Oilee Kreppen, has the sword. Mr. Kreppen, may we see the sword, please."

"Most certainly," said Mr. Kreppen with a broad grin. "It has been in our family for a very, very long time. I only found out about the significance of it, ha-ha, today."

"Well," said the reporter, "you are indeed a very lucky man. Because of that sword, when it is fully authenticated, you will be king."

"That is something I look forward to very much," said Mr. Kreppen. "I look forward to being able to help serve the people of Gütenberg more fully. Your worries are my worries, your challenges are my challenges, your successes are my success, and your money is...I definitely look forward to helping our people."

"Yes, well, thank you, Mr. Kreppen," said the reporter. "And what is to become of the former King Straunsee and his lovely daughters?"

"The nation of Kerblatti has agreed to take them as exiles—I mean, guests," said Mr. Kreppen.

*   *   *

Katrina, Robert, and Kimberly were having problems of their own. The castle was heavily guarded, with new guards arriving every minute. The youths made it into the dungeon area just before a new set of guards was posted at the main entry door. There were also roving guards patrolling the underground halls near the cells. Try as they might, they could find no sign of Maria or Tim.

Katrina, Kimberly, and Robert were stuck in the dungeon area for quite a while. They were getting desperate when there was a sudden bustle in the courtyard that drew the door guards away. The youths used the opportunity to slip out the door and dash for the carriage room. They were almost there when one of the guards spotted them.

"Stop!" shouted the guard. "Come on," he said to a guard with him, "that looks like one of the Straunsee girls."

The two men ran after Katrina's group. "Halt!" the guard shouted.

Katrina led Kimberly and Robert around a corner and

directly for the secret passage door. They had no sooner closed the door behind them than the guards ran into the room.

"Where'd they go?" asked the first guard.

"I don't know," said the second guard, looking around. "Are you sure they came in here?"

"See those wet footprints on the floor over there?" replied the first guard.

"Yes," the second guard replied. "Let's see where they take us."

The guards followed the wet footprints. They led to an area of the floor covered with scattered straw. The first guard got down on his hands and knees to investigate. "Here's one," he said, pointing out a footprint. "And here's another. They seem to be heading toward that wall over there."

Inside the secret passageway, Katrina led the way to the rendezvous point they had agreed to meet Sarina's group at earlier. When they arrived, nobody was there.

"Something's gone wrong," said Kimberly. "Jonathan is usually very prompt."

"We're way late," said Robert.

"Yeah, but they would have left us a note or something," said Kimberly.

They waited a few minutes, left a note themselves, and set out to search for Sarina's group. They climbed the stairs to the Straunsee residence. After looking through the slits in the wall and not seeing anyone, Katrina carefully slipped out of the secret passageway to investigate further.

"Be careful," whispered Robert.

"I will," Katrina whispered back. "Thank you."

Katrina tiptoed over to the hallway and peeked around the corner. There were no guards. She carefully approached her father's room; the door was open, so she stepped in. "Father," she whispered. There was no reply. "Father," she whispered a little more loudly.

"No guards and the door is open," thought Katrina. "They've taken him somewhere."

Katrina quickly retraced her steps to the secret passage door, closed it behind her, and said, "Robert, nobody's here."

"Back at the dungeon area, I overheard one of the guards mention something about a meeting in the Great Hall," said Robert. "Maybe they've taken him there."

"Let us check," said Katrina.

*   *   *

"Sir," said a guard sitting in front of a computer screen in a black electronic surveillance van in the courtyard, "someone has just entered King Straunsee's room."

"Get some personnel over there to investigate. It may be one of his missing daughters."

"Yes sir," said the guard.

*   *   *

Katrina led Robert and Kimberly through the secret passageway toward the Great Hall.

"I'm sure glad you know where you're going," Robert said with a grin. "I could get lost in all these tunnels."

"This was part of our playground," Katrina replied.

When they got to the stairs leading up to the Great Hall, they quietly climbed them and followed the narrow tunnel inside the large stone wall. There were several well-concealed slits that enabled them to look into the Great Hall without being seen.

"There's father," whispered Katrina. "He's up at the front platform. And that imposter, Mr. Kreppen, is sitting beside him. I'm sure father is not sitting there of his own accord."

Robert walked farther along the passage to a new spying slit to try to locate Lindy, Jonathan, and Sarina. From his new vantage point, Robert could overhear two women guards talking.

"We've got those kids in the armory," said the first woman. "Mr. Kreppen says to keep them hostage there until after the coronation, then we can dispose of them."

"Okay," said the second woman. "By the way, you haven't told me what your position in the new government is going to be?"

"Oh, me? I'm going to be over *Child Protection*," the first woman replied.

Robert rushed back to Katrina and Kimberly and said, "I just overheard two guards. They're holding some 'kids' in the armory."

"It must be Sarina and Jonathan," said Katrina. "Let's go see."

Katrina quickly led Robert and Kimberly back to the fork in the passage and proceeded on toward the armory. When they got there, they carefully looked over the large room from their vantage point in the secret passage.

"I don't see them anywhere," said Kimberly. "Are you sure they said the armory?"

"Yes," said Robert. "Katrina, there's a guard standing watch at that door over there. Where does that go to?"

"It's a storage room," said Katrina.

"That must be where they're holding them," said Robert. "Does this passage go there?"

"No," said Katrina. "We just have one secret door in this

room. It's over there behind those suits of armor."

"We'll have to distract the guards," said Robert, glancing at Katrina.

"I'll make them think I'm Sarina and that I've escaped," said Katrina. "That will throw them off-balance."

"It's too dangerous," said Kimberly. "I'm sure they're armed. We'll figure out another way."

"We don't have enough time," said Katrina. "They're going to crown that creep, Kreppen, and then we'll all be killed or put in a prison somewhere. No, we've got to do something now!"

CHAPTER 11

Coronation

"Kimberly," said Robert, "Katrina and I will draw their attention so you can get over there to open that storeroom door."

Kimberly nodded and whispered, "Be careful, Robert."

"Will do, Kimbo," said Robert. "And don't worry, we'll find Tim and Maria, too."

The armory was a large, "T" shaped room. It had racks and shelves on the wall which were filled with swords, crossbows, muskets, lances, and longbows. There were free-standing racks and tables lined up in the middle of the room that held suits of armor, longbows, more swords, and many other ancient weapons. There were even a few small cannons on display.

Katrina led the youths to the secret door and silently opened it wide enough to slip through. Katrina and Robert quietly made their way to the far side of the room while Kimberly tiptoed for the storeroom.

Dropping to their hands and knees and crawling along the floor behind a longbow display rack, Robert and Katrina spied Kimberly getting into place near the storage room. Robert stopped when he saw a new guard enter the armory. At the last minute, Kimberly saw him, too, and ducked down behind a sword display case. The new guard was heading directly for

Kimberly's hiding place.

"Distraction time," whispered Robert, staying hunched over as he rose to his feet. He grabbed a longbow and hurled it toward the other side of the room. It hit a far rack, bounced off, and fell noisily to the floor.

"What was that?" called out one of the guards.

Robert grabbed another bow and threw it across the room.

"There it is again!" said a guard. "Karl, check it out."

The guard that was heading toward Kimberly's hiding place turned and headed in Robert's direction.

Robert grabbed a cannon ball and hurled it toward the opposite side of the room. It hit a tall rack and knocked it over. The swords it held went crashing and clanging to the floor. Every guard in the armory, including the one at the storage room door, rushed over to investigate.

With the guards away, Kimberly ran for the storage room door and turned its handle. It was locked.

Kimberly looked around in desperation, spied a large battle axe mounted on the wall, and tried to take it down. The axe was heavier than she expected. She lost her grip on the axe and it fell to the floor with a loud *CLANG!*

Robert grabbed another cannon ball and chucked it as hard as he could. It hit a display table and smashed through its top. The guards rushed to the area. Robert grabbed another cannon ball and readied it. He saw Kimberly raising the battle axe, getting ready to chop the door open and tried to time his next throw. As Kimberly swung downward with the axe, Robert launched the cannon ball. *SMASH!*

Kimberly swung again. Robert launched another cannon ball, this time bowling style. It rolled swiftly and hit the foot of one of the guards, bowling him over. "Get them, get them, somebody's over there!" the guard yelled.

Meanwhile, Katrina had nearly made it to the light switches when one of the guards saw her blond hair. "It's that Straunsee girl, she's escaped!" the woman shouted. "Use your billy clubs. We don't want to interfere with our new king's coronation ceremony.

Clubs in hands, the guards headed in Katrina's direction.

Katrina reached the light switches and turned them off just as Kimberly broke through the storeroom door and pulled it open. Inside, Kimberly spied Jonathan, Sarina, and Lindy just as the lights went off.

Sarina saw Kimberly hesitate. "Grab hands and follow me," Sarina whispered loudly. "I know my way in the dark."

Sarina grabbed Jonathan's hand and swiftly led the way to the secret passage door.

The guards were zeroing in on Katrina's light switch location. One of them found a flashlight and switched it on. Robert threw another lance across the room to slow them. It whooshed by one of the guards in the dark and smacked into a stack of displayed swords. The guard scrambled to get clear as the swords came crashing to the floor.

"Go help father!" Katrina shouted to the others from across the dimly-lit room.

Caught in the flashlight's beam midway across the room, Jonathan, Sarina, Lindy and Kimberly each grabbed a sword from a rack and beelined it for the secret door.

"Those kids have escaped!" shouted a guard.

Sarina reached the secret door and opened it. Kimberly, Lindy, and Jonathan followed her and closed the door behind them.

"They've got your father in the Great Room," said Kimberly. "They're trying to make him turn over the kingship."

Katrina glanced around and then dashed for the secret

tunnel door. She was halfway there when she tripped on a piece of broken shelf and went sprawling on the stone floor. Rising to her knees, she found her way blocked by a pair of boots. Looking up, she saw one of the guards, billy club in hand, menacingly looking down at her.

"Miss Straunsee," declared the guard angrily, "I do not know how you escaped but you will not escape again. He raised his arm to strike her when a resounding *CLONK!* sound filled the room.

The guard collapsed to the floor, leaving Robert standing there, still holding onto an armored knight's boot.

"Thanks," whispered Katrina with relief.

"Come on," Robert whispered, dropping the boot and pulling her up. "Let's get to the passage."

They raced for the secret door. The other guards were closing in behind them. Turning a corner, Katrina triggered the door and she and Robert fell through the opening as the door closed behind them. Seconds later, they could hear footsteps and loud voices outside.

Katrina and Robert carefully and quietly scooted down the tunnel to increase the distance between themselves and the shouting guards. After fifteen meters, they got to their feet and hurried down the passage to the Great Room.

"Thank you for your help," whispered Katrina, still catching her breath as they ran.

"Sure," said Robert, "let's go help your father."

Katrina led Robert along the passage to the Great Room. As they approached the room, they could hear the booming of loudspeakers playing the Gütenberg national anthem, the people standing to sing it, and then it grew silent.

"And now, the moment we all have been waiting for," announced a distinguished-looking man at the podium.

"Gütenberg is about to receive a new king."

Mr. Kreppen was all smiles, nodding to different heads of state and other dignitaries located on the stand and in the audience.

"Mr. Oilee Kreepen, I mean, Kreppen, would you please come to the podium with your king-sword."

Mr. Kreppen bowed and walked up to the microphone. "May I just say," he said, "that it has been a magnificent pleasure to serve you as your President of the Legislature. I now look forward to serving you as your king. We have worked together for many wonderful years and, believe me when I say, that I have many more wonderful plans on the horizon. Thank you."

The audience broke out clapping, some more enthusiastic than others. Some didn't clap at all.

"Now, Mr. Oilee Kreppen, we—."

"Excuse me," said a young man, standing up in the audience. He wore no fancy suit, but he had a sword resting horizontally across his left arm. "Excuse me," Jonathan Wright said again, making his way up to the podium. "I have the one and only, true, king-sword. Do not listen to Mr. Kreppen as his is an obvious forgery. I am the *real* king."

"What?!" said the man at the lectern.

"I have the real sword. *I* am the real king," said Jonathan matter-of-factly.

The announcer looked at Mr. Kreppen.

"Obviously a fake," said Mr. Kreppen.

"True, true," called out a young lady's voice from the other side of the room. "They are definitely *both* fakes. I have the king-sword. I am the real queen. If you will look at my sword you will find the rest are *imposters!*"

There was an audible murmur from the crowd.

"This is most unusual," said the announcer. "King

Straunsee, what do you have to say about this?"

The two guards behind King Straunsee held their guns to his back as the audience looked on. The king appeared to faint. As he did so, he fell backwards into his chair, causing it to tip backwards as well. As the king flipped over backwards, he kicked the two guards squarely in their chests. The guards sailed backwards, losing their guns as they went.

King Straunsee was on the guards before they could recover. He snatched up a gun and held them at gunpoint. "Mr. Kreppen," shouted out King Straunsee, "is a liar. He stole that sword from my family and has been holding my family hostage. Seize him!"

Several of the guards, confused, got up to arrest Mr. Kreppen.

"I am the real king," blurted out Mr. Kreppen, backing away from the podium. "Take Straunsee to the prison!"

"You are insane for power!" yelled King Straunsee.

Wild-eyed, Kreppen yelled back at King Straunsee. "I warned you about your family," he said. "Now they will pay the price for your insubordination!"

Amid gasps from the audience, Mr. Kreppen leaped down from the stand and ran for the armory room. A chair was thrown in front of King Straunsee's path and he fell hard near the podium. Kimberly and Lindy rushed over to help him.

Jonathan and Sarina raced on in pursuit of Mr. Kreppen. The audience members rose to their feet in confusion and many people got in the youths' path. Finally breaking free, the youths raced down the hallway and entered the armory. The room, still a mess, seemed deserted. As Sarina and Jonathan, swords in hand, reached the middle of the room, the door behind them closed. Turning around, they spied two of Kreppen's men.

Sarina and Jonathan took a few more steps but found their

way barred by Mr. Kreppen and two additional thugs at the far side of the room. Each had their sword drawn.

"Welcome, Princess Straunsee," said Mr. Kreppen with a sweeping, bowing gesture and a mocking grin. "I expect your father will be here soon to rescue you."

Sarina unsheathed her sword and threw its sheath clear. Jonathan, standing beside her, did the same.

"Jonathan," said Sarina under her breath, "these men are all expert swordfighters. I have seen them at the meets."

"I figured as much," Jonathan replied.

"Go get help," said Sarina.

"And leave you to face these guys alone? Not on your life," Jonathan said.

"Jonathan, they're pros," said Sarina.

"And so are you," said Jonathan. "I'm not leaving you."

"You're crazy," Sarina said.

"I know," Jonathan replied with a grin. "I feel like I'm at a track meet or something."

"A what?"

"You know, the shot put, the javelin throw," Jonathan replied.

As the three swordfighters approached threateningly, Jonathan rushed over to a rack, grabbed a lance, and threw it at Mr. Kreppen. He ducked as it whooshed by.

"I'm going to make my season record on the shot put," Jonathan said crazily as he grabbed up a cannon ball and threw it in the men's direction. It missed them but also threw them onto the defensive. Jonathan grabbed another and hurled it at them.

"Stop him!" ordered Mr. Kreppen.

The two men lunged at Jonathan. He grabbed up another lance and swung it wildly at them like a baseball or cricket bat.

They ducked. He swung again. Out of the corner of his eye, Jonathan saw Mr. Kreppen engaging Sarina in a duel. Their sword blades slashing through the air. Jonathan hit one of the men smack on the shoulder and knocked him over. Seizing the opportunity, he grabbed another cannon ball and launched it at the second man. It hit him in the stomach and knocked him backwards; his sword went flying.

One of the guards at the door rushed forward to tackle Jonathan.

"Look out!" shouted Sarina.

Jonathan turned to see the man coming and lowered his shoulder for the blow. At the last second, Jonathan dodged to the side and the man went crashing into a nearby rack. Swords and lances flew in every direction. Jonathan ran toward another rack to get more things to throw. A sword-armed guard blocked Jonathan's way from the lances and cannonballs.

Snatching up a sword, Jonathan raced for Sarina's side.

"Long time, no see," said Jonathan with a determined smile.

"Parry until you get a sure shot," Sarina directed. "They're trying to get our backs to the wall."

Mr. Kreppen and the three men kept driving Sarina and Jonathan back. Out of the corner of his eye, behind the men, Jonathan saw Katrina and Robert exit from the secret tunnel. They both grabbed longbows and headed for Mr. Kreppen and another guard, swinging as they went. **WHACK!** They hit them from behind and knocked them to the floor. The guard fell against a stack of shelves, the knights' helmets on them tumbled down upon him.

The guard regained his sword, clambered back to his feet, and turned to fight Robert and Katrina while Mr. Kreppen slithered away.

Katrina and Robert swung their longbows wildly with all

their might as the guard chopped at them. The bows shattered under the man's sword and Katrina and Robert fell back, grabbing swords as they went. They found they were no match for the man and fell back more. Robert grabbed a lance and swung it at the man. It glanced off his shoulder and lodged in a shelf. The guard knocked Katrina's sword from her hands and was closing in for the kill. Robert grabbed up a battle axe and swung wildly at the man, causing him to retreat for a moment. King Straunsee entered the far side of the room with several faithful castle guards. Kreppen's guards ran to attack them.

King Straunsee sprang into action. Grabbing a sword, he leapt upon his children's attackers. He was everywhere at once. The youths stepped back to watch his skill. He took Sarina's attacker in two thrusts, knocking the sword out of his hand and punching him to the floor. He turned to the man attacking Jonathan and did the same. The guard that had been attacking Katrina and Robert lunged at him. King Straunsee, fire in his eyes, struck the sword from his hand and plowed over him.

"Where's Kreppen?" King Straunsee shouted.

Robert saw a movement by the bowmen's rack. It was Kreppen. He had a crossbow in his arms, aimed at Katrina's heart, and he was just squeezing the trigger.

CHAPTER 12

Escape

"Look out!" Robert shouted, leaping for Katrina and knocking her down. The swift, short arrow narrowly missed her and plunged deeply into the wood paneling behind her.

King Straunsee grabbed for a dagger and threw it at Kreppen. The knife hit the crossbow, shattering it and tearing it from Kreppen's hands.

Sword in hand, King Straunsee tore after Kreppen. "You are the cause of all this evil!" he shouted. "Stop now!"

Kreppen shrieked and ran for a nearby exit, his guards fleeing after him. The power-greedy man switched on his phone and yelled into it, "Get the helicopters ready!"

Kreppen and his men raced toward the third castle tower and the heliport just beyond. King Straunsee, his two daughters, the four Wright cousins, and his loyal friends and guards tore after them. The snow was slick outside as they ran up the first flight of stairs, raced along the top of the wall and down another flight of stairs. The sound of helicopter engines running reverberated in the distance.

Kreppen glanced over his shoulder and saw King Straunsee's group pursuing him. He punched his phone. "Deploy the sharpshooters," he called out. "Tell them to fire at the second group that arrives."

"Copy," replied Eva Gelb. "I'm on my way." She quickly radioed to the head of the sharpshooters. Four men, dressed in black tactical fatigues, climbed out of one of the helicopters and took strategic places around the helipad. Through their automatic rifles' night vision scopes, they could see Kreppen's group making their way along the second walkway. They spied Straunsee's group close behind. The groups momentarily disappeared behind a castle tower.

Kreppen's group split up. Eva Gelb had just shown up and led some of Kreppen's guards toward the helicopters. Robert, Katrina, Kimberly, and several others followed Eva. Kreppen and two of his men headed for a shortcut through the castle's ballroom. Swords in hand, King Straunsee, Sarina and Jonathan raced after them.

Kreppen and his men burst through the doors of the ballroom and ducked to the side to ambush their followers. Straunsee chose another door forty feet away to enter, switched on the lights, and spied them. "Who are you waiting for, Kreppen?" he called out.

"You!" spat back Mr. Kreppen. "You've wrecked my plans, now I'll wreck you!"

"You will never threaten my family or my country again," said King Straunsee.

Kreppen and his two henchmen approached King Straunsee, Sarina, and Jonathan.

"You are no match for my skills," Kreppen said. "My men and I are the top swordfighters in the land."

"Prepare to learn from the masters," said Sarina, readying her sword.

Kreppen and his men were soon upon King Straunsee, Sarina, and Jonathan. Kreppen's group were indeed good. Kreppen fought with King Straunsee and his two guards took on Jonathan and Sarina.

Sarina's opponent eagerly approached her. Sarina assumed a defensive stance.

"Missy," said her opponent, "you are *way* out of your league."

Sarina suddenly thrust and slapped his sword hand with her sword. The man recoiled in pain and threw his sword to his other hand. "Missy," he said menacingly, "you're in way over your head. Don't mess with the big boys or you'll get yourself hurt."

"I was taught by the best," Sarina said with fire in her eyes. "Now back off or you're going to get yourself hurt. *And don't call me missy!*"

"I gave you fair warning," said the man angrily. "Now you're going to pay for your insolence." The man charged and their swordfight began.

Jonathan fought his opponent as best he could but he was overwhelmed almost from the start. If it wasn't for King Straunsee's help, he would have been finished off. The king fought furiously both Kreppen and Jonathan's attacker. With a sudden lunge, King Straunsee knocked Jonathan's attacker over and sent the man's sword sliding across the room. Jonathan raced forward and pointed his sword to the prostrate man's chest. He would make sure that the man did not get back into the fight.

Kreppen pressed his attack. King Straunsee momentarily took the defensive and then pushed back. Sarina was holding her own, but the man she was fighting had greater strength and was wearing her down. King Straunsee fought hard against Kreppen and sent him reeling back. The king took the opening and turned on Sarina's assailant. He hit him hard on the shoulder and on his arm, knocking the sword from his grasp and forcing him to the floor.

Sarina lunged and held the man captive at the point of her sword. "Thank you, Father," said Sarina, breathing heavily and wiping the perspiration from her brow.

"That's what fathers are for," replied King Straunsee.

Kreppen lunged at King Straunsee. King Straunsee dodged and engaged the famous swordfighter. Standing guard over their captives, Sarina and Jonathan watched King Straunsee and Kreppen duel.

"You are skilled," said King Straunsee, matching Kreppen blow-for-blow, "but you fight for the wrong cause."

"I *will* be king," said Kreppen, pressing the attack.

The two men fought furiously, their blades striking again and again, the clashes ringing through the air. As they fought, faithful Straunsee Castle guards and supporters started to filter into the ballroom. The fight was gaining quite an audience.

Kreppen and the king parried and thrust, both men sweating hard. Jonathan had castle guards take over their two captives and he and Sarina prepared to help King Straunsee.

"Stay back," said King Straunsee firmly. "I will finish this myself!"

King Straunsee and Kreppen fought back and forth, their blades flashing in the light of the overhead chandeliers. Kreppen was good, there was no doubt about that. But each time he thrust at King Straunsee, the king turned it back on him. Straunsee forced him back farther and farther. Finally, with a mighty stroke, King Straunsee sliced Kreppen's blade in two. Kreppen turned to flee but found his back against a wall. King Straunsee leveled his sword against Kreppen and shouted angrily, "Don't you *ever* mess with my family again!"

King Straunsee shouted to his guards, "Take this man away before he makes me finish him off!"

As his guards rushed forward, King Straunsee called out,

"Sarina, Jonathan, let us go find the young ones!"

*   *   *

Slipping and sliding, Eva Gelb and her followers ran for the helicopters. The four sharpshooters were ready to take out Gelb's pursuers. The first sharpshooter raised his rifle to take aim.

SLAM! The sharpshooter was hit on the left side of his head by a snowball. He wiped it off, quickly glanced around, and went to aim again. *SLAM!* A second snowball hit him on the right side of his face. He lowered his rifle, looking for his unseen attacker. *WHAM!* An icy snowball hit him in the face!

"What's going on?" the man called out, his voice drowned out by the whirr of the helicopter.

A second man began aiming and a snowball hit him firmly on the cheek. He turned to see where it came from and *SMACK!* He got hit in the face. He wiped the snow from his face and prepared to aim again. *WHACK!* There was a rock in it, this time. It stung like crazy.

The other men started to raise their guns and they were immediately pelted with fierce snowballs. The men started backing up toward their helicopter. "Can you see where they're coming from?" asked one of the men.

"No," replied a second man, "but imagine what they could do with bullets."

The four men immediately ran for their helicopter and climbed aboard. "Get us out of here!" The leader called out to the pilot.

"Mr. Kreppen isn't going to like this," the pilot replied.

"Who cares, just get us out of here!" said the leader.

They could now see Eva Gelb approaching, screaming at

them to stop. The pilot revved his helicopter's engine. Eva Gelb and the others raced for the second helicopter. Gelb was hit by a barrage of snowballs, these ones had rocks in them, too. She slipped, slid, and fell flat on her back. When she looked up, she found several very perturbed policemen staring her in the face.

"Well, what are you waiting for?" yelled Eva Gelb. "Help me up!"

"We don't work for you, Miss Gelb," said the closest policeman, "we've come to get you."

"What? What are you talking about? I'm with the new king. You work for me. Now, go get Straunsee before I have you thrown in jail."

"We are *Straunsee Castle* policemen," said the officer. "Your capital guard is in the dungeon."

"But I am going to be queen!" Gelb insisted furiously.

The chief policeman signaled for the helicopter pilots to shut-down their engines and all personnel to disembark. The pilots did so along with the four-member security team.

"Miss Eva Gelb," said the policeman, "you are under arrest."

The policemen lifted Miss Gelb to her feet and handcuffed her.

"Where are you taking me?" Eva Gelb demanded.

"For tonight," the policeman replied, "you'll have the special privilege of staying in the castle dungeon with your cohorts. Don't worry, you'll probably get new scenery tomorrow."

After Eva Gelb and her followers were taken away, two youths stepped out of the shadows.

"Tim!" said Kimberly.

"Maria!" said Katrina.

"Brrr, our hands are freezing from all those snowballs," said Maria. "Does anybody have a handwarmer?"

Katrina and the Wright cousins immediately rushed over

and hugged Maria and Tim as King Straunsee, Sarina, and Jonathan arrived on the scene and joined in the hug.

"Welcome back, Maria and Timothy," said King Straunsee cheerfully. "Thank goodness you are okay!"

*   *   *

Mr. Kreppen, Eva Gelb, and their followers spent the night in the cells of the Straunsee Castle dungeon. All were very eager to get out of the dungeon as they had been visited by the "ghosts" of the castle during much of the night.

Miss Eva Gelb and Mr. Oilee Kreppen, particularly had a bad night of it. It seems that when they were first introduced into the holding cell, they were confronted by a small, black and white kitty. It wasn't a kitty exactly, it was, well, more of a skunk. A very irritated one at that.

"Don't move, don't say a word," said Mr. Kreppen.

"Ah-ah-ah," said one of the guards, trying to stop a sneeze.

"Don't you dare," said Miss Gelb.

"Ah-*CHOO*!" sneezed the guard.

Miss Gelb and Mr. Kreppen held their noses, but it did no good. By the time they were retrieved from the room, they smelled so foully they had to be soaked in tomato juice before they could be whisked away in a prisoner shuttle van to Trelbloff Prison. They were put in isolated cells, of course, to protect the other prisoners. It would take several weeks for their "sweet perfume" to wear off.

The castle police got a confession out of Eva Gelb. She told them that she had discovered an old document hidden in the wall at Rhunfeld Castle. It told of a king-sword, or king-maker sword, as Mr. Kreppen called it. Kreppen used the storyline to design the successful *Sword of Smorganvue* video game. At first, the project was designed to make Rhunfeld Castle more popular as a tourist destination. Kreppen got a cut of the money from Eva. But when Kreppen realized the story might be real, he changed the game to trick people into helping him find the real sword so he could make himself king.

Gütenberg was still in a state of serious crises. According to law, its leader, the king, had to have the king-sword. To make matters worse, nobody knew what the sword actually looked like. There were a thousand and ten swords in Straunsee Castle alone. Which one was it or was it even one of them? Was it the new, velvet-wrapped sword the youths had found and Kreppen had stolen?

It was agreed the next morning, by an emergency session of the legislative and judicial branches of government, that King Alexander Straunsee should stay on, at least until the king-sword and its owner were found.

The capital guards were removed from Straunsee Castle, their status to be determined later. The castle police force and guards, released from the dungeons, helped to clean-up the armory and made sure the threats from Mr. Kreppen and his group were countered and stopped. Everybody pitched in.

"We've still got a dilemma," said Mr. Gervar, the octogenarian and keeper of the castle's ancient records, late that afternoon in the Straunsee home. "Until that sword is found, there is not going to be peace in Gütenberg."

"Nor at this castle," said King Straunsee's chief of castle guard.

"I have been unsuccessful in finding the king-sword," said King Straunsee, "what would you suggest?"

In the next room, Sarina, Katrina, Maria, and the five Wright cousins were all ears.

It was silent for the moment and Mr. Gervar spoke up.

"There was something in the records your Sarina brought me about the king-sword," he said. "They give a description of the sword but I have seen none like it." Mr. Gervar took a piece of paper and pencil from his binder and began to sketch. "It has a scabbard like thus," he said. "The hilt is rounded here at this point in a most distinct way, like this. There are engravings here and here. It was used in the battle of Trepid-smorf."

"Can we see, too?" asked Sarina, entering the room.

"Certainly," said King Straunsee. "The more help, the better."

The youths gathered around to look at the drawings. Lindy's eyes widened. "Hey, wait a minute," she said, "that looks kind of like the rusted sword I found down near the mountain tunnel. It has a handle like that and there's some engraving on it, too."

"Do you still have it?" asked King Straunsee.

"Yes," replied Lindy. "It's in my backpack in my room. I'll go get it!"

Lindy raced off to get the sword. When she got to the room, she dug under her bed and pulled out the backpack she had used several days before. The sword was gone!

Then Lindy remembered she had set it in a corner of the closet. She pulled back a travel bag and there, leaning against the corner, was the sword. It was a rusty, beat up old sword, but it was a beautiful sight.

Lindy retrieved the sword and ran back to where the other cousins and the Straunsees were. She handed the sword to King Straunsee. The king and Mr. Gervar took the sword over to the light and studied it. The Straunsee girls and the Wright cousins watched, too.

"See, there's some writing," Lindy pointed out.

Mr. Gervar cleaned the sword with a damp washcloth and

said, "There does seem to be some engraving here. Let's see." He paused a moment and said excitedly. "Look here, Alexander, it talks about the bearer of the sword. 'He who bears this sword defeated the Trunnelts at Trepid-smorf. He is king."

King Straunsee suddenly had a tough time speaking. He cleared his throat and handed the sword to Lindy. "You are the bearer of the sword," he said. "You now have the throne. It makes you Queen of Gütenberg."

"Me, Queen of Gütenberg? I...wow...me, queen?" said Lindy, blushing. "I'm no queen. I don't even have any royal ancestors."

"What about me?" said Tim. "I have a twin sister that's a princess, I think?"

"Tim, stay out of this," said Kimberly. "Show respect for Queen Lindy."

"Queen Lindy?" said Tim. "But she's just our cousin."

Wide-eyed and with a surprised grin, Lindy glanced at each of the cousins, at Katrina, Sarina, Mr. Gervar, the police chief, and finally back at King Alexander Straunsee. "King Straunsee," she began, "you're the real king. This sword doesn't make you a king. That's who you are inside. I would never want to take that away from you."

Lindy handed the sword back to King Straunsee, who smiled gratefully.

"There is more to you of true nobility than you realize," said the king. He looked at the sword, turning it over in his hands, studying its features. "Could it be the same?" he wondered aloud. The hilt was badly weathered, the broken blade rusty. He froze when he saw the familiar inscription on the handguard: "To Charlotte Sutherlee, with all my heart, Alexander."

"Father," said Sarina, pointing toward the hilt, "why does it have mother's name on it?"

"Because it is the sword of a queen," King Straunsee said

with moist eyes. "I gave it to your mother as an engagement present when we were to be married. It had been in our family for generations. She always did enjoy practicing our fencing on the castle wall, just as you and Jonathan."

"That's why you were so worried about my sword," said Sarina. "You lost this one over the wall, too, didn't you, Father?"

"Yes," said King Straunsee. "It was starting to rain. Your mother wanted to just practice five minutes more. I accidentally knocked the sword from her hand. We never found it, until now."

King Straunsee glanced up warm-heartedly at Lindy. "Thank you, Miss Lindy Wright," he said. "For restoring the sword of Sutherlee. I, my family, and our country owe you much."

"You're very welcome, Your Majesty," said Lindy with a blushing smile. "Keep fighting the good fight."

CHAPTER 13

Snowmen

Maria slept soundly through the night. Her sisters, Katrina and Sarina, accused her of snoring sometimes, but she didn't that night. She was too tired. She woke up bright and early the next morning and knocked on Katrina's door. "I'm hungry," she said.

"There's cereal in the cupboard," said Katrina.

"Do we have any Crunchy Pops?" asked Maria.

"I don't know," Katrina replied. "I'll be up in a little while. I need to get some more sleep."

Maria next knocked on Sarina's door and walked in. "Do you want to eat breakfast with me?" asked Maria.

"What?" said Sarina. "Maybe later." She rolled over and went back to sleep, too.

Maria next knocked on Lindy's door. "Hi," she said. "Want to eat some breakfast?"

"Sure, Maria," said Lindy with a waking-up smile. "Give me a minute and I'll get dressed."

Lindy quickly slipped on her day clothes and followed Maria over to the kitchen. On the way, Maria told Lindy about how she and Tim had met in the dungeon and the fun they had had haunting the Kreppen guards and Miss Gelb there.

"You should have heard them run," said Maria. "I haven't

had that much fun since I don't know when. Do you have a twin brother?"

"Yes," Lindy said. "His name is Robert."

"Oh, *Robert*," said Maria. "My sister has told me about him." She clapped her hand over her mouth. "Oh, please forget I said that. Sometimes I spill the beans too much."

"Maria?" said Lindy, looking at her curiously. "Why do I get this crazy feeling...you remind me of someone."

When Sarina, Katrina, and the other Wright cousins got up, they ate a hearty breakfast and went out on the balcony to take in the beautiful, snowy mountain scenery. It was cold enough to see their breath.

Katrina asked Lindy to follow her back into the family room. "So, Lindy," she said curiously, "please tell me about Robert. What's he like?"

The question took Lindy by surprise. "Well," she said matter-of-factly, "he's kind of a smart, sensitive guy. Pretty easy going, fun, you know how twins are. He's a good buddy."

"Is he a good guy?" asked Katrina.

"Nobody better," Lindy said with a smile. "Why do you ask?"

"Oh, nothing," said Katrina. "He just seems really nice."

"He is," said Lindy. "He's a good, decent, smart, nice guy." She leaned over to Katrina and whispered, "Would you like his email address?"

"Thanks, I've already got it," Katrina replied with a grin. "He was on Jonathan's 'sender' list."

"You do have competition, you know," Lindy said. "Marci Franklin likes him, too."

"I know," Katrina replied. "We'll see how it goes. I mean, we're still in high school and all. A lot can happen in the next several years. But he seems like a really good guy."

Maria opened the porch door and stuck her head in.

"Katrina and Lindy," she said, "Jonathan and Sarina have invited us all to go out and build snowmen. Want to come?"

"Sure," said Katrina, "let's go."

The youths bundled up in warm snow clothes and went out into the courtyard to play in the snow. They had a wonderful time building snowmen, snow dogs, and snow cats. Tim even built a snow spaceship. He was putting a tail fin on it when he accidentally knocked over Maria and Katrina's snowgirl. From then on, it was a running snowball fight with Tim, Kimberly, Jonathan and Sarina on one side, and Maria, Katrina, Lindy and Robert on the other. By the time they were done, not a single snow sculpture was left standing and the youths were soaked from head-to-toe.

"Welp, Sarina," said Jonathan with a grin, "there's only one remedy for this."

"What's that?" asked Sarina.

"Let's go build a smooshy-smooshy snowman!"

"Mush!" said Tim, and he fell over in the snow.

CHAPTER 14

Tim Meets His Match?

A few mornings later, the Wright cousins were leaving for America. They packed their bags and thanked the Straunsees profusely for their kindness and generosity. The Straunsees thanked the Wrights for their vital help in stabilizing their country's government.

"And a very special thanks to you again, Queen Lindy," said King Straunsee.

Lindy blushed and said, "You're welcome, your Majesty."

As Robert and Katrina hugged, she thanked him again for protecting her from Mr. Kreppen and the others.

It was a tearful good-bye for Sarina and Jonathan. "We'll see you again, soon," said Jonathan with an affectionate grin. "You just take good care of yourself, you hear?"

"I will, my friend," Sarina said, giving him an extra squeeze.

Sarina noticed that Maria and Tim didn't hug each other good-bye. "Well, Maria," she whispered, "at least shake his hand."

"Come on, Tim," said Jonathan, "at least shake hands with Maria."

Tim and Maria both reached out to shake the other's hand but pulled back. "Cooties!" they said at the same time.

"No way!" said Tim.

"Yes, you do," said Maria. "You have cooties so bad it makes the sidewalks crunch."

"I do not," said Tim, caught off-guard. "Only girls have cooties."

"We do not," said Maria adamantly. "Tim Wrights have cooties."

"Maria Straunsees do so have cooties. Just ask my sister, Kimberly," said Tim.

"I said no such thing," said Kimberly. "Tim, you keep me out of this."

Jonathan stepped up beside Tim and Sarina stepped up beside Maria. "You must shake hands," they both said.

"Us?" said Maria and Tim.

"Yes. The Wrights cannot leave until you shake hands," said Sarina. "Wait a minute," she added with a grin, "that's not all that bad."

"Stare match," said Maria. "The one who blinks first, has to shake hands first."

"I'm in," said Tim, taking up the challenge. "Ready, go!"

The older youths watched as Tim and Maria started their staring contest.

"My sister watches too many movies," said Sarina.

"Tim plays too many video games," said Jonathan.

Thirty seconds, a minute, ninety seconds, two minutes. Tim and Maria's eyes were beginning to get itchy and burny but neither would give in. A fly landed on Tim's nose; he still refused to blink. Maria took a deep breath and blew into Tim's eyes. Tim blinked.

"I won!" said Maria. "I won. Nanny nanny nanny goose!"

"No fair. You can't call nanny nanny nanny goose unless you're holding your breath," said Tim.

"Enough," said Kimberly. "Tim, now you shake her hand or

else I'll call Mom to have you *hug* Maria good-bye."

"You wouldn't," said Tim.

"Oh yes I would," said Kimberly, pulling her phone out of her back pocket.

"Okay, okay," said Tim. "If you're going to use the nuclear option, I'll...shake hands."

Tim extended his hand toward Maria and they both reluctantly shook hands. Kimberly and Sarina both snapped pictures with their phones.

"No fair," said Tim, glancing momentarily at Maria. "We've been set up!"

"Don't I know it," Maria replied. "What would you suggest, twin brother dear?"

"Arrgh, *sisters!*" said Tim.

The SECRET of TRIFID CASTLE

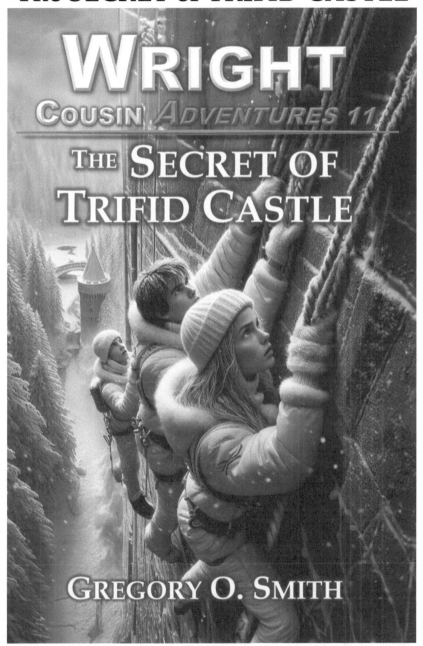

GREGORY O. SMITH

"Finally," said Kimberly, "Timothy Wright wasn't able to sneak his spy guys on our new front cover!"

"But what about the smiley faces?" Lindy replied. "And the helicopter?"

"That helicopter *does* look awfully familiar," said Kimberly. "Do you think it means something?"

"Do the names *Kimosoggy* and *Toronto* mean anything to you?" said Lindy.

Kimberly's eyes grew wide. "We're in *big* trouble!"

The SECRET of
TRIFID CASTLE

The SECRET of TRIFID CASTLE

Gregory O. Smith

Dedication

This book is dedicated to children, youth, and adults who
like mystery, adventure, and spy stuff. *Have fun!*
And, to my patient editors, Lisa Smith, Anne R. Smith,
and Dorothy Smith

Author's Note

Writing a book is always a big learning
experience for me, both technologically and
people-wise. Just when I think I've got Tim
and the Wright cousins figured out, they say or do something
that totally surprises me. *The Secret of Trifid Castle* is no
exception.

Keep an eye out for Robert and Tim's new glasses, Mr.
Gervar, and GearSpy1. If only we'd had GearSpy1 around when
I was a kid, playing hide-and-seek would have been a whole new
adventure!

Good luck and have a blast with the Wright cousins as they
work to discover *THE SECRET OF TRIFID CASTLE!*

~ Gregory O. Smith

CHAPTER 1

Plane Trouble

After saying good-bye to the Straunsee family in Gütenberg, the five Wright cousins spent a week visiting some of the beautiful countries of eastern Europe. They especially liked the amazing mountains and the common peoples' kindness. The Wright cousins checked their luggage in at the airport and boarded an airliner for their flight back to America.

"It'll be nice to finally get back home and unpack," said Robert as the cousins stepped onto the plane.

"Yes, and isn't it great to know that there are good, decent people all over the world," said his seventeen-year-old, twin sister, Lindy.

"That's for sure," agreed Robert, patting his stomach, "and good food, too. I wish we could take more of their bread and sausage with us."

"Mom said on the phone that she has a homemade peach pie waiting for us when we get back," said Lindy.

"Did she mention vanilla ice cream, too?" asked Robert.

"Yes, I believe she did," Lindy replied with a smile.

"Well, what are we waiting for?" Robert said with a grin. "Let's get home!"

The cousins found their assigned seats and sat down. Robert and his two cousins, Jonathan and Tim, sat together. Lindy and her cousin, Kimberly, were in the row in front of them.

"I can't wait to check out the B-17 and B-24 airplane projects," said Jonathan. "I'm sure looking forward to actually being able to fly them."

"Me too," said fourteen-year-old Tim.

"Not until after you're twenty, no, make that twenty-five," said Kimberly, leaning back in her seat. "It's too dangerous."

"Aw, Kimberly," Tim replied, "I got the spaceplane down safely, didn't I?"

"Yeah, and I still don't know how you pulled that one off," said Kimberly.

"Pure skill and talent," said Tim with a playful smile.

The passengers were instructed to put on their seatbelts and the plane began to taxi out onto the runway. Tim glanced out the window and spied several other planes around the airport. Some were propeller driven and others were jet aircraft. He could see some of the repair and maintenance hangars on the far side of the runway.

"Hold on, Tim, here we go," said Kimberly, her knuckles growing white as she gripped the armrests tightly.

"Take-off is my favorite part; you can really feel the power of the engines," Tim replied, noting that Kimberly was getting a little uptight. "Aw, Kimberly, don't' worry about it. Just imagine you're on that new rollercoaster ride back home. Oh, wait a minute, you didn't do so well on that one. Well, just close your eyes and go to sleep. I'll wake you up when we're up at about 20,000 feet."

"Sleep?" said Kimberly. "Like I'm really going to be able to do that."

The plane lifted off the ground and banked toward the west

in a long turn. "USA, here we come!" said Tim. "Kimberly, why are you turning green?"

The cousins were soon over high, snow-covered mountains. They could see ice covered lakes far below. The plane was headed into a snowstorm.

"Please keep your seatbelts on and return your seats to their upright positions," announced a stewardess. "We may experience some turbulence."

In the cockpit of the airliner, the two pilots eyed their instrument panels. Instructions had just come over the radio for them to proceed to Cidronfeld Airport.

"Copy," said the pilot. "Would you please repeat that again?"

"Proceed to Cidronfeld," the voice repeated.

"That is not in our flight plan," said the pilot.

"There is an especially dangerous storm building over the western mountains. Proceed to Cidronfeld. We have already notified them to expect you."

The pilot and his co-pilot glanced at each other. "Cidronfeld it is," replied the pilot. "We're going to have a lot of unhappy passengers on our hands."

"Better safe than sorry," said the controller.

After alerting the flight crew, the pilot made the announcement over the plane's intercom. There was much grumbling amongst the passengers.

"Cidronfeld?" said Tim. "Where's that?"

Kimberly quickly looked it up on her phone and said, "It's in the country of Gütenberg."

All eyes immediately went to Jonathan. Jonathan's girlfriend, Sarina, lived there. Her father, His Royal Majesty Alexander Straunsee, was the king of Gütenberg.

"Don't look at me, guys," said Jonathan with a growing grin, "I didn't do it."

"Sure," said Tim. "and I thought we had left all that mushy stuff behind."

"Me too," said Robert. "And I was looking forward to my mom's homemade peach pie with ice cream."

"The pilot said it was due to a fierce storm," said Kimberly.

"Yeah," teased Tim. "Jonathan's broken heart for having to be away from Sarina."

"I think Tim did it so he could see Maria again," countered Jonathan.

"No way," Tim replied. "Wait a minute, maybe Robert wants to see Katrina again. Oooooooo, Katrina."

"She might like me, but that doesn't mean I like her...more than, well, regular," Robert replied.

"Oooooooo, regular," teased Tim.

"Tim, you are such a nut," said Kimberly.

The plane hit turbulence and began to shake. The cousins looked outside to see the wings flapping up and down.

"Look at that, Kimberly," said Tim. "This plane flies like a duck."

"That's not very funny, Tim," Kimberly replied, holding onto her seat and starting to turn green again. "I don't like this turbulence stuff."

"Just ignore it," said Tim. "It's not like the wing is going to fall off or something. Wait, Kimberly, did you see that? Part of the wing flap just cracked!"

"That's not funny," Kimberly replied, holding onto her seatbelt.

"Oh my goodness, a big piece of the wing just broke off," said Tim.

"That was ice," said Robert. "Our wings are starting to ice up. The de-icers must not be working. The ice wrecks the airfoil efficiency of the wings because the airflow changes. They'll have to take us down to a lower elevation to melt off more of the ice."

True to Robert's prediction, the pilots soon descended to a lower altitude. After several minutes there, large chunks of ice began peeling off the wings.

"Ladies and gentlemen," said the pilot's voice over the speakers. "You will note that the seatbelt light is still on. Please remain seated. We will be arriving at Cidronfeld Airport in about twenty-five minutes. We thank you for flying with Transbergian Airlines today. We wish you a pleasant stay in Gütenberg. For those of you who will be traveling on to other destinations, the airlines is working on your connecting flights."

"That means everybody," said Kimberly. "Cidronfeld wasn't a scheduled stop on our flight."

"Well, maybe we could do a little sightseeing in Gütenberg," suggested Jonathan with a smile. "Maybe even visit Straunsee Castle or something."

"Tim," said Kimberly, "do me a favor: roll up the airline magazine in front of you and bop Jonathan on the head."

"Really?" said Tim, quickly grabbing up a magazine.

"Hey, wait a minute," said Jonathan. "I was just kidding."

"Sure," replied Tim.

There was snow covering the ground as their plane touched down. Everyone disembarked from the plane as ground crews arrived to investigate the de-icing boot problems. The cousins were directed to the Transbergian Airlines booth to complete their flight re-routing plans. While waiting in line, the cousins watched national and international news on wall-mounted television screens. On one of the screens, there was a lady reporter, speaking in Gütenbergian.

"Robert, what's she saying?" asked Tim.

"She's saying that a small plane crashed this morning near Veilet Lake," Robert replied.

The screen switched to another reporter. "What's he talking about?" asked Tim.

"There's been a four-alarm fire in an office building at the capital," said Robert.

"Wow," Tim asked, "I wonder how it started?"

"The reporter says they believe it was arson," Robert replied.

The next scene showed a reporter talking with a family who had recently built a seven-foot-tall igloo in their backyard.

"What's that?" asked Tim, staring at the screen.

"The children have been studying wilderness survival in school and their family is going to sleep overnight in their igloo. The mother isn't so sure about it, but all the kids are excited."

"How do you know their language so well?" said Tim, still staring at the screen.

"From our last visit," said Robert.

"Boy, you must have talked with Katrina a whole lot," said Tim, looking at him for a moment.

"Well, actually," said Robert, "they have captions in English at the bottom of the screen. Read it for yourself."

"Oh," said Tim, "I thought those were just stock market things."

The picture switched to a man standing in front of the Legislative building in the Gütenbergian capital of Alpenglow. His manner seemed upset.

"We have just received reports that there is a faction in the capital—about one-third of the legislators and half of the lower judges—who are rebelling against King Straunsee's leadership. The rebels want to change the law to make the President of the Legislature, the Honorable Mr. Oilee Kreppen, the new king of Gütenberg. There are angry protesters both in and outside the capital building, shouting and threatening that if they don't get their way, they will appeal to a foreign military power to forcefully put Mr. Kreppen on the throne. In other news, the whereabouts of His Royal Majesty, King Alexander Straunsee, and his family is still a mystery. Rumors are flying that the king is off skiing somewhere. King Straunsee, come home, your country needs you! Where are you in this time of national danger?"

Jaws dropped. The cousins looked at each other.

"What?" said Jonathan. "We just saw the Straunsees a week ago."

"How did Kreppen get out of jail?" asked Kimberly. "We had him cold. He was sent to prison with Eva Gelb and all the others who threatened King Straunsee and his family during our *Sword of Sutherlee* adventure."

"Forget the plane tickets home," said Jonathan. "We've got to find out what's going on here. Sarina and her family need our help!"

CHAPTER 2

Straunsee Castle

The Wright cousins stepped to the side and held a quick planning huddle. They decided to rent a car and drive to Straunsee Castle to see what they could do to help. Having faced Mr. Kreppen previously, they knew it would not be an easy task. Kreppen was power-hungry and ruthless.

The Wright cousins found a car rental agency at the airport and studied their options. The man at the desk enthusiastically steered them toward a white, 4-wheel-drive SUV. He *insisted* it was the right car for them. They could not leave without it. Tim liked the car because it had cool-looking, big tires. It also seemed to have all the latest electronic gadgets and then some.

The cousins were just loading their luggage aboard their newly rented SUV when a hostess from the airlines came dashing in. "Oh, I'm so glad I caught you," she said. "You forgot some of your luggage."

The cousins took one look at the two briefcases she was carrying and told her they weren't theirs.

"Aren't you the Wrights?" she asked, glancing down at the tags on the two cases. "This one says it belongs to Robert Wright and this one says Tim Wright. Which of you is Robert and which of you is Tim?"

"I am," said Robert and Tim at the same time.

"Well, here, please take your luggage," said the hostess with an encouraging smile and holding out the two briefcases toward the boys.

Robert and Tim each took a briefcase and began to look them over.

"These aren't ours," said Robert, looking up. "We didn't have any luggage like this."

"Is that your name and address listed on the tag?" asked the woman with a determined smile.

Robert looked at the tag. It did have his name and address on it, in his writing, no less. "Yes," he replied. "That's my information."

"And yours?" smiled the hostess, looking at Tim.

"Yes," said Tim, looking a little embarrassed.

"It's nice to meet you both. Please take your luggage with you. Believe me," the hostess said with a relieved smile, "the last thing we need around here is more luggage."

The hostess quickly turned and left.

"Tim, did you and Robert buy some new luggage without us knowing it?" asked Kimberly after the woman was gone.

"Not that I remember," said Tim.

"Just put them in the car and we'll figure it out later," said Jonathan as they packed the rest of their luggage into the SUV.

Before leaving Cidronfeld, the Wright cousins purchased food and other supplies. They ate as they drove, completely forgetting about the two briefcases. The SUV's studded tires handled the snowy roads very well. They arrived at the castle within two hours and found it occupied.

"Welcome back," said the guard at the castle gate, recognizing the cousins.

"Have the Straunsees returned?" asked Jonathan.

"No, we haven't heard a word from them," the guard replied. The guard opened the gate and the cousins drove on into the castle courtyard.

When the cousins knocked on the front door of the Straunsee residence, they were greeted by a maid. She welcomed them in, also recognizing them from their previous visit.

Aside from the maid, the Straunsee home was very quiet. Too quiet. To the cousins, it felt strange walking into the Straunsee home and not seeing the smiling faces of Sarina, Katrina, Maria, and King Straunsee. The maid told them that the Straunsee family had disappeared. Nobody had seen them for over three days. She also told them that Mr. Kreppen and his followers had been released from prison, on bail, by a judge the week before. The maid took pride in the fact that Kreppen "had not dared come near the castle since his release."

"Why, if I ever saw that criminal again," said the woman, "I'd let him know what was what!"

"Where is Kreppen now?" asked Jonathan.

"He and his other crumazoids are raising trouble at the capital," the maid replied.

"Boy, we leave and everything falls apart," Tim whispered to Robert.

"Yes," Robert whispered back, "I thought Kreppen was in cold storage for good."

"It's lonely around here without the Straunsees," said the maid. "Would you like a snack or anything?"

"Thank you very much but we've already eaten," said Jonathan, speaking for the cousins. "Any idea where the Straunsees may have gone?"

"None," said the maid. "But I hope they come back soon. I miss them already."

The Wright cousins left the Straunsee's residence and quickly walked through the courtyard to visit with Mr. Gervar, the octogenarian record keeper of the castle, in his office.

"Welcome back," said Mr. Gervar, looking up from the large, old architectural drawings he had spread out across a table.

"Hi," replied the cousins, walking over to Mr. Gervar.

"What are you doing?" Tim asked.

"Oh, just looking at some old castle plans," said Mr. Gervar. "I'm trying to preserve them for future generations."

"We want to help the Straunsees," said Jonathan. "Do you know where they are?"

"The whole kingdom is looking for them," said Mr. Gervar. "I'm sorry, but I cannot help you. These are hard times in Gütenberg. I recommend you leave for America before you get caught up in our struggles."

"We're already caught up," said Jonathan. "We want to help the Straunsees."

"Take the next plane and leave," said Mr. Gervar. He paused for a moment, his brow wrinkling. "I can only tell you this, because you are their friends," he continued, "some of the Straunsee girls are safe. I do not know where King Straunsee is. That is all I can tell you. Now go!"

"Thank you, Mr. Gervar," said Jonathan. "We will take your advice as soon as we can."

The cousins were almost to the front door when Mr. Gervar called them back. "There's something you may be able to do," he said. "Alexander once told me your parents are communications experts. This Kreppen fellow has a lot of money behind him. *Stop the money, and you will stop Kreppen.*"

"How do we do that?" asked Robert.

"Communications," replied Mr. Gervar. "If you can find out who's supplying the money, shut them down or get them mad at Kreppen."

"Divide and conquer?" said Robert.

"Yes," said Mr. Gervar. "That's the strategy King Straunsee's great-grandfather used at the battle of Giller-smorf. He was totally outnumbered, so he sent spies to cause distrust among the invading armies. They got them so mad that they wound up attacking each other instead of Straunsee's army." Mr. Gervar noted that Lindy was studying the drawings and said, "Well, if you will excuse me, I need to put these drawings back away."

Mr. Gervar carefully but quickly gathered up the drawings, carried them over to a tall, dark green cabinet, and laid them flat in a wide drawer. He closed and locked the drawer. As he did so, he saw someone peering in a side window.

"Kids," Mr. Gervar said, "I must make some phone calls."

"Oh, sure, thanks, Mr. Gervar," said Jonathan. "We've got to be going, anyway."

"Keep the Straunsees in your prayers," said Mr. Gervar. "These are hard times for their family. They and our country really need help."

"We will," said Jonathan. "And if you come across anything else we can do, please let us know."

The five cousins said good-bye and walked out of the old archives room. They talked briefly in the snowy courtyard near their car.

"Jonathan, what do you think Mr. Gervar is up to?" asked Kimberly.

"What do you mean?"

"Well, he's worried," continued Kimberly. "It was written all over his face."

"I didn't see any words on his face," said Tim.

"I didn't mean *written* written," Kimberly replied. "I meant his mannerisms, body language."

"Like shaving cream and a moustache," said Tim.

Kimberly scrunched her nose at him.

"I think Mr. Gervar knows where the Straunsees are," said Jonathan, "but he is probably afraid it might endanger them if he tells us anything more."

"I think the Straunsee girls are still here," said Lindy. "Some of those plans Mr. Gervar had out were for this castle. I got a good look at them."

"Really?" said Robert, grateful for his twin sister's photographic memory.

"Yes," said Lindy. "The plans..." Lindy closed her eyes for a moment to concentrate. "The architect's inscription mentioned an underground addition to the castle back in the mid-1930s."

"Before World War 2?" said Robert.

"Yes. They built a special place under this castle to protect the royal family," continued Lindy. "It connects to the secret passages."

"Then why didn't we see it when we were here before?" asked Tim.

"We weren't looking for it," Lindy replied.

"We can use the secret door to the passages in the old carriage house Katrina showed us two weeks ago," said Robert.

"Well what are we waiting for?" Jonathan said. "Let's get going!"

The cousins hurried over to the carriage house and after a bit of trouble, located the well-hidden secret door there. Triggering its concealed latch, they pushed it open, switched on their lights, and ducked through the low portal into the tunnel.

"It's darker in here than I remember," said Kimberly as they closed the door behind them.

"Secret passages are always dark," said Tim. "And a little bit spooky."

"Tim, now is not the time to start with the spooky stuff," Kimberly replied.

"Yeah, but you know how it is. The monsters always like to hide and get you in the secret passageways," said Tim.

"Timothy Wright, you know as well as I do that there's no such thing as monsters," Kimberly replied, looking around herself a bit uneasily.

"Oh yeah? Then what's that thing over there?" asked Tim, pointing at a dark shape farther down the tunnel.

Kimberly quickly shined her light. "It's—it's just a—Timothy Wright, you stop that. You know it's just a rock!"

"Lindy," said Jonathan, "you lead the way. You remember the plans better than the rest of us."

"I think we should let Tim take the lead," suggested Kimberly.

"No, it's okay, really, I don't mind," Tim said quickly. "Lindy will do a great job."

Lindy set out in the lead. The tunnel was tall enough to stand in without hitting their heads. It led them toward the end of the castle where the Straunsees lived. They came to a fork in the tunnel. Remembering the drawings, Lindy took the right fork. She led them another fifty feet and paused. "It should be right around here," she said.

Lindy closed her eyes and focused on the picture in her mind. "It will be on that wall over there," she said, pointing to the opposite side.

The cousins started examining the solid rock wall. "I don't see anything," said Tim. "Are you sure it's this side?"

"Tim, it's Lindy," Robert said. "She never forgets."

"Oh yeah," said Tim, kicking the base of the wall, "but this rock's as solid as a—."

Tim never finished his sentence. There was a scraping sound as a hidden door swung inward, revealing a new, dark passageway. Tim scooted back from the opening. "Here,

Kimberly," he said with some trepidation, "you can go first."

"No, really, that's okay," Kimberly replied. "I'm good."

After shining their lights around the inside of the new tunnel, Jonathan led the cousins into it. The tunnel continued for twenty-five feet and ended abruptly at a strong, steel door set in place with concrete. It looked very old and dusty.

The cousins examined the door but they couldn't see any way to open it. Tim leaned against the wall on the right. As he did so, a loud buzzer sounded.

Surprised, Tim quickly pulled back his arm. He looked closer and found a button hidden in the wall. He pushed on it and the buzzer sounded again. "Hey, this is fun," he said, pushing the button several times more. *BUZZ! BUZZ! BUZZ!*

"Tim, you stop that!" said Kimberly.

BUZZ! BUZZ!

Kimberly finally had to pull Tim's hand away from the button to stop him.

A moment later, the cousins heard a clicking sound and the steel door swung open inward, away from them. As it did so, bright light poured into the passage the cousins were in, momentarily blinding them.

"Maria?" said Tim, shielding his eyes.

CHAPTER 3

Lights

"Hurry in, twin brother," Maria said with a smile. "Mrs. Olsen, my chaperone, says I'm not supposed to open this door but I saw you through the peep hole and knew it was you guys."

Ever since Tim had first met thirteen-year-old Maria, she had called him her "twin brother." Nobody knew why. It was a mystery.

The cousins quickly slipped past the massive, foot-thick steel door and into the light beyond. They found themselves in a narrow, well-lit hallway.

"I'm so glad you've come," said Maria, her eyes suddenly tearing-up and her voice faltering. She hurriedly closed the steel door behind them. "Do you know where my father or sisters are?"

"They're not here?" asked Jonathan.

"No," Maria replied. "Just the Olsens and me. Father left a message for us to stay down here."

Lindy hugged Maria. "It's going to be okay," she said, patting her on the back. "We're here to help."

"Thank you," said Maria, wiping her eyes and taking a deep breath. "Let me show you around our family bunker."

"Bunker?" said Tim, his eyes lighting up, "Cool!"

Maria led the cousins into the living room and introduced

the Wright cousins to her chaperones, Mrs. Maren Olsen and her husband, Olaf Olsen. Mrs. Olsen remembered the Wrights from when they had rescued Sarina Straunsee at Fort Courage. She welcomed them graciously.

"Now," said Mrs. Olsen, "we have more people. During times like this, more is better."

Maria showed the Wright cousins around the bunker. Deep underground, built in solid rock, it had no windows to let in natural sunlight. Its lights and filtered air circulation system used electricity from the castle. If that failed, there were back-up generators and battery power. The bunker had a finely designed, comfortable living room, family room, kitchen, bedrooms, bathrooms, exercise room, large storerooms of food and water, and more. It also had an extremely complete, futuristic audio-visual communications room. Robert and Jonathan studied the equipment with great interest. One of the large video screens had an interactive map of Gütenberg. There were a few green lights blinking in various parts of the country. One of the green lights changed, blinking yellow every few seconds.

"Boy, our parents would have a hay-day with this," said Robert.

"What's that over there?" asked Tim, looking back through the doorway and down the hall.

"That's our little theater," said Maria. "Would you like to see it?"

"Sure, I guess,' said Tim. "Come on, Robert."

Maria led Tim, Robert, and the other cousins to the theater room. As they entered, they spied numerous chairs, tables, and couches. There was a large screen at the far end of the room.

"We get a whole lot of cartoons," said Maria. "Twenty-four hours a day if we want."

"Really?" said Tim, obviously impressed. "Wow, when can

we start?"

"Wait a minute, Tim," said Jonathan, "we've got to take care of some business first."

"But Jonathan," said Tim, "we're talking some serious cartoons here!"

While Maria and Tim sat down to watch cartoons, the rest of the Wright cousins talked with Mr. and Mrs. Olsen in the living room about where the Straunsees might be.

"All I know is that Alexander contacted us, asking us to stay here with Maria," said Mr. Olsen. "We've had to stay down here with the children a few times before, when there has been political unrest or military threats. Alexander said he needed to stay at the capital to work with the legislature on a critical new law. And then he got word that Sarina and Katrina had disappeared."

"Sarina and Katrina were missing before King Straunsee?" asked Jonathan.

"Oh yes," answered Mrs. Olsen. "You know how those two girls are, strongheaded and all. They had gone shopping in Flewdur after the incident."

"Incident? Wait," said Jonathan, "I think you'd better tell us what happened from the start."

"It was a few days after you left," Mrs. Olsen explained. "The day someone broke into Alexander's office in the capital. I saw Sarina in the courtyard. She said that you had messaged her that you were coming back this week and would be visiting for a few days before your flight back to America. She was so excited. She wanted to get some new, pretty blouses and clothes to wear for when you came back. That's why they went to Flewdur."

"She's so pretty," said Jonathan, blushing slightly when he realized what he had just said. "She didn't need to get any new clothes just on my account."

Kimberly eyed him suspiciously and said, "Jonathan, I thought you said you didn't organize our coming back here."

"I didn't plan this. How could I?" said Jonathan. "My phone went missing at the airport, remember? I didn't get it back until last Friday. A janitor found it. Somebody had purged its history and thrown it into a trash can."

"Then how did Sarina get the message?" asked Kimberly.

"I don't know, but let's see if we can find out," Jonathan replied, taking out his phone and requesting an online history. He scrolled down through the messages. "Here's one," he said a minute later, reading through it and finally looking up. "And it was sent to Sarina's phone, too. The only problem is, I didn't write it."

"Somebody used your phone to send that message to Sarina?" said Robert. "That's weird. Everybody but us knew we were coming back here, and we only came because of the plane trouble. How did they know we were going to have plane trouble?"

"That is rather unusual," said Mr. Olsen. "It's almost as if someone planned for the plane to have trouble."

"Yes, but who?" said Mrs. Olsen.

"Whom," said Tim, just entering the living room. "*Whom* is the proper word."

"Thank you, Tim," said Kimberly. "I thought you were watching cartoons."

"I am. I'm just on my way to the kitchen to get some snacks," Tim replied.

"Where's Maria?" asked Kimberly.

"She's holding down the cartoon 'pause button' on the remote," said Tim. "It doesn't work right and we don't want to miss any of the cartoons."

Tim soon returned with a full plate of cheese and crackers

and two cups of milk. "Remember, *whom* is the proper word," he said.

"Thank you, Mr. Timothy Wright, now you can go back to your cartoons," said Kimberly.

"Mr. and Mrs. Olsen, if you don't mind, we're going to look at the communications room again. Our parents are pros at that type of stuff and they've taught us a little bit about it," said Jonathan.

"I think that would be all right, don't you, Olaf?" asked Mrs. Olsen.

"I think so," said Mr. Olsen. "Anything you can do to help the Straunsees would be much appreciated. We don't want to stay down here for the rest of our lives if we don't have to."

Jonathan, Lindy, Robert and Kimberly headed for the communications room. They were soon seated in comfortable, rolling office chairs, trying to decipher what was being displayed on the large screen before them.

"This seems to be tracking things," said Robert. "There are some surveillance cameras we have access to."

Robert hit a few buttons and a landing strip and airplane hangars appeared on the screen.

"An airport?" said Jonathan. "Do you have any idea where it is?"

Robert searched through several screens. When he tried to locate it on the map, the only screen it brought up was "ACCESS DENIED."

Jonathan found a screen showing an office. Behind the desk was the national coat of arms of Gütenberg.

"That might be King Straunsee's office," said Kimberly, looking over Jonathan's shoulder.

Jonathan zoomed in on a window in the office. "That must be the capital building out there," he said. "I think you're right,

144

Kimberly."

"What about the map screen with all the green lights on it?" asked Lindy. "What do you think the blinking green lights mean?"

"Good question," said Robert. He and Lindy both studied the screen.

"They're not changing location," said Lindy. "So, they don't seem to be aircraft, boats, or cars."

"Not unless they're parked," said Robert. "Maybe they're towns or something?"

"True," said Lindy. "But why would they be blinking?"

"Where are we on the map?" called out Tim's voice from behind them.

The cousins turned around to see Tim and Maria standing just inside the doorway.

"I thought you guys were watching cartoons," said Robert.

"No, the pause button got stuck and we couldn't get them started again," Tim replied. "They're not as much fun when the pictures don't move."

"Maria, do you know what the green and yellow blinking lights on this map screen mean?" asked Lindy.

"No," Maria replied. "My father never told me. We don't come down here very often."

"Where's your castle on the map?" asked Robert.

Maria studied the map and pointed, "Right here, this green light right here that's blinking."

"But none of them move," said Lindy.

"Hey, what's this?" said Kimberly, retrieving a necklace from a rack. "This is pretty."

"That's our family necklace," said Maria. "Each of us girls have one. Father always insists we have them with us."

"Let me see it," said Jonathan. "That looks like the one

Sarina was wearing when we first met."

Maria handed Jonathan the necklace.

"No," Jonathan said, studying it more closely, "this one's a little bulkier and has a small button on it."

"After Sarina was kidnapped at Fort Courage, Father gave us these. He said we were to press that little button when we needed help," said Maria.

Acting on a hunch, Jonathan pushed on the small, hidden button and the blinking green light on the map at Straunsee castle turned to bright yellow. When he stopped, the blinking yellow light turned back to green. He did it again with the same results. "It seems to be some kind of sending beacon," he said. "It locates where you are on the map. Ingenious."

Jonathan pushed the button again and the map light blinked yellow again.

"You're right," said Robert. "Then the green and yellow light could be where King Straunsee, Katrina, and Sarina are."

CHAPTER 4

Maps

The cousins quickly looked up the location of the yellow blinking light and wrote it down. It was the town of Flewdur, a city in the valley.

"Sarina and Katrina went shopping at Flewdur," said Maria.

"I wonder if there's a mobile tracking device," said Robert, "Your dad must have something like that."

The cousins started looking through the drawers. Inside a tall cabinet were several electronic devices. Robert pulled one of them out and switched it on. "Okay," he said, "try pushing the 'help' button."

Jonathan pushed the button and a light started showing up on the device screen Robert was holding. "Straunsee Castle," it said.

Robert walked into the living room and they tried it again with the same result. "Good," said Robert, returning to the communications room. "This will do. It's a directional locator to find the necklace. Wow, Maria, your father has some really first-rate spy stuff in here."

Maria smiled and said, "Father likes electronics."

The youths heard a loud, staticky sound coming from the theater room. "Maybe the cartoons are back on," said Tim. He rushed over to see, but instead of cartoons there was a large rally being broadcast. "Hey guys, come here," Tim called out. "It's that creepazoid Kreppen."

The cousins rushed into the theater room. "This is the only thing on the channels right now," said Tim.

The screen showed a large protest rally in the capital of Gütenberg. Thousands of people were in the streets. The cameras zoomed in on Mr. Oilee Kreppen, standing on a balcony, his voice blasting away on a large microphone system.

"King Straunsee is gone!" shouted Mr. Kreppen into the microphone. "He has fled. I was unjustly held in prison, but the judges have ruled correctly and I have been released. Where are you now, my accuser Straunsee? Are you out with your family skiing in another country. Why don't you have the courage to speak up, Alexander Straunsee? I'll tell you, because you are no longer fit to rule Gütenberg."

Mr. Kreppen smiled arrogantly. "Who do you want to rule over you now?" he called out again. "Who will be your leader?"

The audience began chanting, "Kreppen, Kreppen, Kreppen!"

"I have been your humble president of the Legislature," Kreppen began. "You have trusted me and I have fulfilled my duty. It has been a pleasure to serve you so well and I would humbly accept the kingship."

"Kreppen, Kreppen, Kreppen," chanted the crowd. "We want Kreppen!"

"Those people are idiots to follow him," said Mr. Olsen. "Kreppen is a dangerous liar. He's behind King Straunsee's disappearance, I just know it."

The cousins turned around to see that Maria and the Olsens were watching the screen as well. Maria, near tears, shut off the TV.

Mr. Olsen spoke up again, "Kreppen has long been stealing from Gütenberg and he wants to steal more. He is now trying to steal the kingship. His ways will turn us into a third-world country."

"What can we do?" asked Mrs. Olsen.

"We can't call the police, that's for certain," Mr. Olsen replied. "Kreppen's supporters have infiltrated all of our police and capital guard. He's got somebody with huge amounts of money and personnel backing him."

"Follow me," said Jonathan, leading the group over into the communications room. One of the green light locations was still blinking yellow. "That must be them," said Jonathan. "That's got to be them. Sarina, Katrina, and maybe King Straunsee are at Flewdur. We've got to help them!"

"Jonathan, I would go if I could," said Mr. Olsen, "but I have promised Alexander we would stay here with Maria. I would suggest you talk to Mr. Gervar to find our helicopter pilot and have him fly you to see who is at Flewdur."

Tim started to say "whom" again but Kimberly saw it coming and elbowed him a good one in the ribs.

"Good thinking," said Jonathan. "Maria, may we take some of this spy gear with us?"

"Take all you want," Maria replied. "Just please find my father and sisters."

"Will do," Jonathan said with a determined smile. "And don't worry, we'll find them."

Jonathan nodded at Robert and Robert retrieved the locator device. The cousins tried to contact their parents in America to let them know they were okay. After several attempts, they were finally able to leave a message on their home answering machines.

"Let's go track down that helicopter pilot," said Jonathan, looking at the other cousins.

"Maybe Tim should stay here," said Kimberly with concern.

"I want to come along, too," said Tim.

"No, Tim," said Kimberly. "I told Mom I'd keep you safe, and that's what I'm going to do."

"But Kimberly, I can help. I can get into smaller places than you guys if I need to."

"No," said Kimberly. "You're staying here. You can keep Maria company. We'll call you when we find out anything."

"Better stay here in the bunker this time, sport," said Jonathan, patting Tim's shoulder. "We'll be back as quick as we can. You man home base here. If you find out anything else we need to know, call us. You've still got your dollar store phone, don't you?"

Tim reluctantly said "okay" and watched as the rest of the cousins walked out of the communications room.

"You want to watch some more cartoons?" said Maria.

"No thanks," Tim replied. "Not right now."

"I know what you mean," said Maria. "I wish I could go, too. They're going to need our help. Mr. Kreppen is a rotten crumazoid. He's got all kinds of bad stuff planned. The only way we're going to stop him is to scare him to death. He's a real coward at heart."

After leaving the bunker and the secret passage, Jonathan, Kimberly, Robert, and Lindy went to talk with Mr. Gervar. As before, he was leaning over another large architectural drawing, this time looking through a large magnifying glass.

"Mr. Gervar, sir?" said Jonathan.

"Yes," the octogenarian replied, looking up from the drawing.

Lindy noted the drawing was labelled "The Fortress of Trifid Mount" and studied it for a moment.

"Mr. Gervar," continued Jonathan, "do you know where the Straunsee's helicopter pilot is?"

"In prison, where he belongs," said Mr. Gervar.

"They haven't gotten a new one yet?" asked Robert.

"Haven't had time, for goodness sakes," replied Mr. Gervar. "Things are going on much too quickly in this country as it is."

"Do you know anybody who could fly the helicopter? It would really speed up our search for the Straunsees," said Jonathan.

"I used to fly," said Mr. Gervar, "but I haven't flown one of those copters in years." He looked at the four youths. "We'd have to figure out the new controls. Would you like me to fly you?"

"But you haven't flown in years," said Kimberly. "We wouldn't want to put you out or anything."

"It could be fun though," said Robert.

"Thanks for the offer, Mr. Gervar," said Jonathan. "We'll use our rented SUV. Come on you guys, we've got to hit the road."

"By the way," said Mr. Gervar, "how is Maria?"

"Fine," said Kimberly without thinking. "I mean, I think she's fine."

"Good," Mr. Gervar said with a smile. "Godspeed you on your venture."

"Thank you," replied the cousins.

The four cousins hurriedly walked out to their rented SUV. There was a light snow falling. They turned on the defroster, cleared the snow off the windshield, and climbed in. As they were driving to Flewdur, the cousins heard a strange noise in the back of the car.

"What was that?" asked Lindy, turning to look behind her.

"It sounded like a bear or something," said Kimberly. "There it goes again. Jonathan, pull over and stop. There's something in the back of the car!"

Jonathan quickly pulled over onto a paved siding and the cousins carefully probed to see what kind of animal had gotten in. Lifting a backpack and a blanket out of the way, they spied Tim sound asleep, snoring like an idling chainsaw.

"Tim!" said Kimberly, shaking him awake. "What are you doing here?!"

CHAPTER 5

Rescue Mission

"Trying to get some sleep," said Tim, rubbing his eyes.

"You were snoring. What are you doing here?" asked Kimberly again.

"I so do not snore," Tim replied groggily. "It must have been you, Kimberly."

"I have *not* been asleep," said Kimberly. "You can ask Lindy."

"How do you know?" Tim said, yawning. "Well, anyways, it wasn't me."

"Tim, you are so busted," said Kimberly. "When we get back to America, you'll see."

"We're too far down the road to take him back," said Jonathan, shaking his head.

The cousins were on the snowy road again, driving toward Flewdur. Tim climbed up into the seat and sat between Kimberly and Lindy. A short while later, all three of them heard another growling sound in the back.

"What now?" said Kimberly. "Tim, are you snoring again?"

"I told you, it wasn't me," Tim replied. "It's Maria."

"Maria?" said Kimberly and Lindy at the same time. Jonathan pulled onto a paved siding again.

The Wright cousins saw another blanket in the back move. Maria's head appeared. "Did somebody call my name?" she asked.

"Ooooooo, Tim," Kimberly scolded. "You were *so* not supposed to come, and you brought Maria, too? Mom and Dad are going to ground you for a year!"

"Again?" said Tim.

"He didn't bring me," said Maria. "*I* brought him. I didn't know what car you were driving. I want to help find my father and sisters, too. It's lonely in that old bunker without them."

"Tim," whispered Robert from the front seat, "I thought you said two weeks ago she had cooties?"

"She does," said Tim, leaning forward and whispering. "We drew a line down the middle of the car. As long as each of us stay on our own side, we won't get cooties."

"I guess that works," said Robert matter-of-factly.

"We've got to phone the Olsens to let them know Maria's with us," said Kimberly. "They'll be scared cold."

"I left them a note on the door, the refrigerator, and the dining room table," said Maria. "I didn't want them to worry."

"Kimberly, Maria says she and I are twins. Is that so?" asked Tim.

"I don't know," said Kimberly. "You sure act like it sometimes."

Kimberly looked back and forth at Tim and Maria. "Goodness," she finally said, shaking her head tiredly, "now I've got two of you to worry about keeping alive until you're in your twenties!"

As Maria was crawling forward into the rear seat, she hit her knee on the cousins' luggage. "Ouch," she said, "what's in these two briefcases?"

"We don't know," Tim replied, suddenly remembering the cases. "We just got them at the airport."

"But it has your name on it," said Maria. Tim tried to shush her.

"Why?" Maria whispered back.

"It might be schoolwork from my schoolteacher in America, Mrs. Grindley," whispered Tim. "She told me if I wasn't back on time, she was going to send me my homework to do. We were supposed to be back in class this week."

"I thought so," said Kimberly, listening in on their conversation. "Tim, we'd better open up that briefcase. Mrs. Grindley must have sent it two weeks ago. We've got to get you going on it. It's homework time!"

"Sorry," said Maria with honest compassion to Tim, "I didn't know."

"It's okay," said Tim. "Robert, do you want yours, too?"

"Thank you, *Timbo*," Robert said like a condemned man. "We can both do our homework together. *Ugh!*"

Maria handed both briefcases forward. All the youths got seated again and Jonathan pulled back out onto the road.

"It doesn't say who sent it," said Kimberly, looking it over and trying to get it open.

"Here, let me see it," said Tim.

Robert and Tim both studied the briefcases. "Hey," said Tim, "this thing has a wristband so you can't lose it at an airport. That's kind of cool. Let's see if it works."

Tim pulled the band out from the handle and slipped it around his wrist. It clicked. "Hey, what's going on?" he said, trying to get the wristband off his arm.

"Here's a latch," said Robert, twisting the handle on his briefcase. The handle clicked and the briefcase opened slightly. With the case sitting on his lap, Robert opened it up to look inside. "Sunglasses," he said in relief, "and I don't see any homework."

"That's great news," said Tim from the backseat, still trying to get the wristband off.

Robert told Tim how to open his briefcase, which he successfully did a moment later. His, too, held sunglasses. Tim pushed on a small, red button on the inside of the briefcase. A serious voice began speaking: "Thank you, Kimosoggy and Toronto, for accepting this most difficult assignment..."

"Close it up, close it up," said Kimberly. "It means trouble!" She tried to close the case, but Tim blocked her hand.

"Your TOP-SECRET PRIORITY ALPHA MISSION is to proceed to Tri—"

"T-SPAM!" said Tim and Robert excitedly at the same time.

Kimberly slammed Tim's briefcase closed before it could say anything more.

"Kimberly," protested Tim, "why did you do that? It's a T-SPAM!"

Tim reopened the briefcase. It was quiet so he pushed the button again. This time it didn't say anything. He glanced sideways at Kimberly in irritation and pushed the button again multiple times. It didn't repeat the message.

"See what you did," said Tim. "Now we're never going to know what our T-SPAM is!"

"Good," said Kimberly, "we don't want to get caught up in that stuff again."

"But Kimberly, it was a T-SPAM," Tim complained. "It was urgent. We haven't had one of those since that MMERMS thing at Lake Pinecone"

"No," said Kimberly. "We're going to find the Straunsees and help them. We're not going to get tangled up in any international espionage spy stuff again. We had spy equipment flyers coming out our ears for six months after that. Everybody wanted to sell us a super spy camera or a laser thing or flying boots. We even had to change our email accounts because of the all the spams. No, Tim, we've got to stay focused right now."

"Golly gee whiz," said Tim with disappointment, "you sure know how to take the fun out of stuff."

"Better we stay alive than have fun," said Kimberly.

"You've got to admit, though, it was kind of fun being secret agents," said Tim.

"Yeah, but then you guys will start thinking about making your broccoli bombs and diving in to...no, we've got to stay focused," said Kimberly.

"Broccoli bombs aren't such a bad idea," said Tim. "Robert and I have been thinking on a way to improve the recipe."

While Tim and Kimberly were talking, Robert was curiously, quietly looking over the things in his briefcase. A small card inside instructed that they "get these attaché cases into the hands of America's top two secret agents, Kimosoggy and Toronto."

Robert's attaché didn't have a recording button like Tim's did, but it did seem to have some other cool items. He didn't announce it out loud just now; he didn't want to worry Kimberly. The things in the briefcase meant serious things were going on in the spy world.

"Remind me again what T-SPAM means?" asked Jonathan.

"Top-Secret Priority Alpha Mission," Lindy replied.

Robert tried on the sunglasses. He found them to be auto-adjusting ones that would change according to the light. When he looked outside, the bright snow didn't blind him. When he looked down at his feet in the shadows, he could see them just as well. Did the glasses have the same button features as they did before? He felt for the familiar button but didn't find it. In fact, the glasses just seemed to be regular, auto-adjusting glasses.

"Rats," mumbled Robert, "I wish I could see what these glasses can do."

Robert had no sooner said it when all kinds of words and

diagrams started appearing in the sunglass lenses: range; temperature; passive night vision; dangers; countdown; available support; potential threats; and more.

"Whoa!" said Robert excitedly. "Tim, try on your glasses."

Tim reached into his briefcase and put on the sunglasses. "So?" said Tim, "what's up? They just seem like regular glasses."

"Try talking," said Robert.

"Okay," said Tim. "What should I say?"

Suddenly, possible word commands started appearing on Tim's glass lenses. "Wow!" he said. "This is cool!" He looked at Kimberly. She didn't look enthused. The glasses labeled Kimberly as a "Threat" and started outlining possible remedies.

"No, no, no," said Tim, speaking to the glasses. "Kimberly is not a threat...sometimes."

"Timothy Wright give me those glasses," said Kimberly. She reached out and took them from his nose. "What's going on?"

Kimberly put on the glasses, looked through them and said, "I don't see anything. These are just like my pink and yellow flower glasses back home."

The frame of the glasses suddenly turned pink with small yellow flowers all over them.

"Tim, what are you laughing at?" asked Kimberly.

"Nothing," said Tim, trying to keep a straight face. "You're right, they *are* kind of like your flowered glasses back home. "Can I have them back, please?"

"That's *may* I have them back, please," said Kimberly.

"*May* I have them back, please," said Tim.

"I guess so," Kimberly replied and handed them back to Tim. As Kimberly took the glasses off her face, they returned to their normal color and design.

Tim was more careful after that. He decided to use Robert's technique and start quietly looking through his briefcase. He slipped the glasses back on and as he would pick up something in the briefcase, the glasses would identify what the object was. "Commlinks," the glasses labelled some small, round metal objects he picked up.

As they drove along the snowy road, the cousins pulled out the food they had packed and ate lunch. "How soon until we get to Flewdur?" asked Tim.

"The signs say it's another ten kilometers," said Jonathan.

"Oh," said Tim. "That means about...let's see, carry the one, divide by..."

"Six miles," Kimberly replied.

"Right," said Tim. "I knew that."

As the cousins drove into Flewdur, they found it to be a very modern city. The buildings were well lit, the streets were wide and had sidewalks. The homes looked cheerful and well cared for.

"What does the direction finder say?" asked Jonathan.

CHAPTER 6

The Mall

"It looks like we've got about two more kilometers to go," Robert replied.

"Just let me know when we need to turn," said Jonathan.

"Okay," said Robert a short time later. "It looks like we'll need to turn to the right soon." He glanced up and then looked back down at the direction-finder. "That next street looks like it might be it."

"Good," said Jonathan, "because we're running out of streets on this side of town."

Jonathan turned right onto the next street. It was a narrower street, but it was still paved, paved with cobblestones.

"This must be an older part of town," said Jonathan. "Where to now?"

"About one kilometer," said Robert. "It's kind of hard to tell."

When they had driven the kilometer, the locator told them to turn left.

"We're getting close," said Robert. "Slow down a little."

The youths were surprised when the road merged into a large parking lot. They found themselves at the back side, the freight dock, of a large shopping center.

"Are Sarina and Katrina in there?" asked Maria.

"We'll know in just a minute," said Jonathan as he drove

around the perimeter of the mall.

There were parking lots on three sides, filled with hundreds of cars. Robert kept his eye on the locator as they drove; it pointed toward the mall the whole time.

Jonathan parked the car near the main entrance to the mall. "I don't know what we're up against here," he said.

Kimberly gave Jonathan the "you need to do something" look. Jonathan asked Tim and Maria to stay hidden in the SUV and "be ready to open the doors if they saw them running out of the mall." Kimberly would stay in the driver's seat with the engine running in case they needed to make a quick getaway.

Robert handed commlinks to Jonathan, Lindy, and Kimberly to put behind their ears and he put one on, too. To their surprise, the commlinks soon turned to the color of their skin. Jonathan, Robert, and Lindy then got out of the car and walked into the mall.

It was a large, brightly lit mall. There were play areas for children and many stores on three different levels.

"Where to now?" asked Jonathan.

Robert glanced down at the locator device he had cupped in his left hand. "That way," he said, pointing down the long mall.

Robert led the way. Jonathan was to his right, Lindy to his left. Trying not to gain any attention, they talked as they went and acted casual. The locator led them toward a large food court. Wonderful smells came from the different food booths there. As they passed the food court, they came to a large, alpine toy store. They were just passing it when Robert glanced down at his locator. It said the beacon was somewhere behind them. The Wright cousins returned to the food court. The locator pointed toward a narrow hallway which led to the outside.

Halfway to the outside doors, Robert stopped, still eyeing the locator, "It says they're right here." The hallway was empty!

"Maybe," said Jonathan, looking around and then at the ceiling. "Maybe it means they're upstairs."

"I hope so," said Robert. "Otherwise we're going to need a ladder to check above those ceiling tiles."

Jonathan, Lindy, and Robert quickly made their way back to the food court.

"It must be lunch time," said Lindy, noting the large numbers of people flowing in. "Gütenbergians seem to be such a happy people."

"King Straunsee has done an excellent job in teaching them about how to stay a free people by teaching them to choose well and to be self-reliant," Jonathan said.

"It helps them keep their *identity* as a people," said Robert.

As Robert said the word "identity", an interesting thing started happening on his glass lenses. Each time Robert now looked at a person, a bracket would appear around the person's face. A second later, a name would appear below the brackets identifying them.

As they made their way through the crowd, Robert glanced at a man walking toward them. The name "Rheynard" appeared on his glasses. "Rheynard," Robert read aloud.

"Yes, hi," the man replied as he walked by. "It is good to see you."

Robert glanced at another person. "Hi, Morgan," he said.

"Hi," the man replied cheerfully. "Excuse me, I've got to get some food before we leave."

Robert glanced to their right and saw a young woman carrying a shopping bag. "Hi, Marta," Robert said cheerfully. The girl smiled, said "hi" back to him, and then looked at him with a "do I know you?" look. Robert grinned back and said, "Say hi to your family for me."

"Yes, certainly," said the young woman, "I will." She left, still trying to figure out who Robert was.

"This is cool," said Robert. "Hi Suzette, nice to see you," he waved to a girl on his left. Suzette waved back.

"Robert," Lindy whispered from behind him, "how do you know those people's names?"

"I just kind of look at them," said Robert. "And I say to myself, now, who does that person look like? And all of a sudden, I see their name. Lindy, why don't you try it?"

"Me?" said Lindy.

"Sure, it seems to work every time," said Robert.

"Okay," said Lindy, hesitantly. She glanced at someone on the far side of the corridor. "Let's see," she said, "that person looks like a Bertha."

Robert glanced over at the lady and her name appeared on his lenses. "Bertha? Lindy, how did you know her name?"

"The way you told me," said Lindy. "This is fun! Let's see, that person coming up looks like a Thomas."

"No," said Robert. "That's Frederick. Hi Frederick," Robert called out and waved.

"Great to see you again," Frederick replied. "How's your family?"

"Very well, thanks," said Robert.

"Robert?" whispered Lindy.

Robert chuckled and whispered back, "My glasses are using some kind of facial ID or something."

"You realize that none of those people have any idea who we are," said Lindy as they headed over toward an escalator.

"Yes," said Robert. "Hi Dantzel," he said as he waved to another young woman wearing cute glasses.

"Robert Wright, it's so wonderful to see you," said the girl, stopping to chat with him. "What are you doing here in Gütenberg?"

"We're, um, visiting some friends," Robert replied, glancing at Lindy for a second and then back at Dantzel.

"Very good," said Dantzel. "How long will you be staying?"

"A few more days, probably," said Robert. "Our flight got re-routed and then we'll be headed home."

"It would be fun if our families could get together again," said Dantzel.

"Yes," said Robert. Lindy tugged on his arm. "Well, Dantzel, we've got to go. It's been so nice seeing you again."

"You too, Robert. Oh, and my brother is going to be so grateful for your help on the go-kart clutch at the castle," Dantzel replied.

"Sure, anytime," said Robert with a smile. "See you later."

"Good-bye," said Dantzel.

"Who was that?" whispered Lindy as they walked away.

"I don't have a clue," said Robert, looking back toward the girl and picking up his pace toward the escalator. "That girl gave me the heebie-jeebies. Let's get out of here."

"Serves you right," said Lindy with a grin. "Now let's go find Katrina and Sarina."

The Wright cousins rode the escalator up to the second floor. They searched the area. Not finding anything again, they rode up to the third floor.

On the third floor, the cousins found several shops open and doing good business. They had just walked past one shop when the locator told them to go back.

"A knife shop?" mumbled Robert. "Why did it have to be knives?"

The cousins studied the front window displays for a moment. It gave them a chance to get a glimpse inside the store before they went in. Robert glanced at the store clerks. "We need to talk," he whispered to Jonathan and Lindy, glancing down at the locator again. "We're close," he said. "The locator's pointing toward the back of the store."

"Okay," whispered Jonathan, taking a deep breath. "Lindy, you stay out front here and tell us if anything is coming our way. Robert and I are going in."

"Be careful," Lindy whispered.

"Will do, Sis," said Robert.

Robert and Jonathan walked into the store as casually as they could and started looking at the merchandise. There were display cases showing off specialized bread knives, cheese knives, meat knives, hunting knives, pocketknives, and more.

"Hey, look at that," said Robert. "There's even a knife to cut ice cream with."

"Yeah, but look at the price. They're over 100 Dollops," Jonathan replied loudly.

The boys split up, looking at the merchandise, all the while making their wandering way toward the back of the store. They spied a door in the middle of the back wall and nonchalantly headed in its direction, looking at the merchandise.

"That knife over there would be nice to get for Mom," Robert said aloud.

"Yes," Jonathan called back. "but will they let us take that on the plane?"

"Good question," said Robert.

A store clerk walked over toward the back room, paused, and headed over toward the two boys.

"Our superior quality knives may be taken on an airliner providing they are properly checked in with your luggage," the clerk said. "I can give you a special deal on it, say thirty-percent off. Would you like to purchase it?"

"No thanks," said Jonathan. "I'd like to look some more."

"No problem," said the man. He eyed Jonathan for a second

and turned to realign some items in a display case. The clerk stayed between Robert and Jonathan and the closed back room door. Try as they might, they couldn't slip past him.

"Wow, look at that knife," said Robert, pointing to a very fancy stainless steel, salad slicing knife. He whispered to Jonathan, "I think he's getting suspicious."

"Hey, look at that set," said Jonathan, pointing at a beautiful walnut case full of knives. He and Robert walked back toward the middle of the store to look it over. The clerk watched them and followed, keeping within fifteen feet of them.

A woman clerk came over to talk with the youths. "You have very fine taste in culinary instruments," she said. "That set is most appreciated by our finest chefs."

"It is very nice," Robert replied casually. "How much does it cost, Murtha?"

"Murtha?" thought Robert, cringing inside. "Why did I have to use her name?"

"Thank you for asking," Murtha replied. "It is 7,400 Dollops." She noted the surprised look on Robert's face. "We do have an installment payment plan if you would like. If you will follow me, I can make the arrangements."

Murtha was just turning toward the sales counter when a loud, banging sound came from the back of the store. Murtha and three other store clerks rushed toward the rear door.

"Can we help?" called out Jonathan as he and Robert headed after them.

"No, keep back," Murtha replied insistently. "Only our store personnel are allowed to go back there."

Jonathan and Robert continued to follow them. Murtha reached the door first and opened it only partially to look in. A very powerful jet of water hit her on the left shoulder and threw her against the door. The door swung open wide as water began spraying through the doorway.

"Get back out here," Lindy's excited voice called out over the Wright's commlink system. "Sarina and Katrina just came out of the next store over!"

CHAPTER 7

Special Delivery

Jonathan and Robert immediately turned and ran for the front of the store.

"The girls are gone!" screamed Murtha's voice from behind them. "Ferdd, Thommern, close the shop!"

The two clerks leaped into action. They saw Robert and Jonathan coming and ran to intercept them. The Wrights hit them at a full run and bowled them over. The two boys made it out of the store just before the front doors closed.

"Lindy, where are you now?" called out Jonathan over the commlink as they entered the main mall.

"I'm chasing after Sarina and Katrina. I haven't been able to catch them yet. They're heading for the central escalators," Lindy called back, breathing hard. "Boy, can those Straunsee girls run!"

The boys spied Lindy and took off running after her. "Keep Sarina in your sight," Jonathan called out over the commlink. Robert had to sprint hard to keep up with him.

Lindy reached the top of the escalators. She could see Sarina and Katrina leaping down the escalator two-steps-at-a-time. "And I thought I was in good shape," puffed Lindy on the commlink radio. "Jonathan, I don't know how you ever caught up with her...Sarina!"

Sarina and Katrina leapt onto the platform at the bottom of the first escalator and ran around to start going down the next escalator below it. Lindy raced after them. "Sarina, Katrina," she called out. "Wait for me!"

The girls didn't hear her.

"Sarina!" Lindy yelled, "wait for me!"

Hearing her name, Sarina looked back at the escalator they had just exited and saw Lindy near the bottom of it.

"Lindy!" Sarina shouted back in recognition. She and Katrina stopped long enough for Lindy to catch up with them. "Follow me," said Lindy as she raced past them. "We've got a car."

Both Straunsee girls took out after Lindy. A knife whizzed by them and stuck in a nearby pillar. The girls didn't take the time to see where it came from. They leapt down the next escalator even faster and made it to the main floor.

"This way," called out Lindy. The girls sprinted after her for the main mall entry doors.

"Start the car!" Lindy shouted over the commlink.

"Already going," replied Kimberly. "We'll pick you up out front."

Lindy could hear the running feet of Sarina and Katrina right behind her. The three girls pushed through the front mall doors into the vestibule area and threw open the outside doors. They were free!

The bright snow outside blinded Lindy momentarily. She spied Kimberly in the SUV and the three girls ran for it. As they climbed into the car, the Straunsee girls spied their younger sister. "Maria!" they called out happily. Katrina climbed into the back seat with Maria and Tim, Sarina slid into the middle seat, and Lindy rushed around to the front passenger seat.

Jonathan and Robert were in a bit of a pickle. They had

several store clerks chasing them, and the clerks liked knives. Each time the boys would turn suddenly to follow Lindy, a knife would whisk by and sink into a wall or a floor. They were just one step ahead of being shish kebabbed.

"Can you believe them throwing all those expensive knives at us?" Robert called out.

"Don't you dare stop to collect any of them," Kimberly broke in over the commlink.

"You don't have to worry about that, Sis," Jonathan called back, their feet pounding. "I'll take swords any day."

The boys made it down to the main floor and sprinted for the main entrance. Three knives pinged off the concrete floor behind them and went sliding. Jonathan and Robert burst through the outer doors, spied their waiting SUV, and dove in through the open car doorways.

"Get us out of here!" said Jonathan.

Two knife store clerks emerged from the mall as the Wright's SUV sped off through the parking lot.

"Hi!" said Jonathan and Sarina to each other at the same time.

"Drive for Trifid," continued Sarina hoarsely. "Hurry!"

"Okay," said Kimberly with a nod. "Lindy, can you get the directions?"

Lindy was riding "shotgun" in the front passenger seat. "Directions for Trifid," she spoke to the car's navigation system. In a moment, the driving route appeared on the dash video screen. "How are we on fuel, Kimberly?"

"Fine," Kimberly replied. "We'll refuel when we get there."

Sarina and Katrina were wet and visibly shaking.

"Let's turn up the heaters," suggested Jonathan.

Maria found car blankets and handed them to her older sisters.

"Sarina are you hungry?" asked Jonathan.

"Yes," said Sarina and Katrina at the same time.

Maria and Tim started passing food forward from the back of the car.

"Thank you," said Sarina, taking a bite of sandwich, "We haven't eaten anything for a day."

"This is good," added Katrina.

Having gotten into the car first, Robert found himself on the bench seat sitting between Jonathan and Sarina, and they were trying to talk around him to each other.

"All right," said Robert finally, "tell you guys what. I'll trade seats with Jonathan."

"Okay," said Jonathan and Sarina at the same time, grinning widely.

Jonathan traded seats with Robert and happily sat down next to Sarina.

"So, how did you get so wet?" asked Jonathan as he clipped on his seatbelt.

"Hold that question," Sarina replied. "First, Jonathan, I want to thank you so much—and all of you—for coming to find us."

"Agreed," said Katrina.

"Second, Lindy, may I borrow your phone please?" Sarina asked. Lindy handed her the phone. Sarina quickly contacted the local police to report to them about their kidnapping by the knife store people. The policeman said they would sweep the area.

After the phone call, Sarina continued eating the food she had been given. The car's heater was really starting to kick in and warm the two girls.

"What happened back there?" asked Jonathan as they sped down the snowy road.

"Katrina and I were doing some clothes shopping at the mall," Sarina explained between bites of food. "A girl came up to us and asked us to take she and her friend's picture in a new store they were opening. It was just two stores down, so we helped them."

"Yes, and the next thing we knew, two guys in the store pulled big knives on us," added Katrina. "They tied us up and put us in a storeroom. Next time, we're going to be more careful about what stores we go into."

"How did you get so wet?" asked Jonathan.

"While we were left alone," said Katrina, "we found a knife and were able to cut our bonds. We cut and kicked a hole in the wall to escape into the next store over. How were we supposed to know it had water pipes in it?"

The Wright cousins and Straunsee girls all laughed.

"I'm sorry, Jonathan," said Sarina, suddenly quieting, "I must look a frightful sight."

"Frightful isn't the word I'd use," Jonathan replied with a grin, "I'd use the word *pretty* or *beautiful*."

"Ugh, here we go again," said Tim from the back seat. "Major mushville!"

"I'm just grateful you were there with this car," said Katrina. "How did you know where we were?"

"Robert used one of your dad's locating devices," Lindy called back from the front seat. "There was a beacon at Flewdur."

"Good job, Robert," said Katrina with a smile.

"Father's at Trifid," said Sarina. "We overheard one of our captors talking about Father being in a Trifid dungeon. They thought we were asleep."

"Kreppen's at the capital right now bragging that your father has abandoned the country," said Robert. "He's trying to take

172

over the government."

"Ooooo, that crumazoid makes me so mad," said Katrina, taking another bite of food. "When is justice going to nail him to the wall?!"

"The police will get him," said Kimberly.

Sarina suddenly looked worried. "There were two policemen in the knife store when we were kidnapped," she said.

"You're right," said Katrina. "I'd forgotten about that."

"And I just called the police to let them know we were free," said Sarina.

The Straunsee sisters looked at each other with concern.

"The Olsen's had mentioned something about the police," said Jonathan. "Let's see, you called the police, but they don't know where you are right now or where we're going."

"They'll probably expect you to go straight back to Straunsee Castle," suggested Robert.

"Yes, keep heading toward Trifid," said Sarina. "We've got to free Father. I don't know who we can trust right now but we've got to free him."

"Without police help?" said Kimberly with concern.

"Um, the knife shop?" reminded Tim.

"We're definitely going to need some help," said Robert, glancing back at Tim. Then he whispered to Tim, "Kimosoggy and Toronto help."

Tim nodded knowingly.

"What did you say?" called back Kimberly from the front.

"Oh, I'm sorry the girls got so soggy," said Robert, knowing Kimberly would probably disapprove of what he was about to do.

Tim slipped Robert's special attaché case forward to him. Robert quietly opened it up. There was a small computer keyboard inside and he quickly and silently started typing a message. "Need climbing gear and special tools to break into fortress. Camo clothes, gloves, masks. Spy extraction gear, ropes..."

Robert glanced up in time to see a new kilometer signpost flash by. Kimberly was driving at a pretty good clip. Soon another signpost streaked by outside the SUV. The kilometer numbers were getting higher. It gave him an idea. He pulled up an overhead view of the road ahead and zoomed in on an area 150 kilometers ahead. There was a small tree near their side of the road, near the kilometer post.

Robert quickly typed in directions, "Leave items in tree," and signed it "Kimosoggy." Tim put in a request of his own and signed out, "Toronto."

Word soon got out that the Straunsee girls had been seen and it was announced on national news.

"Their current whereabouts are unknown," said the reporter. "They were last seen in Flewdur."

A reporter asked Mr. Oilee Kreppen about the matter. "It is a hoax," replied Mr. Kreppen in his office at the capital. "The Straunsees have abandoned us. Mr. Straunsee doesn't have the mettle it takes to lead the country."

After the reporter left, Mr. Kreppen placed a call to Trifid Castle. "The Straunsee girls have escaped. You may expect them within a few hours. Make sure they do not leave."

"Yes, Oilee...Lee," said Eva Gelb's voice on the other end of the line.

Unaware of the "reception" being planned for them, the Wrights and Straunsees discussed plans about how they could rescue King Straunsee. They neared the 314 kilometer post an hour later and Robert asked Kimberly to slow down.

"Why?" asked Kimberly.

"There's a parcel for us in a tree up ahead," Robert replied.

"A what?" said Kimberly.

"Just be ready to stop," Robert said. A snow-covered tree soon appeared in the distance. Robert directed Kimberly to stop near the tree.

"Okay," said Kimberly reluctantly. She slowed and parked, staying on the snow-covered, paved narrow shoulder of the road. Robert jumped out of the car and walked over to the tree. Looking up, he saw a large, waterproof green duffle bag. He hopped up and pulled it down. To his surprise, a second duffle bag came tumbling down and knocked him to the ground.

"I only ordered one," Robert said.

Getting back up, Robert took the bags by their handles and returned to the SUV. The rest of the cousins—except for Tim—looked on in surprise.

"What are those?" asked Katrina.

Robert grinned broadly. "The key to rescuing your dad at Trifid Castle, I hope," he said as he got seated, put on his seatbelt, and opened the duffle bag. "Special delivery for Kimosoggy," said a tag on the handle.

CHAPTER 8

GearSpy1

"Who is Kimosoggy?" asked Sarina, reading the tag.

"You don't want to know," said Kimberly, looking back from the driver's seat.

"Somebody we met a while back," said Jonathan.

Robert looked inside the duffle bag and said, "Good, now we're more ready for Trifid. Let's go."

Kimberly started to protest but Sarina encouraged her to begin driving again, too, so she pulled back out onto the road.

As she drove, Kimberly often glanced into the rearview mirror to see what Robert was up to. She saw him pull out several items of light clothing and a bundle of rope.

"It even has a grappling hook!" said Tim excitedly from the rearmost seat.

"Wow, look at all this neat stuff," said Robert. "They sent it, just like we ordered."

"We're in for it now," mumbled Kimberly from the front seat.

"Any money?" Tim asked.

"Tim, you can't expect them to send all this gear and money, too," said Robert.

"Who's them?" asked Katrina, looking back from the front passenger seat.

"Oh, them," Robert replied. "You know."

"Whom?" said Tim. "You know, the *whoms*; they like to help people out, like roadside assistance and stuff."

"Oh," said Katrina, looking a little puzzled. "I've not been acquainted with them. We usually just have our helicopter pick us up."

An hour and ten minutes later, the cousins' SUV was nearing Trifid. The ground was blanketed in snow, the mountains covered with pines and gray, leafless oaks.

"Trifid Castle is about ten minutes farther," announced Lindy.

As Sarina and Katrina explained to the Wright cousins, Trifid Castle was ancient. It had been built on the top of a steep, rocky mountain by a wide river. It guarded the river crossing there. It had withstood two sieges and three major battles. The Straunsees had visited the castle many times during their youth. They loved playing tag on the old, rugged trails that led from the valley floor up to the castle.

"Does it have any secret passages?" asked Robert.

"Of course," said Sarina. "Any self-respecting castle has to have a few secret passages. That's how castle people survived if their walls were breached."

"Do you know where they are?" asked Jonathan.

"Yes," Sarina said with a smile. "Two from the outside cliffs. We had the original plans to the castle back home. We'll park in the valley near the northern towers. The western side, where the regular road access is, will be much more heavily guarded."

Kimberly drove through several neighborhoods in the valley. The houses, their roofs all wearing a new coat of snow, were lined up close together as if to stay warm. In the distance, on a rocky ridge, the youths could see Trifid Castle. It was old and grey, it's roof's steep. It looked frightful and cold.

"Keep going," directed Katrina.

Kimberly drove along the side of the steep hill. The houses were older here. "There it is," said Katrina. "Park up ahead by that old derelict barn. That will give us access to the trails."

"Why don't we just build a zipline to get into the castle," said Tim. "That would be a lot quicker."

"Only one problem with that," said Robert, "we don't have a zipline cable and the pulley gear."

The sun was just setting as Kimberly parked the SUV. The youths were anxious to find and help King Straunsee.

As Robert opened his car door, to his surprise, his attaché case began beeping. He opened the case and saw blinking LEDs inside. They were part of a small drone system. Robert slipped on his attaché glasses and switched them on. "RECON" appeared on the lenses. "Hey guys," he said, "we can use this drone to scope things out."

They all climbed out of the car. Robert slipped the drone from its controller and prepared to launch. As he fired it up, he was surprised at how quiet it was. There wasn't the usual loud propeller hum. "Must be a new shape of blades," he said. "They don't beat the air so noisily."

The youths gathered curiously around Robert as he moved the drone into RECON mode. The drone flew high into the air and proceeded to make a loop around the castle mountain perimeter and then flew over the castle itself. As it flew, it relayed information to Robert's glasses about possible ways to infiltrate the castle. Infrared located several guards, recently used vehicles, and inhabited areas. When the drone returned, the cousins started getting into their "spy" gear from the duffle bags Robert and Tim had requested.

Tim reached in his duffle bag and pulled out several white, insulated jumpsuits. They were all the same size and very large. Tim held up his jumpsuit to check its length. It was about two feet too tall for him. "Aw, they sent me the wrong size," he said.

"But the tag's kind of cool," said Robert. "It says GearSpy1."

Despite its huge size, Tim tried on his jumpsuit. The sleeves were each about eighteen inches too long. The other youths each had theirs on halfway and couldn't help but laugh at Tim's.

"Tim, you look like a giant starfish," Kimberly whispered with a giggle as she zipped up her own oversized jumpsuit.

"Thank you, thank you," Tim replied with a bow, grinning. As he did so, his jumpsuit seemed to move. "Hey, what's going on?" he said.

Tim's jumpsuit was starting to wiggle and then started to shrink. His sleeves began moving up his arms and the legs, contracting. At the same time, the fabric started to thicken but remained flexible. The other youths watched in amazement.

Lindy noted that the letters on Tim's "GearSpy1" chest pocket logo were starting to fade. She checked her own; it was still solidly lettered.

Unsure of what was going on, Kimberly was about to slip her arms out of the sleeves when her sleeves started to shrink, too. Soon all the youths' jumpsuits were refitting. The fabric was now thick and comfortable.

"We won't need our coats anymore," said Tim enthusiastically. "These jumpsuits are plenty warm."

Tim moved over to the SUV and started to disappear.

"Tim?" said Jonathan, doing a double take. "Are you okay? What's going on?"

"What?" said Tim.

"You're...disappearing," Jonathan replied with concern. He rubbed his eyes and looked again. All but Tim's face and hands had disappeared!

Jonathan stepped toward Tim to investigate. As he neared the SUV, Jonathan, too, started to fade.

"This is really weird," said Robert, holding out his arm to look at it and then glancing around him. "Our jumpsuits are starting to look like...what they're up against?"

Robert stepped walked over to a nearby snow-covered bush. His jumpsuit changed to match the brush and soon blended into it.

"I don't know how it works," said Tim enthusiastically, "but this is cool. Now I can finally win at 'hide-and-go-seek.'"

After getting more acquainted with their new clothing and pulling on the matching GearSpy1 knit caps and gloves, the youths shouldered backpacks and gathered, ready to go.

"Team 1," said Jonathan, "Robert, you, Katrina and Kimberly are hunting for the northwest passage. Team 2, Sarina, Lindy, and I will find the east passage. We don't know what kind of shape the old secret passages are in, so be careful. If you run into trouble, get back here to the car. The secret passages will give us the element of surprise."

Jonathan paused, glancing around at the others. "We can do this, guys," he said. "Keep me updated on your commlink radios. Okay, Sarina, let's go find your father!"

Sarina nodded.

Kimberly noted that Tim and Maria were getting ready to follow them. "Oh, Tim, you and Maria stay and guard the car," she said. "We can't have you guys getting hurt."

"Wait a minute, you aren't going to leave us all alone here, are you?" asked Maria. "Somebody could steal the car and kidnap us."

"It's safer than where we're going," Kimberly replied. "There are armed guards up there and you might get hurt. Hide in the car and lock the doors."

"But what if you guys get captured and they don't capture us?" said Maria. "What are we going to do then?"

"We'll leave you the car keys," said Sarina. "But no driving unless it's a total emergency, okay?"

"Okay," said Maria. "Maybe we can be the getaway car."

"Tim," said Kimberly, "don't you dare drive. Let Maria."

"Are you sure?" said Tim. "I'm a pretty good driver."

"Go carts and bumper cars don't count," said Kimberly.

"But what about spaceplanes?" asked Tim.

"Doesn't count," Kimberly replied. "Sarina said Maria could do it, so let her."

"Okay," said Tim reluctantly.

Kimberly gave the car keys to Maria and she and the others started for the castle.

"So, Maria, what kinds of cars have you driven?" Tim asked as they watched the others leave.

"I haven't," Maria replied. "But ever since Sarina started liking Jonathan so much, she lets me do all kinds of stuff she never used to. She's totally got the smooshies for him."

"You can say that again," said Tim. "Same with Jonathan. Sometimes I even see him just looking out the window and smiling. I think he's gone lulu."

"Cooties," said Maria, shaking her head, "they'll get you every time."

Robert led Team 1 toward the west side of the mountain. Sarina had mentioned a passage coming out there at a rock outcropping about fifty feet below the foot of the castle wall. Team 2's destination was on the east side above the Rystrad River. Its portal, too, was in a large, grey-tan rock outcropping.

Both teams appreciated the shelter that the dense pine forest gave them. There were several paths already beaten in the snow, possibly by large animals. When they could, the teams compared their progress. Robert's team reached their destination first. After surveying the area, they looked in the most likely spots for a secret passage entrance.

"Team 2, this is Team 1. We've not found the hamburger yet," Robert whispered into his commlink.

"Copy. We're still on our way to our location," Jonathan replied. "Thanks for the update."

Several minutes later, Team 2 arrived at their area. There were three possible rock outcroppings in the immediate hillside. Jonathan began looking over one, Sarina the second, just above Jonathan's, and Lindy took the third. They tapped on rocks to see if any seemed loose or hollow but weren't having any success.

"Team 2," Robert radioed, "we think there has been a landslide and the hamburger is buried. Over."

"Copy," Jonathan whispered back. "Look for five minutes more. If you still can't find anything, join us. We've got three possibles over here."

"Roger," said Robert. "Over."

Jonathan and Lindy didn't find any trace of a passageway, so they joined Sarina in searching the middle rock outcropping.

"Somebody's coming!" said Lindy fifteen minutes later. Even though they were virtually unseeable because of their clothing, she, Jonathan, and Sarina ducked under an overhanging rock.

"Can you see who it is?" asked Sarina.

"No, I just saw movement over there in the trees," Lindy replied.

The three youths hunkered down and peered into the darkening forest. As they did so, Sarina felt a warmth in the rocks behind her. "Keep watching," she said to Jonathan, "I want to check on something."

Sarina turned around, took off her glove, and ran her hand along the rocks. Most felt as cold as the mountain air, but there was a warm place, too. She focused on the warmer rocks, running her hand along their edges. Suddenly, she noticed a warm draft of air coming from a crack in the rocks. She felt around the edges. "I've found something," she whispered to Jonathan excitedly.

The youth's headsets crackled. "Team 2, where are you guys?" said Robert.

"Beneath the middle overhang twenty-five feet above you," Jonathan replied.

"Roger, out," said Robert, and he, Katrina, and Kimberly started climbing up to join them.

"Jonathan, this may be the secret tunnel," said Sarina excitedly. "Look at this."

Sarina, Jonathan, and Lindy examined the large rock, trying to see if there was some way around it. They pulled at the edges.

"If it's a door, we'll have to clear some of this dirt away from the bottom of it," said Lindy.

The youths quickly dug with their gloved hands. They soon came to bedrock.

"What did you find?" asked Robert as he and the girls with him reached the small overhang.

"It might be a door," said Jonathan. "Help us see if we can get it open."

The youths first pulled on the left side of the rock. It didn't move. They switched to the right side. This time they were met with success and the rock shifted. They cleared more debris from its base and tried again. The rock pivoted, revealing a long, dark, spider-webby passage!

"Where's Tim when we need him," said Robert.

"Right here," called out a voice right behind them.

Kimberly jumped, letting out a brief shriek before she caught herself. Turning around, she saw Tim's face just appearing at the overhang with Maria's close behind.

"I thought we told you guys to stay with the car," whispered

Kimberly.

"Aw, Kimbo," Tim whispered back, "it's not fair that you get to have all the fun. Besides, Maria has an important message for Sarina."

"What's that?" asked Kimberly.

"I don't want to stay in the car anymore," said Maria. "Besides, when we saw Katrina's group and that other group of soldiers behind them, we thought we'd better warn you."

"They looked like snow troops," said Tim. "They had machine guns and helmets and everything."

CHAPTER 9

Direct Hit

"Where'd they go?" asked Robert.

"I don't know," Tim replied.

"Hurry up and get in here so they don't see you," Jonathan whispered loudly.

Tim and Maria quickly joined the others under the overhanging rock. Jonathan retrieved two small branches broken off from a nearby tree. He handed one to Sarina and kept the other. They switched on their lights and started into the passage, using the branches to knock down the spider webs. It was part cave and part hewn passage and headed slightly upward toward the middle of the castle above. Forty-five feet into the tunnel, they ran into a cave-in, blocking the passage from floor to ceiling.

"Now what?" said Kimberly. "How are we going to get through?"

The youths tried moving some of the rubble out of the way and stacking it along the righthand sidewall. After several minutes of digging, they still had no opening at the ceiling of the tunnel.

"This could be caved-in for hundreds of feet for all we know," said Jonathan. "Our chance for helping Sarina's dad could be running short. I say we need to go back outside and go up over the wall."

"We can't all go," said Kimberly, eyeing Tim and Maria.

"True," said Sarina, "we could go with a group of three or four and the rest could stay here and try to get through this cave-in."

"It should be four," said Jonathan. "Two sets of two that can work together. Who would like to volunteer?"

"I'll go," said Sarina, glancing at Jonathan.

"That's two of us," said Jonathan.

"I'll go," said Robert. "I've got the gear."

"That's three," said Jonathan. "Anybody else want to come?"

There was silence for a moment. Tim was just about to speak up when Kimberly said, "I'll be the fourth. Robert and I can team up."

Tim just about fainted. He couldn't remember when Kimberly had ever volunteered for something like this.

"But what about me?" asked Tim. "I want to be a commando, too."

"You stay here and help Lindy, Maria, and Katrina with the digging," said Kimberly. "I'm going so you can be safer."

"But I've got the grappling hook," said Tim.

"It will be too noisy in the night," said Kimberly. "Besides, you're still totally grounded for not staying at the car."

"I think we'll be better off if we stick together," said Jonathan. "Let's try digging through this stuff for five minutes more and see if we can get through. If we can't, then we'll go over the wall. Agreed?"

"Agreed," said the rest of the group.

Their five minutes was just about up when Robert pulled a big rock out of the pile and several more came tumbling down out of the ceiling. The youths had to scramble to get out of the way as tons of rock slid into the area they had just been clearing, filling the tunnel with dust. When the dust settled, they just saw more rubble from floor to ceiling.

"The wall it is," said Jonathan with certainty.

The youths made their way to the portal of the tunnel and held a quick huddle to plan their next steps. It was dark outside so Robert and Tim handed each person a pair of infrared night vision goggles from their backpacks. Just one of the many items they had gotten from the tree luggage. It was cold outside, but their GearSpy1 clothing helped to ward it off so they didn't feel it.

The youths' new plan called for Jonathan, Sarina, Robert, and Kimberly to scale the wall to get inside the castle. Lindy, Katrina, Maria, and Tim would wait near the foot of the wall for support and to make sure the area there was secure for their return. Robert sent up the spy drone again to reconnoiter the castle. It was programmed with stealth technology and independently showed the youths where guards and other personnel were around the castle proper.

"I wish it could see inside the buildings," said Tim, eyeing the monitor. "And maybe, if we had one of King Straunsee's shoes or something, it could track him down."

"Ah, yes," said Robert, "a tracking drone. We'll have to work on a program to do that when we have time."

"And we could arm it with water cannons," added Tim.

"It's too cold, they would freeze," said Kimberly.

"Then how about lasers?" Tim replied.

"Yes, that would melt the ice," said Maria, nodding her approval.

To conserve batteries, the youths planned to "park" the drone on a vantagepoint in the castle so it could continue to report movements within the castle courtyard. If needed, Tim would fly it for closer inspection.

After readying more gear, the youths set out. The snow was

becoming slicker as the evening temperatures dropped. They had to be especially careful as they made their way along the narrow path. One slip and they would tumble down into the icy river below.

Several minutes later, the youths arrived near the middle of the courtyard's north wall. The location had been selected by the drone. It would give them access to a low, inner wall that would allow them to move along the inside without being seen from most of the yard.

Tim's eyes grew wide as he watched Robert retrieve a rope gun from his backpack, complete with grappling hook on the end, and ready it. The target was a small notch at the top of the wall. Everyone looked anxiously on as Robert aimed and fired. The hook shot skyward, pulling the rope behind it. Up, up it went. Just when it looked like it wasn't going to make it, the grappling hook sailed over the top of the wall and landed inside. It hit the wall's inner walkway with a clink. Robert carefully reeled in the rope. He tugged hard three times to make sure the hook was set and wouldn't slip.

The first stage seemed to have worked, it was time to climb.

Jonathan grasped the rope, preparing to go first. He was about to start climbing when Robert tapped on his shoulder and said, "Just a minute, you'll want this."

Robert slipped a battery-powered device onto the rope and attached it to Jonathan's climbing harness. "Push this button to start and this one to stop," directed Robert. "When you get to the top, send it back down. It's a rope climbing device."

Jonathan pushed the button and the device started to lift him off the ground. "Somehow this feels like cheating," he whispered. When he was ten feet off the ground, he whispered again, "I take that back. This is awesome!"

Robert was the last to ascend the rope with the help of the

"climber." As he did so, he thought he saw movement further along the wall to the east, but by the time he focused on it, he could see no one. Was somebody else scaling the wall?

It was a long fifteen minutes before Jonathan, Kimberly, Sarina, and Robert were assembled in a dark area of the walkway at the top of the castle wall. There's a certain exhilaration when you reach a goal, and the youths felt it.

Robert took out his locating device and dialed it in. "Over there in that direction," he whispered, pointing toward some buildings at the far end of the courtyard. The courtyard was dimly lit except for hooded lights shining over several doorways around the perimeter. It looked like a grey, bland prison. There were armed guards at several of the doorways, including the one the locator device was pointing to.

"We need a diversion to get rid of the guards," whispered Jonathan.

"Maybe we could start a fire or something," said Kimberly. "You know, sabotage."

"We don't have a lighter," said Jonathan.

"We could use the drone to draw them off," said Robert. "You know, fly it down close to them and draw them over to the other side of the courtyard."

"That could work," said Sarina eagerly. "Have you the controller?"

"Yes," Robert replied. He felt his pockets. "No, wait, I gave it to Tim. I've got some smoke grenades though."

"Now you're talking," whispered Jonathan. "When we're in position, throw one near that truck at the other end of the courtyard. Join us after you toss it."

Robert nodded and waited as the other three youths quietly ran to get near the doorway.

"Almost ready," Jonathan whispered over the commlink.

"Okay, we're in position. Throw the smoke grenade."

Robert quietly stood up, pulled the arming pin, and threw the grenade. It sailed over a parked van, smacked on the cobblestone courtyard, and rolled under a truck.

"What was that?" called out one of the guards from across the courtyard.

There was a popping sound as the grenade started burning. Smoke began pouring out from under the vehicle. Robert could now see flames. "One diversion coming up," he said as he ran to join the other youths.

The courtyard guards ran in the opposite direction toward the truck. They were almost to it when the leaky fuel tank caught fire and a big *whoosh* of flames shot skyward.

Robert's glasses helped him see Jonathan and the girls heading for the now-guardless doorway. He reached the stairs about seventy-five yards behind them, leapt down two stairs at a time, and hit the courtyard running. Glancing back, he could see the truck fully engulfed in flames.

As Robert ran past the doorways lining the courtyard, a hand reached out from one of them and yanked him into an unlit side room. The name "Dantzel" appeared on his glass lenses for just a second as he tripped and fell to the floor.

"Get out of here the way you came!" shouted a female voice and the person turned and ran out of the doorway.

Robert's glasses and goggles had flown off his face and gone skidding across the stone floor. He scrambled to his knees and blindly searched for them. He finally located them several feet away and put them back on. He could now see again in the darkness. As he turned toward the courtyard doorway, he could hear the loud sound of helicopters approaching. Soldiers suddenly appeared from the perimeter of the courtyard amid loud, bright explosions.

Robert looked through the open doorway to see two military-type helicopters landing in the courtyard. Soldier-commandos, some repelling down ropes, were disembarking from them before they even touched the ground, throwing stun grenades in many directions. One of the grenades was tossed in Robert's direction; he ducked back into the room as the grenade exploded with a blindingly bright flash and loud concussion.

For a moment, there was yelling in the courtyard as soldiers ran to-and-fro. Shots rang out and Robert stayed where he was. The helicopter rotors kept their loud cadence. Soon there was more yelling of commands. Robert glanced out the doorway and his eyes caught sight of the pilot in the forward helicopter. "Dantzel," said his glasses. The image was burned in Robert's vision. "Dantzel?" he thought. "But this person looks older!"

Confused and stunned by the grenade, Robert saw commandoes emerge from the end of the courtyard. They were rushing a man toward the lead helicopter. "King Alexander Straunsee," said Robert's glasses.

More commandoes emerged, this time carrying three limp youths, Kimberly, Jonathan, and Sarina. Their knit caps were gone, their faces and arms fully visible. The captives were rushed aboard the helicopters. Robert dashed out to try to stop them but another stun grenade exploded in front of him, knocking him backwards to the ground.

The rotors sped faster as the helicopters lifted from the courtyard, leaving a smoky, dusty haze in the air. Robert watched them, stunned, as they leapt skyward and turned west. The truck was still burning. Robert got to his feet and headed for the rope at the wall. He had to get out of there and fast before the castle guards discovered him. With the king gone, the castle was a place to be far away from.

Robert raced up the stairs, his head pounding. The rescue

mission had totally backfired. Not only was the king gone, but Jonathan, Sarina, and Kimberly were gone, too! Who took them and where were they being taken? And who was this Dantzel? And how could she be young and old at the same time?

CHAPTER 10

Vital Fuel

Robert reached the grappling hook and rope and tried to climb over the wall. The motor "climber" was gone. What had he done with it? But the rope was still there. He grasped it with his gloves and tried rappelling down. He was good for the first thirty feet but the rope slipped in his hands and he fell faster. He bounced off the wall and landed in a pile of snow-covered brush at the bottom.

When Robert glanced up, he saw Lindy, Katrina, and Maria crouched around him.

"Where's Tim?" asked Robert.

"Could somebody please get this guy off of me," Tim called out from underneath Robert.

"I thought I landed on a bush," said Robert.

"Yeah, no thanks to these fancy camouflage duds," Tim said. "From now on, I think I'll stick to regular clothes."

"Where's everybody else?" asked Katrina.

"The helicopters took them away," said Robert haltingly. "I couldn't stop them."

"Let's get you back to the car," said Lindy, concerned about her brother. "Can you walk?"

"I think so," said Robert. "We tried, Lindy, but there were commandos."

"We saw the helicopters, too," said Lindy.

Katrina was anxious to find out the fate of her dad and sister. "Robert, do you still have the locator?" she asked as she and Lindy helped Robert to his feet. Robert felt his pockets and said, "Yes." He retrieved it and handed it to Katrina. She switched it on. "Good," she said, "we've got a strong beacon. Probably Sarina's necklace."

Tim switched on the controls for the drone and had it scan the castle courtyard. "Oh wow," he said, "it looks like a hornet's nest in there. There's soldiers all over. We'd better get out of here."

Enjoying being at the controls, Tim next flew the drone—using its infrared night vision—to scout their way along the outside of the castle. "Looks clear," he said.

Tim set out in the lead, using his night vision glasses and the drone. Katrina was next, then Robert, Lindy, and Maria. Robert was a little wobbly at first, Lindy helped him, but after a few minutes he could walk on his own. They retraced their steps along the narrow trail above the Rystrad River.

Tim suddenly motioned for them all to duck down. His night vision glasses had picked up something on the trail up ahead.

"What is it?" whispered Katrina.

"Soldiers," Tim replied. "And they're coming this way!"

The youths spied some bushes on the hillside above them and quickly scrambled up the slope to hide in them. They could hear the soldiers approaching. The soldiers wore white parkas and were carrying submachine guns. The lead soldier was talking by radio. "No sir," he said, "we haven't seen any of their support group yet. We don't know where they came from. We'll let you know if we find anything. Over."

The soldiers stopped on the trail directly below where the youths were hiding. Their pause gave them a chance to study the area. They were about to move forward when a branch Tim was kneeling against suddenly snapped. Katrina grabbed him by the arm to stop him from tumbling down the hillside. The soldiers shined their lights up in the youths' direction.

"Everybody pull your knit caps down over your faces," whispered Lindy.

"Look at those tracks," said one of the soldiers.

"Follow them," said the squad leader. Two soldiers started climbing up the hillside toward where the youths were hiding. They followed the youths' footsteps up toward the bushes and shined their flashlights into the brush. The youths held their breath, praying they wouldn't be seen.

"Something climbed through the brush here," said one of the soldiers.

The soldiers probed, prying branches aside. Their lights were now shining directly on Katrina and Tim.

"We're wasting our time," said the second soldier. "Let's get back down to the others."

The two soldiers turned around and made their way back down the hillside.

"Nothing," reported one of the soldiers to his squad leader. "Someone had been there, but nobody's there now."

With that, the soldiers continued along the trail the youths had just come from.

"Whew," said Lindy, "I thought they'd never leave."

"Tim, they shined their lights right on you and Katrina," whispered Maria after the soldiers had gone.

"Yeah, I take back what I said," Tim whispered. "I think I *do* like these GearSpy1 jumpsuits after all."

"Let's get out of here," said Lindy.

The youths quickly made their way back down to the trail and continued toward their car. A short while later, they were forced to hide under some trees as another helicopter landed at the castle. This time there was no shooting.

When the helicopter was out of sight, the youths started out again.

"Those men who shined the lights on us, and that helicopter," said Katrina. "They were not from our country."

"Katrina, where have they taken Father, Sarina, Kimberly, and Jonathan?" asked Maria with concern.

It was another twenty minutes before the youths reached their car. Lights were out all over Trifid. Here and there, car headlights could be seen but that was all. Nobody wanted to become a target.

Maria gave the keys to Robert, who was feeling better, more alert now. Robert unlocked the car but when they went to open the doors, they were frozen closed. They had to yank the doors open. Robert climbed into the driver's seat, Katrina the front passenger seat, and Tim, Lindy, and Maria sat in the middle of the car.

Robert started the car and waited for the heater and defrosters to begin working. Katrina switched on the locator Robert had given her.

"Where are they now?" asked Robert.

"They're heading northwest," Katrina replied. "I'll guide you."

Once the windshield was clear, Robert pulled out onto the road and headed down the street.

"Take the next right," directed Katrina. "It will take us to the main road."

As the youths pulled out onto the highway, another car pulled out after them.

The locator kept Robert and Katrina up to date on the fastest route. Sometimes the route changed. The helicopter in which

King Straunsee, Kimberly, Jonathan, and Sarina were flying was not traveling in a straight course.

The youths were tired from their castle ordeal. The sun had gone down hours ago. As the car warmed, Tim leaned his head back against his headrest and was soon snoring lightly. Maria, her head resting against Lindy's shoulder, nodded off, too. Lindy soon joined them.

In the front seat, Katrina was trying to help Robert stay awake by keeping up a conversation with him. "I am sorry your visit to our country has not been as Sarina and I had planned," she said.

"You *do* know how to throw a party," Robert replied with a grin, looking straight ahead at the road. "Seriously, though, it has been fun seeing you and your family again. Where do you think the helicopter troops are taking your father?"

"I wish I knew," Katrina replied, glancing down at the locator. "We're still on the fastest road."

Katrina was silent for a moment and said, "It is not right that those foreign soldiers were at Trifid Castle. Mr. Kreppen must be stopped or he will destroy the freedom and government of our country."

Tim's voice interrupted them. "No more pickles on my peanut butter sandwich, please," he called out, talking in his sleep.

Robert and Katrina both chuckled. "That's Tim. He says some pretty crazy things in his sleep, sometimes," said Robert, grinning.

"Maria does as well," Katrina said, smiling also. "Those two are like two birds in a pudding." She paused for a moment and said, "Robert, thank you for helping my family."

"Hey, that's what friends do, right?"

"Yes," said Katrina with a smile, "that's what friends do.

You're a good guy, Robert Wright."

Following the locator's directions, Robert turned off onto a new road heading north through the mountains. The road curved in and out as it followed the canyon. There was little snow on the road itself, but it was piled high off to the sides where the snowplow trucks had thrown it.

Katrina looked back to see how Maria and the others were doing. They were all sleeping soundly. Katrina noticed a car behind them. "Robert," she said, "I think that car might be following us. I saw those same type of headlights behind us half an hour ago."

Robert checked his rearview mirror and sped up a little. The car behind him sped up, too. "You might be right," Robert replied.

Katrina glanced at the locator. "We're supposed to turn right onto a new road in two kilometers," she said.

"If they really are following us," said Robert, "maybe we can lose them there."

The "road" turned out to be a bridge over the river they had been paralleling. Robert drove steadily, acting as if he was going to continue straight. At the last minute, he cut hard to the right. The SUV started sliding sideways. To his surprise, flaming jets suddenly shot out from the left side of the car, helping the SUV around the curve. The car behind them shot past the bridge and kept on going straight.

"They didn't turn to follow us," announced Katrina.

"Yeah, but did you see those blue flames on the side of our car?" said Robert.

"No," Katrina replied, "I was looking at the car behind us. Do you think our car is damaged?"

Robert checked the side mirrors but didn't see any smoke coming from their car. The gauges looked okay. "I don't see any problems," he replied, stepping on the gas pedal just in case there was someone following them. The car leaped forward, throwing Robert and Katrina back against their seats.

"Whoa!" said Robert, seeing the speedometer racing higher.

"EVADE MODE," appeared on the car's instrument panel.

"Robert, don't you think we should slow down a little?" said Katrina, her knuckles turning white on the car's grab handle.

"I'm trying," said Robert. "The gas pedal's stuck to the floor."

Robert steered into a curve. Blue flame jets shot out from the side, keeping the car on the road. Trees alongside were now just blurs.

Katrina was starting to panic. "Robert, please stop going so fast!" she said.

Robert stomped on the brake pedal. "The brakes aren't working either." He tried turning off the ignition key but the car kept going.

Robert and Katrina looked at each other in concern and back at the road ahead. Robert's hands were glued to the steering wheel. At least he could still steer. He glanced at the SUV's navigation screen. "FUEL LOW," it said.

"We're almost out of gas," Robert said. "Then we'll have to stop."

"Thank goodness for that," said Katrina. "Just keep us on the road."

Along with the "FUEL LOW" warning, a map appeared on the car's navigation screen, plotting out the locations of the nearest gas stations. "Katrina, go ahead and pick one," said Robert.

Katrina studied the screen for a moment and tapped one of the locations. The screen changed, focusing on the route she had just picked. Katrina glanced back behind them. There were no cars in sight.

As they closed to within one kilometer of the targeted gas station, the gas pedal released and the SUV began to slow. Robert cautiously turned into the gas station and stopped at a gas pump. The car engine shut off by itself. Weary, Robert and Katrina glanced at each other.

"That was *something*," said Katrina with relief.

"Yes, I'll—I'll get the car fueling and look into what's wrong with the car," Robert said. "Katrina, I want you to know that I normally don't drive like that."

"Sure," said Katrina with a grin.

There was an icy wind blowing as Robert got out of the car. His jumpsuit turned white to match the SUV. The frigid wind woke up the three youths in the back seat. Robert got the nozzle going and glanced up at the fuel pump. A digital screen on the pump caught his eye. An older woman was being interviewed by a news host on the screen. Robert gasped and banged on the car window. "Hey guys, look at this," he said, "that looks like great Aunt Opal!"

CHAPTER 11

The Pilot

Great Aunt Opal was the Wright cousins' somewhat forgetful aunt who had an unusual knack of starting out to go somewhere and accidentally ending up in a totally different place. Her family had given up on trying to figure out how she did it.

"What's great Aunt Opal doing on the gas pump?" said Tim, wiping the sleep from his eyes as he got out of the car to look at the video more closely. Lindy, Maria, and Katrina joined him.

"Ma'am," said the show host on the *Nickel-Saver's Show*, "how do you do it? How have you been able to see so much of the world on so little money?"

"Well, take this trip for example," said great Aunt Opal. "I was just flying down to New York. From the looks of the palm trees around here, I must have landed in Florida."

"Ma'am, this isn't Florida," said the host. "We're in Hawaii."

"Hawaii, oh my," said Aunt Opal. "And I was on my way to Niagara Falls."

"Would you like to say anything to our guests?" asked the interviewer with a chuckle.

"Why, yes, young man, I'd be happy to. Timothy Wright, deary, I know you're out there."

"No I'm not, no I'm not," said Tim, glancing down at his shoelaces and putting his hands over his eyes so she couldn't see him.

"Timothy, dearie, be sure to keep your shoelaces tied. You don't want to trip on them. Oh, and also to my dear young nieces and nephews, the Wright cousins, I've got some more of your favorite Chocolate Garlic-Broccoli Delight. I'll save it for you, sweeties."

"Thank you, ma'am," said the host, grimacing. "I'm sure they will love them."

"Chocolate Garlic-Broccoli Delight?" asked Maria. "That almost sounds good."

"No, it's not, it's terrible with a capital 'T'," Tim replied, holding his nose. "Yucky! Robert, hurry and get us out of here before she figures out where we are and sends it to us!"

Fueling done, the youths were just about to climb into their car when the TV screen picture switched to a royal dance. Robert's GearSpy1 jumpsuit suddenly started reflecting the bow tie and tuxedo of the man on the screen.

Tim laughed, but stopped when a picture of a tuxedo with bow tie suddenly appeared on his jumpsuit, too. "Noooooooo!" he said. "Robert, stop it!"

"Quick," said Robert. "We've got to find a new background picture to change our gear back." He glanced at the screen. An ad showing baby clothes was now appearing.

"Oh no!" said Tim. "Everybody in the car!"

Everyone scrambled into the SUV. By the time Tim had gotten in, the image of a blue baby bib had appeared on the back of his jumpsuit. "All right," said Tim, "what is everybody laughing about?"

"Nothing, Tim," said Lindy with a chuckle, "we're just glad you're so young at heart."

As they were leaving the small town, Katrina spied the same car catching up with them.

"They're back," Katrina announced.

"Again?" said Robert. "I thought we'd left them behind."

Robert cautiously stepped lightly on the gas pedal. The SUV sped up slightly. The car pulled up closer onto their tail. The driver was motioning for them to pull over.

"No way," said Katrina. "Don't do it, Robert. They're probably from Trifid Castle."

The car pulled out into the passing lane to get ahead of the youth's car. "Not on my watch," said Robert, gunning the gas pedal. Blue flames shot out of the rear of the SUV and it surged ahead.

"Wow," said Tim, now thoroughly awake, "this is a great car."

Twenty minutes later, the youths were reaching the outskirts of the next town. Robert glanced at the navigation screen. "There's a shortcut up ahead," he announced. "We just have to go straight instead of turning left."

"Don't even think of it," said Katrina. "It's probably a dirt road, and this time of year it won't be good."

"Okay," said Robert, noting their high speed and stepping on the brakes to slow down. To his amazement, the brakes worked this time. They made the turn. Up ahead, the youths could see flashing lights and two vehicles parked in the roadway.

"It looks like a roadblock," said Robert, slowing the car to look for a way out.

"Robert, that car is still following us," said Lindy.

Robert glanced nervously in the rearview mirror. The youths heard a loud sound thumping overhead. Two bright lights appeared in the sky, spotlighting their car in the dark night. The lights were lowering and a helicopter soon appeared in their headlights. Robert jammed on the brakes and the car skidded toward the copter landing in front of them.

When their car stopped, Katrina said, "It's Father's helicopter," and leapt from the car. Robert got out and chased after her. "Stop, Katrina," he called out. "It might be a trap!"

Katrina made it to the helicopter and pulled open one of its doors. She took one look inside and motioned for the others to join her. "It's okay!" she called out. "It's one of Father's." Then she spoke to the pilot, "Wait while we get our things." In the distance she could see the cars—there were now two of them—still several kilometers away, but they were rapidly approaching.

Katrina rushed back to the cousins' car and directed Robert to pull it onto the shoulder. "Get your things," she said. "It's Mr. Gervar."

The youths quickly retrieved their luggage and supplies from the SUV and locked it, rushed over to the helicopter and climbed aboard. They were several hundred feet in the air as the two pursuing cars pulled up to their parked SUV.

"Ha-ha," laughed Tim, looking down at the cars. "You can't catch me, I'm the gingerbread man."

"Gingerbread man?" said Maria.

"Yeah, you know, the gingerbread cookie that always gets away," Tim replied.

"But he got eaten by the fox, didn't he?" asked Maria.

"Well, yeah, but he got mostly away until that," Tim replied.

"He means we got away just in time," explained Katrina with a relieved smile on her face.

"Got away? What do you mean?" asked Mr. Gervar, the helicopter pilot.

"Those cars were chasing us," Katrina replied. "They've been after us for a while."

"You didn't get away from them," returned the pilot with a

serious grin. "They were told to bring you here."

"They were?" said Katrina, glancing back at Robert.

"Don't worry, Katrina," said the pilot. "They are some of your father's supporters. They've been trying to catch up to you so I could pick you up. We finally had to arrange for the roadblock."

"You mean we've been trying to get away from the good guys all this time?" said Katrina.

Mr. Gervar looked at her and chuckled, "I haven't had this much fun since I found the secret plans to Telvert Castle."

"Have you located Father and Sarina?" asked Katrina. "Soldiers took they and our friends away from Trifid Castle."

"We're not sure," Mr. Gervar replied. "The only word I got was that I was to take you kids to Pallin."

"Pallin?" said Katrina. "What's going on there?"

"We're evacuating the Straunsee Aerospace Works."

"Dad's shops? Why?" said Katrina.

"Kreppen's trying to steal the advanced rocket engine technology. We got word he's in league with somebody named Slagg and they're trying to overthrow the kingdom."

"Slagg?" said Robert, glancing at Lindy. "Do we know him?"

Lindy closed her eyes for a moment to search her photographic memory. "Yes," she said, opening her eyes again. "He's the one that tried to shoot us out of space."

Maria spoke up. "I heard my sister, Allesandra, mention his name a long time ago. She and her friend, Eric Brown, fought against him during the battle of Rheebakken 2.

"Eric Brown?" asked Robert.

"Skip Brown's uncle. We met him at the dinner at Straunsee Castle," informed Lindy, her cheeks turning slightly pink. Skip was the Wright cousins' good friend from Lake Pinecone and a special friend of Lindy.

"Yes, right," said Robert. "I knew that."

The helicopter flight was faster, but it wasn't as smooth as what the cousins had expected. The copter kept banking right and left, as if there was a lot of turbulence. Tim suspected it was Mr. Gervar's out-of-practice flying. He didn't say anything, though, because he didn't want Kimberly elbowing him in the ribs. It took him a while to realize Kimberly wasn't even there.

"Please keep your seatbelts on," Mr. Gervar said. "Katrina, would you please hand out the peanuts."

"Peanuts?" remarked Tim. "Do we get a movie and parachutes, too?" Robert elbowed him a good one in the ribs. "Okay, Kimberly...I mean, Robert," said Tim.

As they flew, the youths began to see other dark shapes in the night sky with red and white flashing beacons. Slipping on their night vision equipment, they could see they were joining other helicopters, military ones. They all seemed to be flying in the same direction.

"Katrina?" asked Robert. "What's Pallin like?"

"It is a small town," Katrina called back from the front seat. "On the outskirts, there's an airport and some military buildings, and my father's aerospace works," Katrina replied.

The military helicopters were flying in formation, low and fast. Mr. Gervar had a challenging time keeping up with them in the smaller engined Straunsee helicopter.

Ahead, the youths could see the golden glow of a small town spread out amongst low hills and mountains. Ten minutes later, an airfield came into view. Looking out into the lit-up sky, the youths could see at least half a dozen helicopters besides the one they were in. Mr. Gervar received directions to fly to the far end of the airfield to land near the large hangar there. As he did so, two large cargo helicopters flew in beside him and landed, too. The youths could see several helicopter gunships circling the base.

As Mr. Gervar set the helicopter down, the youths saw dozens of people, some in uniforms, some in civilian clothes, scrambling about inside and around the large aircraft hangar. Once the rotor blades on the cargo helicopters had stopped, forklifts emerged from the hangar to begin loading the large copters with their precious cargo. Bright, trailer-mounted lights on tall poles lit the immediate area. As the youths stepped down from the Straunsee helicopter, they could feel an urgency in the air.

A civilian in a dark blue parka approached Mr. Gervar and the youths. She introduced herself as Laurel Sorenton. Laurel appeared to be in her mid-forties. Robert could see from the nametag she wore that she worked for the Straunsee Aerospace Works.

"Please follow me," Laurel said. She led them into the large, well-lit hangar. They had to step to the side several times as a forklift or other small vehicle came driving through. "I'm afraid we're a little rushed here tonight," she said. "We've got to get this hangar cleared out before they get here."

CHAPTER 12

Unwelcome Guest

Laurel led Mr. Gervar and the youths over to the left side of the hangar to a small office and ushered them inside. At the far side of the room, a tall, grey-haired man was standing with his back to them, speaking on a phone.

"Father!" said Katrina and Maria at the same time. He turned to see them and immediately set down the phone as they rushed over to him. There were tears shed by all as they warmly embraced.

"But Father, Robert said the helicopter soldiers took you away," said Katrina. "How did you get here?"

"They brought us here," King Straunsee replied. "They're some of our most loyal soldiers."

Katrina led her father over to where Robert, Lindy, and Tim were standing. "Thank you for helping my children," he said to the Wrights.

"Mr. Gervar said you are evacuating your equipment, sir," said Robert. "How can we help?"

"You kids get some food and use the bathrooms," said King Straunsee, "we will then put you to work. Laurel, would you please show them the way?"

"Certainly," said Laurel with a smile. "Follow me."

Laurel Sorenton led the youths out of the office and over to a food station that had been set up in a nearby room. When they got there, they found Jonathan, Sarina, and Kimberly already eating.

Robert and Tim's jumpsuits still had the picture of the bow tie but the rest of the tuxedo had faded. "Wow," said Kimberly, getting up from her chair, "nice clothes, you guys."

Tim ducked behind Robert and said, "Yeah, well, it's all Robert's fault."

"Our jumpsuits kind of malfunctioned," said Robert. "The batteries must have died or something."

The youths all hugged. Tim almost got away without being hugged but Sarina caught sight of him and gave him a good hug, too. The youths quickly filled each other in on what their groups had experienced.

"We got caught in the middle of King Straunsee's rescue," said Kimberly. "We were right there when the concussion grenades exploded. Boy are those things loud. I'm surprised they didn't destroy our eardrums!"

"What did you say?" asked Jonathan.

"I said we got caught in the middle—," Kimberly said again.

"I'm just kidding," said Jonathan with a big grin. "I could hear you okay."

"Brothers!" said Kimberly, shaking her head. "Sarina's dad saw us and had the soldiers haul us out, too."

"They brought us here by helicopter and here we are," said Jonathan. "We tried to tell them about you guys but they couldn't go back to the castle. Kreppen's guards were all over the place and shooting at us."

"We prayed you'd be safe," said Sarina.

"We have been praying for you, too," Katrina replied. "I'm so glad you're okay."

"Boy, you should have seen our car go," said Tim. "Robert totally outran the good guys in our SUV."

"You mean 'bad guys', don't you?" Kimberly said.

"No, we outran the guys that were trying to help us," Tim replied. "And our SUV was awesome. It had booster jets to keep us on the road and go faster. Now that was cool!"

"Really?" said Jonathan.

"It's actually a pretty amazing car," said Robert. "Too bad we had to leave it behind."

Sarina retrieved a jug of milk from the refrigerator and poured a cupful for each of the newcomers.

"Did you guys see those helicopter gunships flying around out there?" Robert asked.

"Yes, do you think we could get to ride in one of them?" asked Tim.

"No thanks," said Kimberly. "I don't want to get mixed up in any maneuvers."

"Kim, these aren't maneuvers," said Jonathan. "They're gearing up for the real thing."

"Jonathan, then we—all of us—really need to get out of here," Kimberly said worriedly.

"We will," Jonathan replied, "but first we've got to help these good people.

The youths quickly ate and reported back to King Straunsee for assignments. He had Laurel take them down into the concrete bunker under the hanger building. Among other things, the bunker housed the computers used for their hi-tech research and those controlling the lathes, mills, and other manufacturing machines.

Laurel and the youths entered the secure elevator to take them down. She stayed with the cousins and Straunsee girls as they joined computer technicians to help catalog and carefully load the computer equipment into specially insulated packing containers.

"Nothing must be lost of Alexander's work," said Laurel.

"Unknown aircraft approaching," announced a voice over some speakers in the main room of the bunker. "Warning, unknown aircraft approaching. Estimated Time of Arrival—20 minutes. Prepare to secure all vital equipment that has not been loaded."

The youths, Laurel, and the technicians hurriedly worked to finish their task. Boxes were closed and latched, wires coiled and bagged, paper documents were sealed in waterproof bags. Robert spied a technician with hard drive equipment and rushed over to help him. The man first tried to shoo him away but then finally accepted his help. Robert dug in wholeheartedly.

"We have to be especially careful with these things," the man said. "They damage very easily."

Robert carefully packed the equipment. The man seemed to be taking longer than necessary, so Robert continued to help him. As they packed, the man kept trying to get Robert to help somewhere else. There were fifteen computer memory units.

"This unit is faulty," said the man. "Let's focus on getting the other fourteen units packed and ready." They went back to packing.

"There's something not right here," thought Robert. "That's one of the primary backup units."

Robert watched the man closely as he worked. The man seemed nervous. Out of the corner of his eye, Robert saw the man slip the boxed fifteenth unit into an olive drab document bag under the table.

"Okay," said the man, "let's get these units to the elevator."

"Sure," Robert said.

Robert and the man made several trips, carrying the gear to the evacuation table nearest the elevator.

"Be careful with those boxes," said the man to Jonathan and Sarina who were preparing to take them up.

There were several olive drab bags under the table where the man had stashed the fifteenth drive. Robert headed back to the table to see what else needed to be done. The technician soon returned. "Are we done over here?" asked Robert.

The man glanced around. A slight grin appeared on his face. "Yes," he said. "Let's get out of here."

"Okay," said Robert, feeling lighter. "With those unidentified aircraft coming, the sooner the better."

"Thanks for your help," said the man. "I felt kind of overwhelmed." The man picked up some boxes and left on the elevator.

Robert suddenly felt bad for suspecting the technician. Jonathan called Robert over to help him with a heavy crate. Working together, they carried it over and rode the elevator up to ground level. The rest of the youths soon joined them. They loaded their boxes onto one of the waiting cargo helicopters. The forklifts had been doing their work well and the two large aircraft were nearly full.

"Fifteen minutes until unidentified aircraft arrival," announced the loudspeakers.

More equipment was quickly loaded into the two large helicopters. Their large rear and side doors were closed and latched shut, and the pilots began speeding up the powerful rotor blades. The blades whipped the softly falling snow into a near tornado as the two massive helicopters lifted into the air and headed north. They were joined by four smaller, olive-green helicopter gunships. They flew off into the dark, snowy night.

After watching the helicopters leave, the youths reentered the large hangar. They hurried down to the bunker, but found the main room now empty except for tables and chairs. They quickly searched each of the other rooms in the small bunker and found similar results.

"I guess we're all done down here," said Jonathan. "Let's go find out what else we can do."

The youths returned to the elevator and rode it back up to ground level. As they entered the hangar, they heard new helicopters approaching. Three foreign-built helicopters, one a gunship, were just arriving from the southeast. They were there for a parley under the symbol of the white flag. The helicopters touched down near the hangar on the landing strip. King Straunsee's guards moved forward to surround the helicopters.

As the helicopters' blades wound down, Mr. Oilee Kreppen and several heavily armed soldiers stepped down onto the tarmac. Captain Landis, one of King Straunsee's men, went to notify the king that Kreppen was there. King Straunsee soon arrived, accompanied by many of his guards as well.

"What do you want, Kreppen?" called out King Straunsee from just inside the large hangar.

"We need to talk," said Mr. Kreppen.

"We can talk well enough here," King Straunsee replied.

"All right," said Mr. Kreppen. "Alexander, for the good of all Gütenberg, our country, I call on you to turn your aerospace works over to me."

"That's quite a demand coming from a thief, kidnapper, and liar," said King Straunsee.

"Name calling will get you nowhere," said Kreppen.

"I call it like it is," said King Straunsee.

Mr. Kreppen shook his head and said, "It is my desire to save you and your family, Alexander." He shielded his eyes from the bright overhead lights with his right hand. "I have it on good authority that a foreign nation will attack us if we don't turn over your aerospace works to them. For the good of our country, our people, and yourself, man, help me so we can appease them by turning it over to them."

"I am well aware that you are in league with Colonel Slagg and his forces," King Straunsee replied. "You have been for some time."

The Wright cousins and the Straunsee girls were watching from inside the hangar as well.

"Katrina," asked Maria, "why is Father talking with him for so long?"

CHAPTER 13

Intercepted

"I think Father is trying to buy time," replied Katrina. "He's giving our cargo helicopters and gunships a chance to get clear of here."

"Alexander," continued Mr. Kreppen, "you and your friends can go free. I will see to it that you are escorted from the country under my protection. Colonel Slagg has promised as much."

"Kreppen, since when did you *ever* keep your word when it mattered?" said King Straunsee. "You go back to your master, Colonel Slagg, and tell him that neither you nor he will get our aerospace works or our country. We know how to fight and we know how to win."

"Alexander, already there are fighter-bomber planes in the air, just waiting my call to fly into Gütenberg air space," Kreppen replied angrily. "Don't let your stubbornness destroy all that we've worked for!" Kreppen paused for a moment and said, "Alexander, you will have twenty minutes after I leave before the bombs arrive. Make your choice."

"What makes you think you're leaving?" said King Straunsee. "I thought we could defend our soil together."

Mr. Kreppen glanced nervously around and nodded toward one of his soldiers.

Out of the corner of his eye, Robert saw the technician he had helped. The man had an olive-green pouch under his arm.

He had been slowly making his way over toward Kreppen. When he saw his chance, he ran the last few steps and handed the bag and whispered something to Kreppen. Kreppen's eyes widened.

"Never mind, Alexander," said Kreppen with a smirk on his face. "We now have what we came for. It seems a patriotic technician has retrieved your data. We will no longer interrupt your fleeing from Gütenberg."

Kreppen and his men quickly backed up to their helicopter and climbed in. King Straunsee's guards kept their weapons trained on them all the while.

"King, do you want us to keep them here?" asked Captain Landis.

"No," replied King Straunsee. "They came under the flag of truce and they shall leave the same way. Besides, I have been informed that they got what they deserve."

"What's that mean?" Maria whispered to Katrina.

"It means Robert switched the computer units on them," Katrina whispered back with a growing grin. "Kreppen just got a box with an empty stapler in it."

"I like Robert," whispered Maria. "He's a good guy."

"Yep, he is," Katrina whispered back. "But that's just between us two girls, all right?"

"Right," said Maria. "If Tim ever found out about it, we'd never hear the end of it."

The youths watched Kreppen's helicopter as it lifted off the tarmac, joined his others, and flew off into the night.

"Attention, everyone!" announced King Straunsee. "We have several twenty-seat passenger planes coming in to take you to safety. Once the planes have landed, we need you to form into lines of twenty and board them in a quick and orderly manner. When the planes are stopped, we will go out to meet them."

The Wrights and the Straunsee girls continued to help in the large hangar. Twenty minutes later, a colonel came up to King Straunsee to report. "We've just got word, Sir, that several bogeys have just crossed over our borders."

"That's what I was afraid of," said King Straunsee. "Kreppen has totally sold us out. Have you notified the interceptor units?"

"Yes," the colonel replied. "They're already in the air."

"Good," said King Straunsee.

Soon the passenger planes arrived. Everyone gathered inside the hangar and anxiously waited until the planes had taxied into position, then they quickly ran for the open doors of the planes. Once a plane was filled, it took off. The Gütenbergian helicopter gunships that had been circling the base had taken turns refueling at the airport and were all now back in the sky, ready to defend.

King Straunsee told his daughters he had to leave for the capital. He had to steady the government. He asked the Wright cousins and his daughters to help each other in the coming days as they would be challenging ones. He had prepared a flight for them to leave the country so they could be safe.

"Father, we don't want to go. We want to stay and help you," said Maria.

"I need you safe," said King Straunsee, hugging Maria. "War is being thrust upon us." He glanced at Jonathan and Robert and said, "*Please protect my daughters. I must fight this evil that is trying to destroy our people and our country.*"

"I love you, Father," said Maria as she hugged her dad. "I wish Allesandra were here."

"Me too, little one," said King Straunsee. "Good-bye now...and listen to your sisters."

"Yes, Father," said Maria, wiping the tears from her eyes.

King Straunsee hugged Sarina and Katrina in turn and then

headed for the helicopter he had come on from Trifid Castle. Robert slipped on his spy glasses so he could see better in the dark. Brackets appeared around the helicopter pilot's face. "Dantzel," it said. He started to head over to the helicopter to find out just who she was, but Katrina grabbed his arm and said, "Come on, we've got to go meet our plane."

"Oh yeah," said Robert, turning away from the helicopter.

Jonathan, Sarina, Kimberly, Lindy, Robert, Katrina, Maria and Tim quickly made their way to the last waiting plane. The snow was falling heavier now. As they ran toward the plane, their view of the large Straunsee Aerospace Works hangar faded from view behind them.

King Straunsee's helicopter was just lifting off as the youths reached their aircraft. It was a twin-engine turboprop plane and was several hundred feet away from the hangar. Jonathan and Sarina waited at the foot of the stairs as the other youths climbed in. All the other personnel had already left. The interior of the plane was dimly lit. Sarina and Jonathan were the last ones aboard. The Gütenbergian helicopter gunships were just leaving.

As Robert went to sit down, his hand brushed something in his back pocket. He retrieved it. It was a double-folded piece of paper. As he unfolded it, he discovered a black-and-white picture of a go-kart. He turned the paper over and discovered some writing in pencil. "Thank you," it said, "for being a dear friend and helping my brother. It looks like your GearSpy1 batteries ran down. You might want to try the 'GearSpy1 Hi-Tech series.' It has more capabilities. D."

"D?" said Robert. He quickly looked out the airplane window to his left, trying to discover who had put the paper in his pocket. All he saw was falling snow and the dim glow from the distant hangar's lights.

"Oh rats," said Robert, suddenly remembering, "Jonathan, I forgot to get that computer backup drive I hid in the bunker. We can't let Kreppen get it. It's in a box under the table."

"I'll go with you," said Jonathan. He turned to Sarina who was already seated and said, "Robert and I have to return to the bunker. We'll be right back."

"But the enemy planes are coming," said Sarina.

"We've still got a few minutes. We'll run," Jonathan replied.

"I'll go with you," said Sarina, reaching to unbuckle her seatbelt.

"Notify the pilots to wait," Jonathan said. "If we're not back in ten minutes, take off without us."

"We're not taking off without you," said Sarina. "Be careful and hurry back."

"I will," said Jonathan, patting her hand.

Robert and Jonathan climbed down out of the plane. In the falling snow, they could see the glow from the hangar and ran for it. When they got there, they quickly made their way over to the elevator. Lights were still shining brightly, but the place was deserted. There was no one in sight.

The elevator door finally opened. They stepped inside and pushed the down button. The elevator seemed to take forever. It finally stopped and the door slowly slid open. The lights were still on down in the bunker, too. It seemed almost surreal; it being lit but not occupied by anyone.

Robert dashed over to the table he and the technician had been working at earlier. He pulled several green bags off a box and quickly looked inside. "Here it is," he said with relief.

"Good, let's get out of here," said Jonathan. "Those planes will be here in about six minutes."

There was a loud thud and the ground suddenly shook. A metallic ringing sound came from the elevator in the next room.

The lights flickered and went off. When they came on a few seconds later, they were dimmer.

"Emergency power," said Jonathan. "That must have been a bomb explosion. We've got to get out of here!"

There was another loud thud, followed by three more. Smoke began pouring from the elevator. There was another thud and rumble. The ground shook and the lights went out again. When they came on, they were only dim, red emergency ones.

"I hope Sarina and everybody are okay," said Jonathan with concern.

The youths waited a moment to see if there would be any more bombs. When it was still and silent, they started for the elevator. They pushed the button. The doors opened, exhaling smoke into the bunker.

"It's not safe to take an elevator in a fire," said Jonathan. "We'll have to find another way out."

"There was a steel door in one of the other rooms," said Robert. "Maybe it leads to some stairs."

The boys quickly found the door and pried it open. Beyond it was a flight of steel stairs. Smoke and dust were pouring in from a vent in the wall. Pulling their t-shirt collars up to cover their nose and mouths to filter the air, the boys headed up the stairs. Reaching a landing, they turned and headed up a second flight. There was a second door, this one heavier and made of concrete and steel. Finding an emergency release lever, they unlatched the door and pulled it open. Smoke and dust were everywhere. They headed up a flight of concrete stairs and arrived at ground surface level. No overhead lights were shining. Part of a smoking, twisted steel beam blocked their way. They carefully stepped around it. Things were totally different now.

Robert shined his light around in shock. "The whole

hangar's been blown away!" he said.

Jonathan glanced around, trying to get his bearings. "Got to get back to the plane," he said and took off running toward what looked like the landing strip. Robert, carrying the computer drive, chased after him. The snow was still falling, heavier now. They reached the main runway but found nothing. "No!" shouted Jonathan. "They can't be. Sarina, Kimberly, Tim, where are you?"

CHAPTER 14

Missing Link

Robert had never seen his cousin so distraught. He suddenly remembered his commlink. He pushed a button. "Lindy, do you read me?" he called out. There was nothing but static. "Lindy," he said louder, "do you read me? Tim, Katrina, Sarina?"

A piece of metal fell over, making a loud clanging sound. Robert's speaker crackled and a faint voice came over the commlink. "Will somebody please stop Tim from playing with the lights."

"Kimberly? Where are you guys?" Robert called out over the radio.

"Robert, is that you?" Kimberly replied. "Oh, thank goodness. Would you please tell Tim—."

"Kimberly, we can't find you," Robert called back. "Are you guys okay?"

"Yes, we're fine, the bombs missed us," said Kimberly. "But we don't have any pilots and Tim thinks he can fly this plane. Would you guys please hurry and get back here. This is an emergency!"

"Turn on the landing lights so we can see you," Jonathan said with a relieved smile.

"Landing lights?" said Kimberly. "No, Tim, that's the wipers. Find the landing lights."

Soon a white glow appeared in the distance, far from where

the boys had thought the plane should be. Jonathan and Robert ran toward it as fast as they could. The snow was getting deeper, more slippery.

As they ran, Robert's glasses started showing new words. "Radio transmission. Hostile source. Possible threat. Radio transmission: One Straunsee aircraft remains at Pallin. Request intercept aircraft."

Robert was trying to run and had to look past the last words on his lenses to focus on the ground. He'd have to look at the rest of the transmission later. "Jonathan," he called out, "somebody's located our airplane."

The boys picked up their pace. They finally reached the airplane's steps and scrambled aboard. The passenger area was empty. There was light shining from the cockpit so they headed there. In the cockpit, they found Sarina, Kimberly, Katrina, Maria, Lindy, and Tim trying to figure out the controls.

"Oh Jonathan," Sarina said, turning to him, "thank goodness you're here. I was so afraid the bombs got you."

"We're going to have company," said Jonathan. "Robert just got a message from his glasses. Everybody move over so Robert and I can try to fly this thing."

"But you're not cleared for flying multiple engine planes yet," said Kimberly with worry in her voice.

"It's better than bombs," said Jonathan, looking at the controls.

"What?" said Kimberly.

"Kimberly," interrupted Sarina, winking understandingly at Jonathan and turning toward the passenger compartment, "let's go get that side door closed."

"*Yes, please* and *thank you*," said Jonathan, plopping down in the pilot's seat. Robert took the copilot's seat beside him.

Jonathan, Robert, Lindy and Tim stayed in the cockpit;

Kimberly and Maria went with Sarina. Lindy found a quick-reference guide on the plane's controls and started thumbing through it, her photographic mind clicking away.

"Here's the preflight sequence," said Lindy, stopping on page twenty-four. She quickly walked Jonathan and Robert through the steps checking all the plane's vital systems. They found a problem with the navigation system.

"That's probably why the pilots left," said Robert. "Let's see if we can fix it."

Lindy found a "System Diagnostic" section and quickly referenced it. Using the plane's onboard computer, Robert and Jonathan ran a series of tests.

"There's something wrong in the track feed," said Robert.

"That's on your side of the plane," said Lindy. "Check the fuse box in the right panel, box 21C."

Robert opened a door and scanned through the fuses. Several looked like they had taken some heat but none were obviously blown. He was about to close the panel when he found an "iffy" fuse. He pulled it out and examined it. The link was blown. "We need a 30 Amp fuse," he announced.

"Jonathan," said Lindy, "there are some fuses to your left in that square cabinet."

Jonathan quickly opened the cabinet and found a set of spares. "Here's one," he said, handing it to Robert.

With Lindy's help, the boys worked through the sequence to fire up the plane's engines and they soon whirred to life. Tim started the windshield wipers so they could see. Lindy was sitting in one of a pair of seats just behind the pilots' seats.

"Looks like we've got it," Jonathan called back over the plane's speaker system. "Sarina, is the outer door secure?"

"Yes, it took a while to get all the snow off the steps," Sarina replied from a few feet behind him as she slipped into a seat beside Lindy. "Jonathan, Robert, and Lindy, you can do this. Let's get out of here."

"Okay, everybody please take your seats and buckle up," said Jonathan with a serious smile. "And please make sure your seats are in their upright positions."

"All right," Tim called forward from the passenger area, "when do we get our sodas and peanuts?"

"Listen to the peanut gallery," said Jonathan, grinning nervously as he ran up the engines. "Okay, here we go."

"This is my favorite part of flying," the four youths in the front overheard Tim say. "Kimberly, isn't this great? Oh yeah, I forgot."

Robert checked the external lights as Jonathan released the brakes. The plane began creeping forward. Jonathan taxied out onto the snow-covered runway and turned into the wind. Visibility was poor with the falling snow but the avionics were working well now. Jonathan pushed on the engines' throttles. The plane's propellers spun faster as it sped down the runway and took off into the cold night air.

"Wow," said Jonathan, looking out into the snowy night, "this plane flies easier than I thought it would."

"Yeah," said Robert with a relieved smile, "thank goodness for the autopilot functions."

Lindy continued to check the operating manual while Robert studied the onboard computer.

"So far, so good," said Jonathan to the three youths around him. They were now high above the earth, cruising over snow-covered mountains. As they left Pallin, it felt as if they were leaving their troubles behind. The plane was warm and comfortable, sheltering them from the subzero temperatures outside. They were alive, and even more important, they were *FREE*.

"Next stop—," Jonathan called out over the speaker system.

A stern voice over the pilots' headphones interrupted Jonathan. "Turboprop aircraft, you *will* proceed to Grausfeld in the Brattslagg region."

"Grausfeld?" said Jonathan. "Who is this?"

"You will do as I command or you will be shot down," the voice demanded.

"Grausfeld?" Sarina said, picking up a set of headphones. "Let me talk with them."

Jonathan held his hand over his microphone. "No, Sarina, they mustn't know you are here."

"Straunsees, you cannot hide from us," the pilot said. "We know you are aboard that plane. Mr. Kreppen has arranged for the escort of five fighter jets to *properly* see you *safely* to Grausfeld."

"We are not at war with your country," Sarina said. "It is against international law for you to order us around in this manner."

"We have you in our crosshairs. Do not disobey our orders," said the voice. "You will fly with us to our airbase or we will shoot you down!"

"Then you would be guilty of murder, sir," Jonathan replied.

Jonathan momentarily switched off the microphone so they could talk.

"Don't do what they say," said Sarina defiantly.

"They're not going to get you or any of us," said Jonathan. "Everybody, hold on tight!"

Jonathan quickly dove the plane down toward the rugged mountains below. "If they're going to shoot us down," he said, "we can at least make it harder for them."

"Turboprop plane, you won't escape," said the pilot's voice.

"I've got five Mark 6s on the screen," said a young woman's

voice miles away in the sky. "Nearing firing range. They're starting to lock onto the passenger plane carrying my sisters."

Eric Brown jammed the F121LC stealth fighter plane's throttles forward. The hypersonic American plane leaped faster, it's ramjets kicking into full operation.

Allesandra Straunsee, the F121's copilot, broke radio silence: "Attention, please, Mark 6 pilots: You've got nine seconds to eject or we're going to blow you out of the sky. *Nobody* messes with my sisters!"

Allesandra switched over to intercom and said, "Sorry, Eric, that was your pilot job."

"You did well," said Eric, "except that I would have left off the *please.*"

Eric was watching the screen in front of him, desperately trying to get the planes within range of their laser cannons. He saw the passenger plane diving for the ground. "They can't outrun the Mark 6s," he said, still counting the seconds. "Those guys will eat them alive."

Like five cats pouncing on a single mouse, the Mark 6s were turning on Jonathan's plane. It was a matter of seconds now.

"Allesandra," Eric Brown called back. "Lock on the first plane. It's going to be close."

Jonathan's plane rapidly gained speed as it dove toward earth. The canyons below were hazardous; the mountains beside them even more so. There was suddenly a bright flash in the night sky. Robert looked out the side window to see a large explosion on the mountainside to their right.

"What was that?" called out Jonathan.

"I don't know," Robert replied. "Just keep flying and don't run into any mountains."

Another airborne missile swooshed by from the Mark 6s and exploded in front of them. It rocked the small passenger plane and the youths heard several impacts from shrapnel.

"Eject now or you're gone," said Eric over the radio.

"Stay clear," ordered the lead Mark 6 pilot. "This is none of your business. We've got five Marks. Top of the line!"

CHAPTER 15

The Alarm

"You don't have *this*," Eric replied angrily. He squeezed the trigger. Twin laser beams shot out of the F121's wing fronts. They converged on the left wing of the lead Mark 6, blowing one-third of the wing away. The pilot ejected as the plane flared bright yellow and fell toward earth. "Anybody else want to dance?" called out Eric.

The remaining four Mark 6s stubbornly clung onto their prey. "Okay," said Eric, "if you want to play that way."

Allesandra had the new lead Mark 6 targeted. Eric squeezed the trigger and the plane's tail disintegrated. The next plane burst into flames. The last two planes turned tail and ran for Grausfeld.

"Passenger plane, you can come out now. We've got your back," Eric announced over the radio. He heard some loud screams and whoops. "Is everybody okay over there?"

"Eric, tell Allesandra it's us," called back Sarina's voice.

"I know, little sister," Allesandra replied. "We're going to make sure you make it home."

"Thank you, big sis," Sarina replied emotionally. It was Allesandra's turn for a surprise. "Our pilots were gone," added Sarina. "My friend Jonathan is flying our plane."

"Okay, wow, well, tell him to gain a little altitude so you don't run into a mountain," Allesandra replied. She switched over to intercom and said to Eric, "I wish she hadn't told me that. Now *I'm* getting nervous. *Let's get them home!*"

With the aid of Eric Brown and Allesandra, Jonathan and Robert were able to land safely at a secure airbase. The autopilot helped them land in the falling snow without issue. Jonathan was directed to taxi over to a nearby hangar to park the plane. As the youths climbed down out of the aircraft, they noted several holes in the wings and tail. The Mark 6's air-to-air missile had come closer than they thought.

"I think we're in trouble," Maria said.

"They're not going to charge us for the damage, are they?" asked Tim.

"You have flight insurance, don't you?" said Maria.

"No," Tim replied. "But you were flying on it, too."

"I'm covered," said Maria confidently. "I have diplomatic community."

"You mean diplomatic *immunity*, don't you?" Tim said.

"Oh yes, and that too," said Maria. Maria stepped away for a moment to talk to Sarina.

Kimberly took the chance to talk to Tim alone. "Well, Tim, I see you're talking to Maria," she said quietly. "Do you still think she has cooties?"

"I guess not," Tim replied. "She has been awful nice to us."

"Good," said Kimberly, "then you've grown up a little bit more. You're a changed person. You can see a bigger picture now. I'm proud of you, Tim."

"Thank you," said Tim. An alarm started buzzing on his wristwatch.

"What's that for?" asked Kimberly.

"Time's up," said Tim. "Maria and I took a five-minute timeout. Maria has cooties again!"

The area was encompassed by security guards. The youths

were escorted into a secure building near their plane's hangar. There they found a wide assortment of food and other items. Mr. Gervar was there along with the Olsens. As Robert glanced around the large room, he saw some of their luggage on the floor near some dining tables. He took off his spy glasses for a moment to wipe the lenses and put them back on again. As he did so, he saw someone carrying some familiar looking duffel bags of the *Kimosoggy* type. A set of brackets appeared on his lenses for just a moment as the person left the room. "Dantzel," it said. Was she dropping them off or picking them up? Robert was just about to run after her, but Katrina, smiling, grabbed his arm and said, "Come on, Robert, let's go get some of the good food they've prepared for us."

"But what about Tim's and my duffle bags?" said Robert.

"Aw, don't worry about it," Katrina said with a grin. "That's another story."

"I guess it is," said Robert, smiling back at her. "Okay, let's go, I'm starving!"

The CLUE in the MISSING PLANE

"Kimberly," said Jonathan, "how did that smiley face get on the front cover of our book?"

"What?" said Kimberly. "Where?"

The CLUE in the
MISSING PLANE

The CLUE in the
MISSING PLANE

Gregory O. Smith

Dedication

To those who face big challenges and keep on going, trying to make things better and right, and to my three patient editors: Lisa Smith, Anne Smith, and Dorothy Smith.

GREGORY O. SMITH

Author's Note

Years ago, our family went to visit some lava tubes in Idaho. The ground surface was hot and dry, but as we descended into the earth, we discovered water and bright green moss. The air in the old lava tube was cooler. It was like a whole different world down there. These particular tubes had ice in them year-round. One section was so constricted with ice that we had to lay down on our backs and push ourselves along to go further into the tube. The jagged rock ceiling of the tube was just inches above our noses. Further back into the tube, it opened up again. We finally came to a part which was totally blocked with ice. Someone had carved notches in the ice so we could climb up to the top of it and slide down a thirty-foot long chute. We enjoyed sliding down it over and over again. Boy, was it fast!

In this book, the Wright cousins have a similar experience, except theirs might be quite a bit warmer. Will they find hot lava like Tim thinks they will? Can the Wrights discover the secret of the missing plane before it is too late?

Strap on your snow boots and get set for fun as the Wright cousins search for *THE CLUE IN THE MISSING PLANE!*

~ Gregory O. Smith

GREGORY O. SMITH

CHAPTER 1

The Flight

Snow was falling fiercely now. It was early afternoon. The Wright cousins had been in the air for two hours. They were flying over the mountains of southeastern Gütenberg in a twin-engine, turboprop passenger plane. Jonathan Wright was in the pilot's seat, Robert, his cousin, was co-pilot.

"The blizzard's getting worse," said Jonathan. "I can't see a thing."

"We've still got three hundred miles to go," Robert replied, looking out the window into the snowy daylight. "We're going to have to do it all by instrument if it doesn't let up. Why are we doing this flight in this terrible weather anyways?"

"The officer on the phone said this plane was needed at Kalisbehr. They also wanted us 'non-military personnel' off their air force base."

"You'd think they'd be nicer to us," said Robert. "After all we did to help their country at Pallin. If we didn't care about the Straunsees, we'd be out of here right now. By the way, why didn't Katrina and her sisters board the plane with us?"

"I don't think the officer wanted to tell his commander-in-chief, King Straunsee, that his daughters weren't welcome at the base," Jonathan replied.

"But they could have at least let us say good-bye to them," said Robert.

"They were clear on the other side of the base," said Jonathan, shaking his head. "But I know what you mean. With Gütenberg on the brink of war, they should have let us fly Sarina and her sisters to a safer location. Robert, this weather's getting crazy, see if you can find any closer airports."

"Okay," Robert replied. "I'll pull up the electronic charts."

"While you're doing that, I'm going to call in for some help," said Jonathan, switching to the radio. "Air control, this is Charlie-delta-foxtrot-two-five, over."

The plane the cousins were flying in was a civilian model, but it had been upgraded with military-type navigation equipment. It even had IFF—International Friend or Foe—aircraft recognition electronics.

"Air control, this is Charlie-delta-foxtrot-two-five, over. We are caught in a blizzard. We could use some navigational assistance. Over." Jonathan turned up the receiver's volume. There was nothing but static. "Air traffic control, this is Charlie-delta-foxtrot-two-five. Requesting help. Over."

"Jonathan," said Robert, looking at the screen, "somebody's following us."

"What do you mean?"

"We've got something on our tail and according to the IFF it's not friendly," Robert replied. "Look, there's a second one."

Jonathan scanned the electronics, "How long have they been there?"

"I don't know. At first, I thought it was just radar noise from the storm," Robert said.

"Bad time to be trailed by someone," Jonathan said. "Gütenberg could be engulfed in war at any moment and I don't want us to be the first casualties."

Jonathan spoke into his microphone to the other cousins in the plane's passenger compartment, "We've got somebody trailing us. We don't know who they are. Make sure your seatbelts are on tight, we may have to take evasive action."

"In this storm?" Kimberly called forward. "Jonathan, what are we going to do?"

"We'll just sit down and hold on tight," Lindy said from the seat beside her.

"Robert, punch in the TFR," said Jonathan.

"Okay, but it's going to make Kimberly airsick again," Robert replied.

"I hope not," said Jonathan, running up the engine throttles. "Kimberly, have you got your plastic bag?"

"Yes," Kimberly replied. "Tim just gave me one. But please tell me I won't have to use it."

"Just hang on and keep smiling," Jonathan replied.

Robert switched on the TFR—Terrain-following radar. An air force pilot had instructed him how to use it before they took off. TFR would allow their plane to hug the profile of the earth below, keeping them at a safe distance from the ground. They hoped it would make them drop below their pursuers' radar.

The cousins' plane nosed lower and began following the mountainous profile of the ground below.

"Jonathan, there are mountains down there," Kimberly called out worriedly. "And Tim's got homework to do. His handwriting is already too hard to read as it is."

"Thank you, thank you," said fourteen-year-old Tim Wright, seated beside her. "I'm practicing to become a doctor someday."

The cousins were now flying in a narrow canyon, the walls were less than five-hundred feet from each side of the plane. They soon topped a mountain. As they did, a warning suddenly appeared on the instrument panel. They were back in radar range and had just been "painted"—targeted—by someone's weapons system. They dove into the next valley, out of radar range, but not soon enough. An air-to-air missile was locked onto them, following them at an extremely high speed. It slammed into their left engine and blew it to pieces. Kimberly and Lindy screamed as parts of engine and propeller smashed into the fuselage.

Jonathan and Robert fought to stabilize the plane. Smoke and fuel streamed from the left wing. The wing was shaking wildly and bending backward, threatening to collapse. Jonathan steered the plane downward. "Everybody hang on!" he shouted.

As they dropped below the ridges, the snowstorm suddenly let up. Jonathan spotted a flat area clear of brush and trees in the valley below and aimed for it. "This isn't going to be pretty," he called out. "Robert, get the landing gear down."

"We're descending too fast," said Robert.

"I know," Jonathan replied. "I'm doing everything I can, but that left wing isn't going to last much longer."

"The left gear won't lock," said Robert.

The ground was coming at them quickly now. The cousins in the passenger compartment gasped and held on tight as the stricken plane slammed down. The left landing gear collapsed and broke off, taking the left wing with it as the plane skidded across the icy ground. The right landing wheel also collapsed and the plane crunched onto its belly. A large snowbank loomed ahead. They smacked into it and plowed on through. The plane came to a grinding halt thirty feet from large rocks and trees.

"I can smell fuel!" shouted Lindy.

"Me too," said Jonathan, releasing his seatbelt harness and leaping into action. "Everybody grab your gear and get out of the plane," he yelled. "This thing could explode any second!"

The youths grabbed their backpacks, forced open the side door, and scrambled to get clear of the plane. Two fighter jets shrieked overhead and shot past them.

"They'll be back," Jonathan yelled, "run for it!"

Through the falling snow, the cousins saw a stone building in the distance and rushed toward it. The snow on the ground was now knee-high. Jonathan broke trail, lunging at times into even deeper drifts.

The Wright cousins were halfway to the building when the jets returned. Two large explosions rocked the area around the cousins' plane. The ground shook and trembled like an earthquake. The noise of the explosions echoed away, but the earth beneath the cousins' feet kept trembling.

Breaking through a tall snowdrift, the cousins found themselves on smooth ice. Behind them, they heard a high-pitched, eerie cracking noise working its way toward them. They were running on an ice-covered lake!

CHAPTER 2

Into the Storm

"Get to the building!" shouted Jonathan, redoubling his efforts as he plowed into another tall snowdrift.

Racing for high ground, the cousins could hear the sharp reports of the ice cracking behind them. "We're almost there," shouted Jonathan. There was a loud **CRACK!**

Jonathan and the others leapt for a tall bank of snow as the ice shattered and sunk under their feet. The cousins landed in a tangled heap just beyond the water's edge. They had reached the shore!

Their chests heaving, the Wrights crawled up the bank on their hands and knees to get away from the water's edge. The ice continued to crack. Something strange was happening: the ice appeared to be sinking in places.

"Is everybody okay?" called out Jonathan.

"Let's get out of here," said Kimberly, shivering.

The cousins scrambled up to the stone building. To their dismay, it was old and abandoned. It was missing its windows, doors, and roof. Its floor was buried under several feet of snow.

"So much for a warm reception," said Tim.

"There's another building over there," said Robert, pointing toward a distant structure. "Maybe it's in better shape."

The cousins made their way to the other structure but found

it also roofless and filled with snow. As Lindy and Robert walked around the side of the old building, they spied a third building.

The youths, eager to find shelter from the blowing snow, hurried over to the next building. It appeared to be in much better condition than the others and still had its roof and windows in place. It was L-shaped. They hurried up to the front and peered inside one of the windows, rubbing the glass to clean it.

"Hey, there's a boat in there," said Lindy.

"And there's a wood-burning stove over in that corner," Robert said excitedly. "Now we just need some wood."

"A wood stove?" said Tim, shivering. "S-sounds good to me."

Robert tried the front door beside him; it was locked. He peered through the window again, spotted another door in the left wall, and slipped around to investigate it while the others were still looking in through the windows.

The second wooden door on the leeward side was slightly open. Robert glanced in; there was snow on the floor that had blown in through the crack.

"Hello," Robert called out. "Anybody home?" He pushed the door open more and stepped cautiously into the dimly lit room. "Hello?" he called out a second time. Still no answer. He closed the door behind him and walked over to the front door. He studied it for a moment, figured out how to unlock it, and tried to pull it open.

"Tim," Robert called out through the door, "push on the door. It's frozen in place."

Outside, Tim put his shoulder into the door and pushed as hard as he could. Robert tugged on the inside. The door suddenly broke loose and Tim came flying through the doorway, spinning Robert around. They both landed on an old upside-down, dust covered rowboat with a resounding *THUNK!*

Jonathan, Kimberly, and Lindy rushed in to see if the boys were okay. Other than a sore elbow, Tim seemed fine.

Jonathan closed the door to stop more snow from blowing in and the youths looked over their new surroundings. The room looked as if it hadn't been occupied for over fifty years. In fact, there was a newspaper on the floor that proved that point.

"We can't just stay here without permission," said Kimberly.

"Kimberly, you can stay out there in the snow if you want to," said Jonathan, "but I don't want to freeze to death."

"Point well taken," said Tim, standing up from the boat. "I vote we get out of the blizzard. We can pay for room service later."

"But it's somebody's property," Kimberly insisted. "We can't just barge in without permission."

"Kimberly," said Jonathan, "we've just had our plane shot down and crashed. We're not interlopers. This is an emergency."

"Yeah," added Tim, "and if we died, they'd have to bury us and then we wouldn't be able to pay the rent."

"Point well made," said Robert.

"Point well taken," said Tim.

"What's this point stuff?" said Kimberly. "Since when did you guys become lawyers?"

"Yesterday," said Tim, "remember when you said you were going to have Mom and Dad lay down the law for me. So, I decided to become a lawyer. Good thinking, huh?"

"Lousy," Kimberly replied with a slight smile, "but let's see if we can get this place warmed up."

As the cousins examined the room, they could hear the wind howling outside. "Thank goodness we're not still out in that," said Lindy.

The cousins checked their phones; to their dismay, there was no reception.

"Jonathan, let's get that wood stove going," said Robert.

The two youths looked the stove over to make sure it was safe to use. Meanwhile, Lindy checked out the boat, Tim retrieved and ate a granola bar from his backpack, and Kimberly started looking for wood.

"The stove's chimney seems to be in decent shape," said Robert.

"And there's still ashes in the stove so it must still be usable," added Jonathan.

"There's only one problem," said Robert, glancing around the room. "No wood."

"We might have to burn the boat," said Kimberly.

"Wouldn't that be trespassing or something?" said Tim.

"It's an emergency situation," Kimberly replied, her teeth chattering a little. "There's an axe over there leaning against the wall. We could use that to chop it up."

"We can't do it," said Lindy.

"Why not?" said Tim. "It's an emergency. Our lives are more important than the boat. Law number 20564-B."

"Yes, and we're going to freeze to death here if we don't do something," Kimberly said.

"We can't chop up the boat and burn it," said Lindy. "It's made of aluminum."

Robert noted that the room seemed warmer than it should be, even though the stove had not been fired up for probably years. He walked around the room, trying to find out why. In the corner opposite the stove, he found a thick board on the floor. It felt unusually warm. Lifting an edge to peek underneath it, he discovered it to be a large hatch. "Hey, you guys," he called out, "look at this!"

Robert lifted the hatch and leaned it against the wall. As he did so, a warm gust of air bathed his face.

"What is it?" called out Lindy.

CHAPTER 3

Warmth?

The rest of the cousins quickly gathered around Robert as he shined his flashlight down into the large hole in the floor. They saw dark, stone steps leading down into the ground.

"That warm air sure feels good," said Lindy. "Where do you think it goes?"

"The dungeon," said Tim. "It's so warm down there, maybe there's a dragon or monster or something. We need some pepper."

"Tim, have you been reading scary books again?" said Kimberly. "You know how reading scary books or watching scary movies always makes you afraid of the dark."

"Only *Tom and the Sneezy Monster*," said Tim. "Tom, the boy hero, always uses pepper to make the monsters sneeze so he can get away."

"Tim, now where are we going to find some pepper around here?" replied Kimberly. "Oh, now look what you've done. You've got me mixed up in your crazy ideas."

"I've got a pepper shaker in my backpack," said Tim.

"You guys can keep talking if you want to," said Robert, stepping down onto the first step of the secret stairway. "I'm going to find out where this goes."

The rest of the cousins joined him, even Tim. The upper

part of the passage was lined with rocks set in concrete, but as the cousins continued down, they could see old pick marks in the rock walls. The passage had been hand-hewn through solid rock. Tim had his pepper shaker ready.

The stairs headed straight for fifteen feet and then turned to the right. Droplets of moisture clung to the ceiling. The deeper the cousins went, the warmer the air temperature and rock walls became. An old iron water pipe, fastened to the right wall by iron straps, followed the course. The tunnel turned right again and opened into a large room about fifteen feet by twenty feet. A thirty-inch diameter shaft was dug into the middle of the floor. It was filled with water up to about two feet from its top. The iron pipe turned down the shaft and disappeared into the water.

"It must be a water well," said Robert as he leaned over to touch the water. "It's got to be eighty degrees or more."

"Be careful not to fall in there," said Kimberly.

The cousins stayed down in the warm room for over half an hour, basking in the warmth and discussing their situation.

"I was just thinking," said Tim with a happy chuckle as they got warm. "I'm glad there aren't any monsters down here. I brought the wrong kind of pepper. For monsters, you're supposed to have jalapeño."

"And who says books don't have an influence on you," said Kimberly, her toes finally thawing.

A gurgling sound started rising from the well. First, the warm water began to lower and then it reversed and began to rise and flow into the room. The water turned cold.

The cousins dashed to the stairs to keep from getting wet as cold water rose and covered the floor of the rock room. Soon, the first step disappeared into the water, then the second, and then the third. The cousins were about to turn and run up the stairs, but the water began slurping down the well and the warm water returned. The water gushed up so fast it shot up and blasted on the ceiling above the hole. Steam gurgled with the water. The warm water stopped, followed by a geyser of cold water, quickly filling the room again. The cousins had to bound up the stairs to get out of the way. The cycle repeated itself several more times before the water stopped gurgling and the well emptied of all visible water. Steam rose sporadically from the well, but the water was gone.

For dinner that night, the cousins ate granola bars and other snacks from their carry-on packs. They had learned to keep food, water, and other things on hand not only for comfort, but out of necessity. They never knew what emergency might be happening next and they needed to be ready for it.

The cousins spent a fitful night's sleep in the stairway to keep warm. They tried several times to reach someone by phone but their phones still had no service. The storm was evidently playing havoc with communications all over Gütenberg.

The Wright cousins woke up bright and early the next morning. The sky was clear and blue, the ground was covered with several more feet of newly fallen snow. The air was cold and crisp as the cousins stepped out of the building to view their surroundings. The mountains were white. The distant trees looked like stacked marshmallows. There was a high, snow-covered conical peak to the northwest of them. Their plane had crashed to the southeast or east of where the cousins now stood, but they could see no evidence of it. Everything was covered with a thick new layer of snow. It had been cold in the night as the snow was still powdery and sparkled with ice crystals.

The cousins, remembering the breaking ice episode of the day before, didn't dare try to reach their plane. It would be too dangerous to try to cross that ice again. They had no idea of the size or shape of the lake, or the depth of it. They were alive and they wanted to keep it that way.

The youths kept the stairway hatch open to try to keep the stone building warm. The warm air had returned to the well, though the water was still nowhere to be seen.

About 9 o'clock in the morning, Jonathan finally got through to Sarina by phone. "Oh, Jonathan," said Sarina, "thank goodness it's you! Are you guys okay? Where are you? My father has had search and rescue out looking for you all night long. They couldn't find any trace of you or your plane."

"We're all okay, just a little shaken," Jonathan said. "We were shot down by two fighter jets."

Sarina's end of the phone was quiet for a moment, and then she said in a choked-up voice, "Oh Jonathan, I'm so sorry! I'm so glad you're all okay...you're all alive. I'll get help out there for you. Do you know where you are? Never mind, I'll have them track down your phone location. I'll call you back in ten minutes with the details. If you don't hear from me, call me. Wait, I might not be able to reach you. Never mind, just stay on the phone. I'll use Katrina's phone."

"Thank you," said Jonathan.

Jonathan listened as Sarina phoned around to make the arrangements. Sarina talked to her father, King Straunsee. She talked to the air force. Jonathan was impressed, for as easy going and casual as she was, Sarina was an excellent organizer.

"Okay," said Sarina, finally picking up her phone again. "I hope your phone batteries are strong. The air force is sending up an AWAC plane to coordinate efforts and a squadron of fighter jets to secure your region. I've got your parents tracking your phone so our helicopters can find you. By the way, how is your phone charge?"

"48%," said Jonathan.

"Good. Keep it on."

"Thank you for your help, Sarina," said Jonathan.

"You take care," said Sarina. "Help is on the way. We'll track down who did this to you. I love you, my special friend. Get your gear together because we're going to bring you home."

Jonathan was eighteen. He had never told a girl he loved her, except maybe his mom or his sister, but that was his own family. He had never told a girl, a girl friend, that. It was too sacred, too special, it meant too much. He just stood there, holding the phone to his ear, not saying a thing. Thoughts just flying through his head.

"Jonathan, are you okay?" Sarina asked a moment later. "Is your phone still working? Are you there?"

"Um, yes," said Jonathan. "I..." He paused a moment. "Sarina? I...love you, too, my special friend."

"Mush and smooshies," said Tim's voice from behind him.

Jonathan turned around to see Tim and the other cousins standing there. He didn't know how long they had been there, but from the smiles on their faces, they had heard at least the last part of his conversation.

"Sorry," said Kimberly, "we didn't mean to eavesdrop. We wanted to hear what you'd found out."

Jonathan felt his face turning red.

"She's a sweet, good girl," Kimberly said with a large grin. "I approve."

"Yes, she is," Jonathan replied.

"Okay, what's going on?" said Sarina over the phone.

"Everybody just heard the last part of our conversation," Jonathan explained, his face turning redder.

"Good!" said Sarina loudly. "And now that they're all grinning, tell them I love them, too, *even* Tim. Now you guys watch for those helicopters because they should be there soon!"

"Thank you, Sarina," said Jonathan.

"Thank your parents, too," said Sarina. "They're the ones that located your phone."

"Are they listening, too?" asked Jonathan.

"Hi, Jonathan," said Jonathan's mom, Rebecca Wright.

"Anybody else?"

"You guys are so sweet," said Aunt Connie Wright.

Great Aunt Opal chimed in, "You know, dearie, I was engaged to be married when I was eighteen, just like you. I heartily recommend it. Oh, and by the way, please make sure that Timothy has properly tied his shoelaces."

"We're not getting engaged, yet, Aunt Opal," said Jonathan. "We're just friends...um, special friends." Grinning with embarrassment, Jonathan shook his head and said, "I can't believe this. Okay, everybody close your ears so I can talk with Sarina all by myself."

"Okay," came several replies.

"Sarina," began Jonathan, "you know they're never going to let us forget about this."

"I know," Sarina replied happily with tears in her eyes, "But don't worry, neither will I."

"Um," said Tim, "are we done yet? I'm getting tired of holding my fingers in my ears."

CHAPTER 4

Arrival

Soon the Wright cousins could see the contrails of fighter jets high above them in the air. Then they could hear the *rop-rop* of three helicopters approaching. The cousins walked out into the snow and flagged them in. Two gunship helicopters and one squad carrier type. There was a large, flat area behind the building the cousins had stayed in, away from the lake. Jonathan and Robert guided the personnel helicopter to land there. When the pilot signaled it was clear, the Wright cousins grabbed their gear and ran toward it through the snow. The copilot helped them aboard. Once they were all strapped in, the helicopter took off and headed north.

As they flew, the cousins could see multiple jets running interference for them. King Straunsee and his daughter, Sarina, had made sure nothing would happen to the cousins during their return flight.

They arrived at a large, very busy air force base near the town of Kleinstattz. Aircraft were being armed for the possible war. After a quick meal, the Kleinstattz Air Force Base commander and several other military personnel interviewed the Wright cousins, particularly pilots Jonathan and Robert, about their experience during their flight and the attack. They asked about the types of aircraft involved, radio transmissions, any warnings they might have received, tactics used during the attack, weapons used, and so on. The military was also eager to recover the turboprop plane's "black box" flight recorder for the electronic information it had recorded. It could help document the unprovoked attack. That would be important, especially on the international scene.

The interviews took several hours and then, finally, the cousins were cleared to leave Kleinstattz Air Force Base. An armored, chauffeured SUV with bulletproof glass arrived to take the cousins to meet the Straunsees in a nearby town. The SUV was just about to pass through the base exit gate when word arrived at the guard post that they were needed back at the base commander's office.

"What can you tell me about where you crashed the turboprop?" asked Commander Trelland, after the cousins had all gotten seated.

"It was snowing. We crash-landed on a clear, snow-covered area on the valley floor," replied Jonathan.

"Yes," added Robert, "we stopped about thirty feet or so from a bunch of big trees."

"There was a lake nearby," said Lindy. "After our plane was bombed, the ice on the lake started cracking. We barely made it to the stone buildings. We almost fell into the lake."

"And it was really, really cold," said Tim. "Kimberly's lips were turning blue."

"Thank you, Tim," mumbled Kimberly. "I don't think he needed to know that."

"Interesting," said Commander Trelland. "And how far would you estimate the crash site was from the buildings where you stayed overnight?"

"Maybe two-hundred yards or so," Jonathan guesstimated. "It was hard to tell. The snow was falling really hard as we crossed the ice."

"About 185 meters," added Kimberly, doing the math. "Why do you ask?"

The commander looked at each of the cousins. "You seem like nice kids," he said. "Be honest with me, how did you get into that valley?"

"In the turboprop plane," said Jonathan and Robert at the same time. "We had been directed to fly it to Kalisbehr by the officer at the other air force base."

"We have been looking into your story," said Commander Trelland. "No one on the base had authorized you to fly the plane. There were no control tower clearances for takeoff given and no flight plan. Please, tell me the truth now."

The youths' faces started turning red with embarrassment.

"We are telling you the truth," Jonathan said. "If you want proof, the airplane is there where we left it. It was bombed, but they weren't direct hits. The fuselage and tail were still there after the bombing. They must have straddled it."

"I wish I could believe you," said the commander, "but my personnel haven't found any evidence of the plane."

"What?!" said the cousins in shock.

"It's there," said Robert. "It's over where we told you. We're not lying!"

"Tell me, now, we don't look kindly on this kind of prank," Commander Trelland continued. "How did you get into that remote valley? By snowmobile? Were you helicopter skiing?"

The cousins looked at each other in disbelief.

"We were flying to Kalisbehr," said Jonathan. "We were caught in a blizzard. Two jets—the IFF told us they were enemies—chased us, shot a missile at us that blew our left engine apart. We crash-landed in that valley you found us in. Now I don't know why you can't see the plane, but it's there. You look for it and you will find it."

"We have," said Commander Trelland, "with six helicopters. We've combed over every square meter of that valley. There is no plane. And besides, one of our enemy's missiles wouldn't have just damaged your engine; it would have taken the wing off your plane. A turboprop plane like that is not built to withstand that kind of attack."

"But we were using TFR," said Robert. "They couldn't get a good shot at us."

"Or they had it set on 'stun'," added Tim. "Like in space."

"Your *civilian* plane had TFR and IFF?" Commander Trelland asked incredulously, ignoring Tim's remark.

"Yes," said Robert and Jonathan at the same time.

"Those are only allowed on our military planes," said the commander.

"It's the same plane we flew from Pallin," said Jonathan.

"And what were you doing there?" asked Commander Trelland.

"Look, sir, we're telling you the truth," said Lindy. "Why are you treating us this way?"

"Because a lot of time, personnel, and resources, have been used to find you and bring you here. If you were not friends of the Straunsee family, you would be in the stockade behind bars right now. Now, how good of friends are you of the royal family?"

The interview was interrupted by a sharp knock on the door and a soldier came into the room. He handed the commander a piece of paper, which the commander read. He finally looked up. "King Straunsee wishes you to be free to go," Commander Trelland said rather reluctantly. "He's in a precarious position right now. He's taking a big gamble on setting you free, but...you may go."

"Thank you, sir," said Jonathan, standing up quickly. "Come on you guys, we need to leave."

"This won't be your last visit with me," said Commander Trelland. "Until we find your supposed plane, I'll have to keep your passports."

The cousins' jaws dropped. Giving up their passports meant they wouldn't be able to leave the country or get back into the United States. Commander Trelland would not let them go, however, until they had surrendered their passports to him. The Wright cousins reluctantly gave them to him, shouldered their backpacks, and left to go in the SUV.

"Why did he take our passports?" asked Tim.

"The possibility of war gets people on edge," said Kimberly. "People do a lot of things they normally wouldn't do. Jonathan, what are we going to do?"

"Let's get off this base and go talk to the Straunsees. Maybe we'll have to find the plane for them, I don't know."

The cousins dejectedly climbed into the armored SUV. The chauffeur drove up to the main base gate and this time received permission to leave. They were grateful to finally get off the base.

"Well," said Tim, "I guess we'll just have to get new passports."

"It's not that easy," said Kimberly. "They don't like to issue duplicate ones."

"I wish I *could* get a new passport," said Lindy, brushing her hair back. "I took a *really* bad picture."

"Me too," Kimberly agreed. "Their lighting was totally wrong."

The chauffeured drive to Twillidyr gave the cousins an opportunity to rest a while and then they started discussing their predicament. They talked quietly amongst themselves as they rode along.

"How could the plane just vanish like that?" asked Kimberly.

"Maybe somebody stole it," said Tim.

"We would have heard something," said Jonathan.

"Not if they took it out by snowmobile," said Tim.

"The air force would have seen the tracks," said Robert. "Besides, they don't make any snowmobiles big enough to take out a plane that size."

"Maybe they were space alien snowmobiles," said Tim. "They do stuff like that, you know."

"They do not," countered Kimberly, "and you know it."

"Maybe it was a big cargo helicopter that came and got it," Robert said.

"Yeah, a big space alien cargo helicopter," added Tim. "That could do it."

"You and your space aliens," said Kimberly, "Tim, I'm going to have Mom stop you from watching all those crazy space movies."

"Aw gee whiz, Kimberly, I was just teasing," said Tim, glancing up at the driver's rearview mirror. "Why does the driver keep looking at us that way?"

"Who?" asked Kimberly.

CHAPTER 5

Driven

"Our driver," whispered Tim. "I think he's spying on us."

"He's just doing his job and keeping an eye on traffic. Don't mind him," said Kimberly.

But Tim did mind. He kept watching the rearview mirror out of the corner of his eye. Each time the driver looked at he and the other cousins in the rearview mirror, Tim turned and stared back at him. The driver began to tug at his own shirt collar. Tim did the same. The driver began to sweat, Tim did the same.

"Timothy Wright, what are you doing?" called out Kimberly.

"Just sticking my tongue out at the driver," Tim replied.

"That's not nice," said Kimberly.

"He did it first," said Tim.

Kimberly glanced at the driver in the rearview mirror. The driver had a focused, nonchalant look on his face. When Kimberly looked away, the driver chuckled to himself.

"Robert," said Lindy, "you're about to lose that paper from your pocket."

"What paper?" Robert replied. He felt his pocket and a small, double-folded piece of paper fell onto the car seat beside him. He picked it up and looked it over. The handwriting was a lot neater than his. "Hey guys, listen to this," he said, reading aloud:

"*Vital. Retrieve black box, green plane data drum, Pallin computer backup. Glasses Xlcr, Dantz.*"

"Dantz?" said Robert, looking around. "Dantzel?"

"Who?" asked Kimberly.

"She's the mystery girl Robert and I ran into at Flewdur Mall," Lindy replied. "Robert saw her again at Trifid Castle and Pallin. She left a note in Robert's pocket at Pallin, remember?"

"Yes, and she knew about the GearSpy1 clothes we used at Trifid Castle," added Robert. "I've seen her a few times from a distance with my spy sunglasses, but she always disappears before I can catch up with her."

"Maybe she's a ghost," said Tim.

"Tim," said Kimberly indignantly, "she is *not* a ghost."

"How do you know," said Tim. "have you ever seen her?"

"No," Kimberly said. "And besides, you can't see ghosts."

"Well," said Tim, "if you've never seen a ghost and you've never seen Dantzel, then she must be a ghost. I rest my case."

"Timothy Wright," said Kimberly, "that does not make any sense and you know it."

"Hold it, hold it," said Jonathan, shaking his head with a grin. "Let's focus on the note."

"Right," said Robert, glancing back at the note. "*Black box, green plane data drum, Pallin computer backup. Glasses Xlcr, Dantz*"

"Planes have a 'black box' that records their flight data," said Jonathan. "The authorities always try to get it when a plane crashes to see why it crashed. The green plane data drum, the glasses Xlcr, I don't know what they are."

"The Pallin computer backup," Robert remembered, "it's on the plane, too. We forgot to give it to King Straunsee."

"Maybe all of it's in the plane," said Lindy.

"Kreppen—that guy that's trying to take over Gütenberg—

wants that computer information really bad," said Robert. "Slagg said he would help overthrow King Straunsee and make Kreppen king if Kreppen gave him the Straunsee Aerospace Works hi-lift rocket engine designs."

"We can't let Kreppen get that computer stuff," said Tim. "That guy's a total creep."

"We've got to get it first and get it back to the Straunsees," said Jonathan. "It's the least we can do for Sarina and her family after all they've done for us. Kreppen's a threat to all of us, to all the decent people in Gütenberg."

The rest of the cousins agreed.

Unable to figure out exactly what "data drum" and "Xlcr" meant, the cousins spent the rest of the car ride making plans about returning to the crashed turboprop plane site.

"The thing I don't understand," said Jonathan, "is why couldn't the air force find our crashed plane?"

"Don't worry," said Robert with a smile, glancing at his twin sister. "We've got our secret weapon. We've got Lindy and her photographic memory. We'll find it. Lindy, you saw where we landed, right?"

"Yes," smiled Lindy, closing her eyes for a moment to see the location. "Rocks, trees, half sunken wooden boat and all."

"Wooden boat?" asked Robert.

"Yes," said Lindy. "It was stuck in the ice near the first boulder."

"Pirates," said Tim with his classic response.

The SUV chauffeur took them to a residence of the Straunsee family called "Alpenhaus". The Wright cousins had never seen it before. The Straunsees stayed at Alpenhaus when they were needing to be nearer Alpenglow, the capitol of Gütenberg. It was on the outskirts of the city and gave King Straunsee a place to get away from the grueling demands of leading the country. A tall security wall surrounded the well-manicured grounds and the two-story Straunsee residence. As they drove up to the complex, large wrought iron gates swung open, permitting them to enter.

The driver drove up to the front of the large house and parked under the porte cochère—the overhead roof extending from the front of the house and over the driveway—which kept the snow from falling on them. As the Wright cousins retrieved their bags from the SUV, the front door of the house opened and a man stepped out to greet the cousins. He wore the uniform of a butler. "You are the Wrights, I presume," said the man.

"Yes," said Jonathan. "We're here to visit the Straunsees."

"Please come in," said the butler.

The Wright cousins, carrying their backpacks, stepped into the entry. The butler closed the door after them and led them to a large greeting area. "Please be seated," said the butler, motioning toward some plush, red velvet chairs.

"Thank you," said Jonathan and the other cousins. The cousins looked around them. A gold and crystal chandelier hung over the middle of the room; its prisms cast beautiful, miniature rainbows upon the walls, ceiling, and floor. Gold-framed paintings of majestic mountain landscapes hung on the walls. Engraved nameplates identified the scenery and the painters. There were also paintings of several of the Straunsee family ancestors. Kings and queens, princesses and princes.

Eighteen-year-old Jonathan was in awe. He had always been the natural leader of the Wright cousins and had helped in their adventures. Ever since Jonathan had met Sarina at Fort Courage, they had been fast friends. Sarina was a nice, modest, kind, sweet and fun seventeen-year-old young woman. The Wrights had stayed with Sarina's family at Straunsee castle. It had been a wonderful adventure and a lot of fun. But sitting here in this gilded room, it hit home just who the Straunsees were. Sarina's father was the king of Gütenberg. The leader. The commander-in-chief of its armed forces. And Sarina was his daughter. Sarina was a princess. Jonathan was a commoner, a young man of no rank or position. And yet....

Jonathan continued to look around the ornate room. It spoke of authority, of power, of tradition and ancient history. Jonathan thought of his own family. He knew who his grandparents were, and some of his extended family, but that was about it. He remembered his great-great Grandpa Jake, the gold miner, but there were a lot of other ancestors he did not even know the names of. All around him, Jonathan could see the dramatic history of Sarina's family. He made a mental note to learn more about his own family history, his ancestors and their stories. Somehow, he knew that would help him keep life more in perspective.

Jonathan and Sarina's family circumstances and responsibilities were so different, and yet, somehow, Sarina, a princess of Gütenberg, possible heir to the throne, took notice of Jonathan. Why did she do that? Why did she befriend him? And yet, she did.

Whatever the future held, Jonathan and Sarina were true friends, and maybe more. Their friendship was growing dearer to each of them with each passing day. They were better people because of it.

The butler reentered the room. "I will show you in now," he said. "Please follow me."

CHAPTER 6

Return

The butler ushered the youths into a library room. The library walls were lined with bookshelves filled with books old and new. An elderly gentleman, his back turned toward them, was studying an old topographic map through the lens of a magnifying glass. The butler excused himself and left the room by the same door they had entered.

The elderly man in the library turned to greet them. The youths were surprised to see it was Mr. Gervar.

"It's the octogenarian guy," Tim elbowed and whispered to Kimberly.

The Wright cousins had first met Mr. Gervar at Straunsee Castle while they were searching for the Sword of Sutherlee. He had flown them in the helicopter to Pallin during the evacuation from Trifid.

Mr. Gervar stood and eagerly shook hands with each of the Wright cousins. "Your timing could not have been more perfect," he said. "The Straunsees are away, but Alexander—King Straunsee—has put me in charge of retrieving the Pallin computer data. If you want to help the Straunsees, this is your opportunity. We need your help in finding your missing plane. It contained some very vital information. We must return you to that valley to help us find it."

"Thank you for believing us about the plane," said Jonathan. "We were beginning to think everybody was crazy around here."

"You're the Wright cousins," said Mr. Gervar. "And I have learned that you always tell the truth."

The cousins nodded gratefully in reply.

Mr. Gervar smiled. "Will you help us?"

"Of course, yes," said the five cousins.

"Thank you," said Mr. Gervar, leading them over to look at the map he had been viewing on the desk. "The area you were in is an old volcanic region," he continued. "Thousands of years ago, it held several active volcanoes. The area is now mostly known for its health-promoting hot springs. The water has a wonderful balance of minerals. When I was a youngster, my family used to visit there often. One place," he said, pointing to a mark on the map, "was known as Cascade Springs. We could swim in the warm water there in the dead of winter, with snow all around, and not get cold."

Kimberly noticed that Mr. Gervar kept tapping his finger on the map as he spoke. She nonchalantly leaned over to see what his finger was pointing to. On the old map was a series of double dashed, medium blue lines which headed in a southeasterly direction from a cluster of several, tiny black squares with one black "L" shape in the middle of them. As she looked more closely, there were several more of the dashed blue lines throughout the valley. The double blue lines seemed to be radiating from a conical shaped mountain to the northwest of the black objects.

"There are fifteen lakes in that valley system alone," Mr. Gervar was saying. "King Straunsee sent me the air force search and rescue report on your recent rescue. You'll start your search where they picked you up. For tonight, you will find rooms prepared for you at the top of the main stairway in the guest wing. You will leave by helicopter at seven in the morning. Thank you for your help and have a good rest."

As the Wright cousins turned to leave, the library door creaked. Tim saw a shadow move at the bottom of the door. He rushed forward to open the door to see who it was. It was heavier than he thought it would be and by the time he got it open, there was nobody to be seen.

"Thank you, Tim," said Kimberly, "that was very thoughtful of you to open the door for us. There may yet be a gentleman inside you after all."

"But I..., aw, never mind," Tim replied.

As Robert stepped through the doorway, Tim whispered, "There's something going on around here. Somebody was just listening at this door."

"Did you see who it was?" Robert whispered back.

"No, but I bet it was the butler," Tim replied. "They *always* do it."

At 5AM the next morning, the cousins were awakened by a loud knock at their doors. "Time to get going," said an enthusiastic man's voice.

The cousins stumbled out of bed, rubbing the sleep out of their eyes.

"I thought we were supposed to get up at 6," Tim complained.

"They must need us to get out there sooner," said Jonathan.

The cousins ate a quick breakfast in the limousine as they were driven to the airport. A helicopter was waiting for them, all warmed up and ready to go. "Welcome aboard," said the pilot. "Please get seated. We've got to hurry and get you out there."

"What's going on?" asked Jonathan.

"Let's just say we've gotten word that there are other groups looking for your airplane," replied the pilot. "The Straunsees are counting on you."

"Okay," said Jonathan, "let's go."

The cousins quickly strapped themselves in. Jonathan noted some equipment stowed in the back of the helicopter cabin: rope, backpacks, ice picks, and other tools. The helicopter quickly lifted off the ground and headed east.

"Wow," said Kimberly, glancing out the left side window. "Look back there at the airport. There's a whole bunch of police cars there now. I wonder what happened."

"Maybe it's 'Police Appreciation Day'," said Tim.

"With flashing lights?" said Kimberly.

"Well, you know, maybe they're appreciating each other and giving each other tickets," Tim said.

"Thank you, Tim," said Kimberly, turning now to look to where they were headed.

Robert noted they were flying lower than normal. The terrain was beginning to become more rugged. Low mountains were giving way to more jagged peaks. After some time, several of the mountains looked more conical.

"Those look like volcanoes down there," said Lindy.

"Yes, this whole area was very volcanic," informed the pilot. "There are still many hot springs. This region used to be well peopled, but the eruption of 1965 made it too dangerous, and all the people moved away."

"Are we near the valley where we crashed?" asked Robert.

"According to the military charts of your journey, we are getting very close," said the pilot as they flew over a snow-covered valley. "Does anything look familiar?"

The cousins, eager to help the Straunsees, were studying the terrain below and ahead. Heavy snow blanketed the area.

"There are the stone buildings!" Tim said excitedly a few moments later, pointing off in the distance. "We stayed in the one down there that still has the roof on it."

The pilot brought the helicopter lower, hovering above the stone building that Tim had identified.

"We were heading north, if I remember right," said Jonathan. We crashed on the east shore of the lake, somewhere over there near the base of those mountains."

"Okay," said the pilot, turning the helicopter slightly to the right and heading toward the area Jonathan had indicated. "We'll look there."

"There should be boulders and trees," added Lindy.

The pilot began flying along the east side of the valley. They made several runs, but to the cousins' surprise, they couldn't find any trees or large rocks.

CHAPTER 7

Help

Lindy closed her eyes. "They have to be there," she said, opening them again. "Large trees, boulders. There was a boat frozen in place, half sunk in the ice."

"Were you on the lake itself?" asked the pilot.

"We were near the edge of it," Lindy replied.

"Maybe the bombs set off an avalanche that buried our plane," said Robert. "When we were running from the plane toward the buildings, we were on the lake. The ice kept cracking under our feet."

"Let's fly back to the buildings. Maybe we can figure out our route from there," suggested Jonathan. "We barely made it to the ground in front of one of the roofless buildings before the ice broke up."

The pilot slowly steered the helicopter over toward the buildings. "Strange," he said as they flew, "look at that ice down there. It's all buckled. Not a smooth lake surface in sight. What did you guys do with all of the water?"

"What do you mean?" asked Jonathan.

"When the ice on a lake cracks, it usually stays pretty much in place," replied the pilot. "It floats on the water. That ice down there isn't sitting on water. It's all sunken down. Much of that ice is sitting on the bottom of the lake."

"We didn't do it," said Tim. "We were just running for our lives."

"Well, *something* drained this lake," said the pilot. "And it wasn't too long ago."

Their conversation was interrupted by a call the pilot received. He looked far to the north and said, "Okay. Anything else? Roger. Over."

The pilot looked thoughtfully at the cousins. "Tell you what," he said, "I've got to set you guys down on the ground. Maybe someplace with a better vantagepoint for you. I've been asked to help the Kleinstattz Air Force Base searchers for about fifteen minutes to shuttle some of their ground troops around."

"The Air Force?" asked Jonathan.

"Yes," replied the pilot with a smile. "You didn't think you're in on this alone, did you? King Straunsee directed Commander Trelland to find your plane at all costs."

"Commander Trelland? So, he did believe us after all," said Robert.

"But what about our passports?" asked Kimberly.

"We find the plane, we get our passports back," Lindy replied.

"I'm not privy to that information," the pilot replied. "I just do as I'm told. I'd better get you Wrights dropped off so I can go help those searching troops."

"Okay," said Jonathan. "We appreciate the ride."

The pilot nodded and headed to the north of the lake. As he did so, the cousins continued to scan the area. North and south, the cousins could see small white objects moving; Commander Trelland's soldiers in snow camouflage searching for the lost plane.

"Wow, that plane must be pretty important," said Tim, still

glancing out of the window next to him.

"Let's just say our enemies would love to get their hands on it," replied the pilot.

Kimberly looked out the left window and spotted more stone structures below. Most were square but there was one L-shaped building amongst them.

"You'll notice that there are a lot of abandoned stone buildings around here," said the pilot, noting the cousins' interest. "Stone is the only thing that holds up to the harsh winter environment."

North of the lake was another group of stone buildings. They were surrounded by white tents and were next to another frozen over lake. There were soldiers scurrying around them and a tall antenna near one of the tents. The cousins could also see several white snowmobiles and a white snowcat.

"I'll get you as close as I can to the top of that tall hill down there," the pilot said. "That should give you a good view of the valley."

"Mind if we take some rope?" asked Jonathan as the pilot prepared to land. "It's really slippery down there and the rope might help us get around more safely."

"Sure," said the pilot. "And take some of that food and other gear, too. I might get stuck shuttling personnel for quite a while. I don't want you guys to get hungry or cold. There's a pack for each of you."

The helicopter whipped up a whirlwind of snow as it set down. Jonathan grabbed a large bundle of rope and handed it to Robert to carry and then grabbed a large backpack for himself.

"You're okay to get out now," directed the pilot. "Use this hand radio if you need to contact me."

"Thanks," said Jonathan, taking the radio and climbing

down out of the helicopter with the other cousins as they put on their backpacks.

"If all goes well, I'll be back in about twenty minutes," said the pilot. "Let me know what you find out."

After the cousins had gotten clear, the helicopter lifted off the ground and headed farther north.

The Wright cousins adjusted the straps on their backpacks and began hiking. Jonathan broke trail through the two-foot-deep snow; the rest of the cousins followed in his footsteps.

"Boy, I'd love to have a good pair of snowshoes about now," said Robert.

When they reached the top of the small hill, the cousins retrieved their binoculars and phone cameras. They scanned to the south, trying to retrace their steps of the days before. Everything looked so different now. As they had learned from their viewing from the helicopter, their tracks had probably been erased by blowing snow.

The cousins did their best to find the place where they had leaped to higher ground as the distant lake's ice was cracking. They found what looked like the location and tried to line it up with its proximity to the old buildings. From there, they scanned the mountains to the east, searching for their crashed plane.

About twenty minutes after the helicopter had gone, the cousins spied divers in wetsuits, standing ready by the east shore. There were several troops in white camouflage coverall uniforms near them.

"Boy, they *really* do want to find that plane," said Robert, looking through his binoculars.

"I wouldn't want to go swimming in that water," said Tim. "It's freezing cold."

"You can't go anyways," Kimberly said. "Mom says stay warm."

"That's fine with me," said Tim. "There's probably not any water left to dive in anyways."

Lindy scanned the area south of the divers. "There are some of the boulders," she announced.

"Are you sure?" asked Kimberly.

"Kimberly, *it's Lindy*," said Robert.

"Oh yeah, right," said Kimberly. "Well, let's call our pilot and tell him. Then we can get out of this frozen place so we all don't die from frostbite. Timothy, your skin is looking fearfully blue. We'd better get you warmed up."

"And what color sunglasses are you wearing again?" asked Tim.

"Blue," Kimberly replied. "Why?"

"I rest my case," said Tim.

"I'll report to the pilot that we found the rocks," said Jonathan, raising the small hand-held radio to his lips. He was just about to squeeze the "push-to-talk" button when Lindy grabbed his arm and said, "Stop!"

"What's wrong?" asked Jonathan, noting the concerned look on Lindy's face.

"Don't contact the pilot," Lindy said, glancing back anxiously at the telephoto picture she had just taken with her phone. "Look at this."

The rest of the cousins gathered round to view. The screen showed a white, military-type snow cat in the background. On its side, in low resolution markings, was an ominous symbol. "That's not King Straunsee's," said Lindy. "It's from Slugdovia."

"Slagg's?" said Jonathan.

"But our pilot seemed like such a nice guy," said Kimberly.

"Yes, and look at all the nice information he got out of us," Lindy replied. "Grandpa Wright says you can trap a lot more flies with honey than you can with vinegar."

"Vinegar or not, we're in deep trouble," said Robert, lowering his binoculars, "there must be at least a hundred of Slagg's snowtroops out there!"

CHAPTER 8

Tents Moment

"Yes, you *are* in deep trouble," said a woman's voice from behind the cousins. "What are you doing out here?"

The cousins turned around to see a snow parka uniformed woman, sergeant by rank, flanked by two other soldiers. They were carrying guns.

"What are you doing on Slugdovian soil?" asked the sergeant.

"Wait a minute," said Jonathan, "we were under the impression this was part of Gütenberg."

"A lot of people make that mistake," the sergeant said. "Follow me. We can help you get back to where you need to be."

The sergeant and other soldiers led the cousins down to a flat area filled with several large, white tents. It was in a different location than the tents the cousins had seen from the helicopter.

"By the way," said the woman as they walked, "I'm Sergeant Windler. What are your names?"

"I'm Jonathan," Jonathan replied.

"We're from the United States," said Tim. "We need to talk to the American embassy. We're trying to go home."

"This is an unusual place to try to do that," said the sergeant, studying each of the youths. "I will need to see your passports."

"We don't have them," said Kimberly.

"That makes it a little harder," said Sergeant Windler. "But we will get you properly taken care of. You needn't worry."

The snowfall was increasing as the group arrived at a large, thick-walled, heated tent. Sergeant Windler escorted the cousins inside where they found several stacks of large olive drab boxes.

"You can wait here until I can make better arrangements for you," said the sergeant with a curt smile. "I will return soon."

Before she left, the sergeant clicked a quick photograph of the five cousins and said, "Please do stay here for your own safety. There has been trouble in this region and we are trying to get to the bottom of it."

The sergeant turned and left, closing the tent door behind her.

"So, Kimberly, is the sergeant vinegar or honey?" asked Tim.

"I'm not sure," Kimberly replied.

Jonathan opened the door to ask the sergeant a question and found his way blocked by two armed soldiers.

"Please stay in the tent for your own safety as you were instructed," said one of the soldiers.

"When will the sergeant be back?" asked Jonathan.

"Soon," replied the man. "Now just sit back and make yourselves comfortable. You have nothing to worry about."

The guard closed the tent door and latched it.

"How do you like that," Kimberly said, "we came all this way out here and they just stick us in this smelly old tent with these smelly green boxes. The heat does feel good, though. Timothy, what are you doing?"

"I'm just sitting back and making myself comfortable, like the guard said," Tim replied, sitting on a folding chair near the tent doorway.

"Oh," said Kimberly, "I guess that's okay." She shrugged her shoulders and walked to the far end of the tent to stand near the heater duct.

Tim leaned back in his chair. As he did so, he could hear the soldiers outside talking quietly amongst themselves.

"The sergeant says we are not to let the kids escape," said the first guard. "They've got something to do with the plane."

"What would a bunch of kids have to do with a military shootdown?" asked the second guard.

"I don't know. You know how sergeants are."

"Yes," said the second guard, "you ask them a question and then they let you run five miles and do pushups for the privilege. If you ask me, this is just a big waste of time. Our jets finished that plane off with bombs. There wouldn't be much left after that. You remember what happened to that fighter jet they were loading with bombs and the bomb went off. They didn't even find a tail wheel from that thing."

"That's because that type of plane doesn't have a tail wheel," said the first man.

"Well, you know what I mean," the second man replied, stomping his boot in the snow. "It was totally blown up except for the black smudge on the ground. And now, to top it all off, they have us looking for computer drives in a vaporized old plane in Gütenberg. If you ask me, it's like trying to find a beetle in a spray rack."

"Don't you mean 'a needle in a haystack'?" asked the first man.

"No, the spray rack," replied the second man. "Remember, that's where we found the airplane's tail wheel."

"But that type of plane doesn't have a tail wheel," the first man said.

The soldiers' conversation turned to food.

Tim quietly got up, motioned for the other cousins to join him at the other end of the tent, and told them what he had heard. "They talked like it was their planes that shot us down," Tim finished.

"That explains a whole lot," whispered Jonathan. "That's a bunch of baloney the sergeant told us about this being Slugdovia; this is Gütenberg."

"And they're after that computer data from the plane. We can't let Slagg and Kreppen get it," Robert whispered. "They'd use it to make everybody in the world their slaves."

"Yeah, but how are we going to find the plane?" asked Tim. "They've already got a gazillion soldiers looking all over to find it."

"The bombs probably caused an avalanche," said Jonathan. "But Lindy, you said you saw the boulders?"

"Do you think the plane fell into one of the bomb craters?" Lindy replied.

"Or just got blown to bits," said Tim.

Kimberly had been unusually quiet. "Lindy," she said, "last night on Mr. Gervar's topographic map, there were some dashed blue lines in this valley. What would that mean?"

Lindy thought for a second and said, "A single dash usually means a seasonal stream. A double dash could mean an underground water tunnel. Do you remember which kind they were?"

Kimberly thought for a moment and said, "I'm pretty sure they were double dash lines. But this area is volcanic. Why would there be water tunnels around here?"

"They could mean lava tubes," Lindy replied. "They're old tunnels that formed when the lava was flowing. The top lava cooled, forming a roof, but the hot lava underneath kept flowing out, leaving a tunnel when it left. Which way did the lines go?"

"East from the cone-shaped mountain. The old volcano. One of the tubes went through an L-shaped building," said

Kimberly. "Just like the one we found the secret well in."

"Then the plane might be down in the lava tube," said Lindy. "That's why the well-thing acted so weirdly. Hot, then cold, and hot again, and all that water shooting up like a geyser. It must have swallowed up the lake and our plane with it."

"If we're going to find it, we've got to get out of here before that sergeant gets back," said Jonathan. "We can cut a hole in the tent wall."

"I've got a pocketknife," said Robert.

"Me too," added Tim.

The tent was ten feet wide by twenty feet long. It was insulated with multilayered walls and had an attached floor. There was snow piled up against the bottom of the walls on the outside.

Robert and Tim selected a spot in the corner farthest away from the tent door, shielded by a stack of boxes, and began cutting a hole in the wall for them to climb through.

"Hey," whispered Robert after two minutes of trying to cut, "this canvas stuff is tough. They must have Kevlar bulletproof fabric in it; it's totally dulling my blades."

"Mine was already dull," said Tim. "Maybe it will make mine sharper."

"Sorry, but I don't think it works that way," said Robert.

While Tim and Robert were cutting the wall, Kimberly kept watch at the door and Jonathan and Lindy started going through the backpacks they had gotten from the helicopter. The cousins needed to be able to travel fast and did not want to carry anything they would not need.

Once the backpacks were lightened, Jonathan and Lindy piled them near their exit hatch, ready to be passed through when Robert and Tim were done.

Instead of a 2-foot by 3-foot door, the cousins had to settle on an eighteen-inch by 20-inch, u-shaped flap. Robert was the first to climb out, followed by Lindy.

Robert quickly slipped over to the corner of the tent and carefully peeked around it; the guards were still there.

Jonathan passed the backpacks out and Lindy slipped hers on as Tim and Kimberly climbed out. There were no windows in the tent. Jonathan switched off the lights and climbed out, too.

As the youths were hurriedly putting on their backpacks, they could hear the whine of vehicles approaching. Robert peeked around the corner of the tent and came running back. "There's a bunch of soldiers arriving on snowmobiles," he warned. "The sergeant lady's on one of them. There are at least seven soldiers and Kreppen."

"Oillee Kreppen?" whispered Jonathan. "That creep that's trying to overthrow King Straunsee and take over Gütenberg is here?"

"He will recognize us for sure. Let's get out of here," whispered Kimberly, turning to run in the other direction.

"No," whispered Jonathan, grabbing her arm. "We can't beat them that way. They'll see our tracks."

"What are we going to do then?" whispered Kimberly, near panicking. "I don't want to see that Kreppen guy again. Jonathan, he tried to kill us!"

"We'll trap them in the tent and take their snowmobiles."

"But we don't have keys," Kimberly said.

"Most old military vehicles don't use keys," said Robert. "You guys get to the snowmobiles and we'll join you once we get the door fixed."

Lindy was watching from the tent corner. The others lined up behind her.

Kreppen and the soldiers hurried over to the tent to secure

the Wright cousins. Kreppen, the old president of the Gütenberg parliament, was particularly eager to capture the youths who had defeated him at Straunsee Castle. Kreppen had even left his snowmobile running.

The group rushed into the tent only to find it totally dark inside.

"Now!" motioned Lindy.

Robert and Jonathan ran for the tent door. The guards were now inside the tent, too, trying to find the lights and the Wright cousins also. Robert and Jonathan closed the tent door and yanked the supporting poles. With a *Phoomph!* the whole tent collapsed!

"How did we do that?" said Jonathan in surprise.

"Beats me," said Robert, "but I'll take it. Let's get out of here."

The youths ran for the snowmobiles and leapt aboard. Jonathan and Kimberly were on one, Robert and Lindy were on a second, and Tim manned the third.

The cousins heard a lot of angry yelling coming from the tent and also sighted a distant squad of soldiers with submachineguns rushing toward them.

"Follow me," said Jonathan, revving his snowmobile's engine.

Desperate to get away and beat Kreppen to the lost plane, the five youths raced out across the snow, heading southwest.

Lindy hung onto her twin brother's waist for stability as they sped along. "Nobody chasing us yet," she called out to Robert.

Lindy kept glancing back and suddenly saw soldiers coming after them. "We've got about a mile on them," she called out to Robert. "There's three snowmobiles chasing us from the north. Four more coming from the east."

CHAPTER 9

Through the Snow

Jonathan had also seen the pursuers. He signaled Robert and Tim to follow him as they sped up over the bouncy terrain. The group from the east was the most concerning; they could cut off the cousins before they reached the stone buildings far to the south by the lake.

Jonathan turned west. They would have to take a more roundabout way along the side of the mountain. Their path was getting more rugged now as Jonathan led the other cousins between two low hills. Some of the snow had piled up in drifts. The cousins plowed right through the powdery snow; the denser snow acted like jumps.

Lindy glanced back again; three more snowmobiles, also driven by soldiers, had joined in the chase.

At full throttle, the snowmobile engines were whining loudly. Jonathan and Kimberly, in the lead, hit a deep snowdrift and punched through the other side. Hitting slick ice on a frozen over lake, they spun out wildly.

Jonathan desperately steered into the turn to regain control. Robert and Tim barely missed his snowmobile as they shot past on the ice. Jonathan and Kimberly finally stopped spinning, caught up with them, and retook the lead.

Grateful for the polarized goggles and ski caps they had

found in the packs, the Wright cousins pushed on. They reached the far side of the lake and bounced up the bank there. Kimberly, hanging onto Jonathan's backpack, glanced back momentarily. There were now ten snowmobiles pursuing them.

The ground sloped upward. They entered a snow-covered pine forest and had to lean side-to-side as they weaved between the trees. The pursuing snowmobiles kept after them.

Flying out of the woods, the cousins spied some snow-covered stone buildings in the distance.

"There's our buildings," Kimberly called out.

"I see them," said Jonathan, suddenly turning down onto a frozen over river.

"What are you doing?" asked Kimberly.

"Trying to ditch our tracks," Jonathan replied.

The rest of the cousins followed them. They traveled for almost half a mile, following the course of the river, and then Jonathan turned to the right and led the cousins up a snow filled ravine. Staying in the ravine, they kept out of sight as they headed toward the old buildings.

Jonathan stopped his snowmobile near the end of the ravine and switched it off. He directed the others to do the same. Then they waited in silence for their pursuers. Through the falling snow, they could hear the sounds of the soldiers' snowmobiles, but they could not see them. The sounds first seemed to be growing louder but after several seconds they grew more faint. A few more moments of anxious listening and the sounds faded off to just the whisper of the wind driving the snow.

"Okay," said Jonathan to the other cousins, "let's go find that plane."

Leaving the snowmobiles in the ravine, the cousins rushed

over to the old stone buildings. The first building had no roof and neither did the second.

The cousins spied the third building and rushed over to it. The roof was still intact. They turned the door latch and pushed hard. The door moved inward only an inch and stopped. Glancing in, the cousins saw that the building was full of snow!

"It sure filled up fast," said Robert. "There must be a window broken on the windy side."

The cousins ran to the next side of the building.

"This isn't our building," said Lindy.

"What?" said Jonathan, studying the building and then looking around. "But there were three buildings."

"Yes," said Lindy, "but they were different than these. And there's no lake nearby, either."

"You're right," said Jonathan. "Where do you think the other ones are?"

"They must be farther south," said Lindy.

The cousins quickly ran back to the ravine. As they ran, they could hear the sound of snowmobiles approaching again. In the distance, there were several gunshots.

"Jonathan, they've got guns," said Kimberly, looking northward with a worried look on her face.

"We've been in tight places before," Jonathan replied. "We Wrights are used to tackling hard things. Now hang on tight and let's get out of here!"

The cousins started their snowmobiles and drove up out of the ravine. Following their compass, they headed south as directly as they could. Along the way, they had to skirt lava outcroppings and boulders. As they came up out of yet another ravine, they turned off their machines to listen for a moment.

"So far, so good," said Jonathan and they started out again.

The cousins were rapidly crossing another flat. The snow was falling lightly again. There were still no buildings in sight.

They were almost to the other side of the flat when Lindy saw a distant helicopter heading their way. "Robert," she called out, "a helicopter's following us."

"Rats," said Robert.

The ground was getting more rugged and the cousins had to slow down to navigate it. The helicopter flew overhead, circled, and then kept over them.

"They must be showing their snowmobile troops where we are," Robert called out to Lindy.

Jonathan turned more west, trying to find cover. They had to keep moving. The cousins hit a section with deeper snow and had to skirt several large rock outcroppings. The helicopter was still dogging them.

The cousins were now making their way along the side of a tall mountain. There were large swaths of pine forests reaching toward its top. The top of the mountain was mostly bare; it rose higher than the cousins could see through the falling snow. It was part of a chain of mountains.

Jonathan led the cousins into a stand of tall, snow-ladened pines, hoping to lose the helicopter. They brushed through ice-covered branches. It was a full minute before they came out the other side. The helicopter spotted them again as they entered another large clearing.

"Go away, helicopter, you big meanie pest!" yelled Tim as they sped across the flat to reach another forested area.

The new pines were closer together. Emerging from them, they sped out into a large, barren area. The ground sloped downward toward the east, giving them a side slope as they headed south. Far down the mountain, they could see several snowmobiles racing up to intercept them.

Kimberly pointed them out to Robert; Robert nodded, so did Tim.

The helicopter pulled ahead of the cousins and swooped down in front of them, trying to cut them off. The cousins ducked as they passed underneath it. The helicopter turned and followed them, trying the tactic again. This time it was closer to the ground.

The cousins veered to the downhill side and sped around it. They were almost to another group of trees. The frozen ground suddenly broke beneath them and the cousins plunged helplessly into a deep, dark pit with big chunks of ice and snow falling in after them.

CHAPTER 10

Alpenhaus

"Andrews, what do you mean the Wright cousins are not here at Alpenhaus?" Sarina Straunsee asked their chief butler. "I was informed they were here and my sister and I have driven half the night to get here."

"I understand, Miss Straunsee, that Mr. Gervar wished for them to go on a helicopter flight," the butler replied. "They left about 7 of the clock this morning."

"What helicopter flight? Where is Mr. Gervar?" Sarina responded.

"Indisposed," said the butler. "For all I know he may well have gone with them."

"Andrews, you know he would do no such thing without telling us," Sarina replied with fire in her eyes. "Come on, Katrina, let's go find him."

Sarina and her twin sister pushed past butler Andrews and headed straight for Mr. Gervar's quarters. When they got there, they found his room disheveled, as if it had been ransacked. Butler Andrews followed them. Sarina pressed the "panic button" on her phone and was answered immediately by security. "Where is Mr. Gervar and why is his room in a shamble?" she demanded.

"We don't know, Princess, our surveillance gear has been

malfunctioning and we are just now getting it back online."

"Get everyone in security to check out Alpenhaus," said Sarina. "And where are the Wright cousins?!"

"They drove out the rear gate at 6AM," said security. "We have video on it."

"Where did they go?" asked Sarina.

"We're bringing it up on our computers now. GPS puts the vehicle they were in at the airport."

"Who has taken them there?" asked Sarina. "Stop them from leaving the airport."

"Yes, Princess," replied security. "We have found Mr. Gervar. He is in the library. He appears to be unconscious. We are sending help."

"We will be right there," Sarina replied.

Sarina and Katrina glanced at butler Andrew's indifferent face in frustration and rushed for the library. Arriving there, they found several people, including a staff doctor, leaning over an old, gray-haired man who was slumped over in a chair. His back was to the girls.

The doctor looked up and said, "He still has a pulse."

"Thank goodness," said Sarina with tears showing in her eyes. "Whoever has done this will pay for their crime."

"What crime?" asked butler Andrews from behind them. "Mr. Gervar would not tell us what we wanted."

"What did you say?" asked Sarina in alarm. "Andrews, you are a traitor, too?"

"I am a realist, Princess," replied butler Andrews. "You girls have lived the spoiled life. It is your turn to be the servant."

"After all our father has done to help you and your family," said Katrina with distaste. "You, too, are willing to trade freedom for some promised, false security?"

"You are both naïve," said the doctor. "Kreppen will follow

through with his promises. Your father no longer has the popular support."

"You lie," said Sarina. "He has the common peoples' backing. You will see. You can never get him to quit."

"He will give up the throne once he knows we have you," stated butler Andrews. "And do not try to escape, we have this compound surrounded."

The group was now almost completely encircling Sarina and Katrina. The girls gasped when they saw that the old man was not really Mr. Gervar at all, but someone dressed up to decoy them in.

Sarina snatched a sword from its rack on the wall and swung it in the butler's direction. Andrews stepped backwards, trying to get out of the way, and fell over one of the other staff members. He backward somersaulted and sprawled out on the floor. Sarina brandished the sword, forcing the others to give ground, then she and Katrina raced for the library door.

"After them!" shouted the butler, rolling over onto his side so he could get to his feet. "After them. If they get away, you shall all be punished."

Sarina and Katrina ran for the front door, only to find the way barred by two security agents.

"You shall not get away this time," hollered butler Andrews from the library doorway.

The girls turned and raced up the main entry stairway. If they could make it to Sarina's room, there was a balcony they could make their way down from and head out the front gate. Reaching Sarina's door, they found it securely locked.

"Go for my room," said Katrina. Both girls turned and ran down the wide hall to Katrina's room. Sarina tried the handle; it too was locked!

"You forget about the latch," said Katrina, ramming the

door with her shoulder and forcing it open. "That strike-plate hasn't worked for years."

The girls closed the door behind them and ran for the small window at the opposite side of the room. Sliding it open, they quickly climbed through and out onto a lower, red tiled roof, closing the window after them. The tiles were snow-covered and slippery. From their vantage point, they could see personnel searching the grounds and men posted at the compound's gateways.

The girls carefully made their way along the roof toward a far wall. A few moments later, the girls heard a helicopter approaching and ducked underneath an overhanging roof. The helicopter soon came into view. It was white with civilian markings. The craft set down on the Straunsee's heliport and six uniformed soldiers leapt down from it. They headed for the facility's large parking garage and the house. The helicopter's blades slowed. How would the girls get free?

"We'll have to force the pilot to take us out of here," said Sarina, still clutching her sword.

The identical twins carefully made their way to a tree, shinnied down it, and swiftly but quietly headed for the helicopter. To avoid being seen, they approached the copter from the right rear side. Staying low, they grasped the rear door latch, opened it, and slipped in behind the pilot. Sarina was about to raise her sword to command the pilot, when the helmeted pilot, seeing them in a rearview cargo mirror, suddenly revved the engine and took off.

Sarina and Katrina were thrown backwards. They flailed about for something to grab onto to avoid falling out the open doorway. The copter banked hard in a turn as several bullets ripped through the door they had just come through. A canteen hanging on the back wall was hit and sprayed water all over the girls.

The helicopter banked the opposite way and the open door slammed closed. The pilot leveled off the copter and beelined it for the eastern mountains.

CHAPTER 11

The Find

Meanwhile, the helicopter pursuing the Wright cousins saw them disappear into a deep hole. It hovered in mid-air to try to locate them again. As they waited, the pilot radioed to Sergeant Windler's soldiers about the snowmobiles' location.

The helicopter was hovering close to the ground, the air from its rotor blades whooshing down onto the snow beneath it. The snow began to move, causing more snow to slide. The tumbling snow soon became an avalanche. The avalanche grew bigger and wider as it went rumbling down the side of the mountain.

"Now look what you have done," said the copilot. "If you had listened to me and gained altitude, we wouldn't be in this mess."

"Tell it to the sergeant," said the pilot.

"I will," said the copilot, "well, maybe I won't."

The two pilots watched in dismay as the avalanche they had caused gained momentum and sped down the mountainside toward their snowmobiling comrades.

Sergeant Windler and the other soldiers spied the avalanche coming toward them and turned tail to try to outrun the massive wave of snow.

On the edge of the avalanche, the Wright cousins were alive

and moving but having an extremely hard time of it. They had broken through a span of icy snow, formed by a blowing, clinging drift that had "roofed" over a narrow ravine. They were stuck under the snow in a snow tunnel as they went barreling down the side of the mountain. To make matters worse, they had to dodge dangerous icicles as they went. They tried to slow down but no matter what they did, the snowmobiles only slid on the icy snow and ice beneath them.

Before the cousins realized it, they were entering a smooth-walled cave. There was still ice on the floor where a stream had frozen, but now the sidewalls and roof were made of rock, created by an ancient lava flow. It was pitch dark except for a light spot in the distance. They reached the light spot area where the rock roof was replaced with snow and careened into another pitch-black tunnel.

Then suddenly there was a solid wall of glowing snow ahead. *Wham!* Jonathan and Kim slammed into it on their snowmobile and shot out into the bright daylight. Robert, Lindy, and Tim were right behind them as they barreled down the side of the mountain on the edge of the avalanche.

The helicopter was just turning mid-air to return to its temporary base for fuel. Out of the corner of his eye, the pilot spied the cousins' progress farther down the mountain. He quickly reported it and hurried back to refuel so he could rejoin the chase.

Jonathan kept his eye out for the soldiers' snowmobiles as he led the cousins down the mountainside. He could see the avalanche in all its terrifying majesty as it rolled rock and tree down the mountain. His sister, Kimberly, held onto him all the tighter.

There were massive boulders ahead protruding from the snow. Jonathan steered a course to the left of them. He caught sight of the helicopter leaving in the distance.

"There's an ice-covered lake down there with stone buildings," Kimberly pointed out to Jonathan.

"I see it," Jonathan nodded.

Jonathan eyed the frozen lake. Then all at once he saw it; an airplane lay trapped in the ice!

Jonathan steered for the plane. He glanced to his left to see if he could find the soldiers' snowmobiles but all he could see were the white, billowing clouds of ice crystals from the avalanche.

Traveling at high speed, the cousins were nearing the foot of the mountain. There was a large outcropping to the right and left. Jonathan steered between them. He immediately realized it was a mistake and hit the brakes. Too late to stop, Jonathan and Kimberly shot over the top of a frozen waterfall and arced downward toward a frozen pond fifteen feet below. Their snowmobile hit the ice and broke through, its nose stuck halfway into the ice and water. Jonathan and Kimberly, with Kimberly still hanging onto his backpack, were catapulted over the handlebars. They landed in a pile of snow and tumbled across the ice, finally stopping in a big snowdrift. Their snowmobile was out of commission.

Robert, on the second snowmobile, saw them disappear and hit the brakes. Tim did the same. They skidded to a stop just in time.

Cutting their machines back to idle, Robert, Lindy, and Tim quickly made their way to the edge of the precipice. They spied the damaged snowmobile and were gratefully relieved to see Jonathan and Kimberly moving, making their way up the left-hand side of the ravine.

Robert cupped his hands and hollered, "We'll back up and come around to get you."

"Okay," Jonathan called back. "Thanks."

Robert, Lindy, and Tim quickly backtracked and made their way carefully out of the ravine. They soon made it down to where Jonathan and Kimberly were waiting and pulled up beside them.

"Can we take on any hitchhikers?" Robert said to Lindy.

"Oh, I suppose so," Lindy replied with a grin, glancing at their two snow-covered cousins. "Are you guys okay?"

"Just some bruises, I think," said Kimberly, rubbing her shoulder.

"Same here," said Jonathan.

"That was quite a plunge," Lindy said. "Thank goodness you guys weren't killed."

Both youths nodded. Jonathan's face brightened and he said, "I think I found the plane."

The cousins quickly regrouped on their remaining two snowmobiles. Kimberly climbed on behind Lindy and Robert. It was a tight fit, so they had to transfer Robert's backpack to Tim's snowmobile. Jonathan took over the driving of Tim's snowmobile with Tim on behind.

"Hitchhikers," grumbled Tim as they started out.

Jonathan again led the way, a little more cautiously this time.

Avalanche ice crystals were still floating in the air as the cousins sped down the mountain slope toward the plane in the frozen lake.

The cousins still had no idea where the enemy soldiers were and realized they could strike at any time. All the cousins could do was pray and keep going. They *had* to get to the plane first.

Nearing the shore of the lake, Jonathan followed it south toward the area where he had seen the plane. They shut down their snowmobiles when they arrived and scrambled over to it. Covered with snow and ice, the wings, fuselage, and tail were bent and broken. Finding the place where the door should be, they dug away at the piled snow with their gloved hands to gain access.

"Listen!" said Lindy.

The cousins stopped. They could hear the distant whine of snowmobiles approaching.

"Don't those creeps ever give up?" said Tim.

"What are we going to do?" asked Kimberly.

"We have to get the Straunsee computer data," said Robert.

"No, we have to leave right now," said Lindy. Robert was about to protest but Lindy looked him straight in the eye, twin talk. "Something's wrong, I can feel it. We have to leave *right now.*"

Robert knew better than to go against his twin sister's intuition. "Lindy's right," he said, the hair beginning to stand up on the back of his neck. "We've got to get out of here!"

Without waiting for any more explanations, the five cousins turned and ran for their snowmobiles. As they did so, there were several bright flashes followed by popping sounds on the east side of the lake.

"Somebody's shooting and it's not BB guns," called out Robert as they ran.

The cousins reached their snowmobiles in record time, climbed aboard, and sped southward. They were not prepared to be a part of any battle.

The cousins were now in a wide part of the valley where the terrain was much more conducive to snowmobiling. After several minutes, they drove up to the top of a small hill to get their bearings. They were looking back toward the airplane they had just left and saw it suddenly flash and explode into flames.

"Whoa," said Tim. "I'm glad we got out of there."

"But what about the computer data?" said Kimberly.

"That wasn't our plane," Robert replied.

"What?" said Tim. "It was sure crashed like our plane."

"I saw one of the wings as we were leaving," said Robert. "That was a jet, ours was a turboprop. Thanks, Lindy, for being sensitive and getting us out of there."

"Thank you for listening to me, brother," Lindy replied. "Now we just need to find *our* plane. It must be in the lava tube."

Hurriedly looking further south, the cousins located some stone buildings that appeared more familiar. Robert gave Lindy his binoculars to check them out. "That's them," she said with a confident smile.

The cousins leapt aboard their snowmobiles and sped for the old stone buildings. As they traveled, the crack of gunfire and resulting explosions began filling the eastern sky.

The cousins spied a snowcat vehicle up ahead and steered well clear of it. As they passed around it, they found it abandoned. It had broken through the ice and gotten stuck. It bore the markings of Slagg's forces.

Jonathan signaled Robert to slow down. They were approaching a creek which fed into the lake. The creek was covered with ice but was still flowing. The ice looked iffy.

"We're going to have to jump it," Jonathan said.

"We'll go first," said Robert.

"No way," said Kimberly, who was hanging onto Lindy who was hanging onto Robert on the snowmobile.

"Follow us," said Jonathan with a grin.

"Yippee!" shouted Tim, holding on tight as Jonathan hit the throttle. Picking up speed, they hit the ice and flew across. Once on the other side, they waited for Robert and the girls to catch up with them.

Robert revved his snowmobile. It shot forward, hit the ice, and sped across. Just as they reached the far side, the ice behind them broke loose and tumbled into the frigid water.

"Yeehaw!" shouted Robert. "one-track-drive!"

Lindy laughed with relief as they raced to catch up with Jonathan. Even Kimberly was smiling.

As the cousins drove toward the stone buildings, Lindy glanced back to see if they were being pursued. A shiny object in the distance caught her attention. "Robert," she called out, "there's a helicopter chasing us again!"

Robert glanced back momentarily to see the new threat. "It's going to be close," he called back to Lindy.

The cousins were beginning to look like frozen snowmen as they raced through the swiftly falling snow.

Jonathan saw the helicopter, too; it was bearing down on them as they neared their destination.

The cousins were getting so close. Jonathan and the others shot past the nearest stone building. They pulled up to the second building, parked under what was left of its dilapidated porch, shut off their snowmobiles, and sprinted for the L-shaped building. They had just ducked under the roof eaves when the helicopter roared overhead.

The cousins turned the door latch but found it frozen. They pounded on it with their fists and shoulders and kicked it. The door finally broke free and swung open. As the cousins slammed the door behind them, it sounded as if the helicopter was coming in for a landing.

Inside the room, the cousins found the aluminum boat and wood stove still there. They scrambled to find something to prop the door closed with. Robert found a fireplace tool and wedged it closed.

"Everybody get to the secret stairway," said Jonathan. "We'll have to camouflage it so they can't find us."

"You really think the plane is down there under the

ground?" asked Kimberly with concern.

"Yes!" said Lindy, Robert, Jonathan, and Tim at the same time.

"Okay, okay," said Kimberly.

Jonathan grabbed an old tarp; Robert grabbed a short steel pipe and an old newspaper and they headed for the stairway. Was there still water in the well?

CHAPTER 12

Wild Flight

"Where are you taking us?" shouted Katrina, hanging onto one of the back seats in the helicopter flying from Alpenhaus.

"Where you are needed," the pilot replied in a young woman's voice. "Now sit down and get yourselves strapped in. The Wrights need you!"

"Who are you and how do you know the Wrights?" Sarina yelled over the high-pitched whine of the engine and roar of the rotor blades.

"My name is Dee," the pilot replied. "It is my business to know the Wrights. They saved my mother."

"Well what are you waiting for?" said Sarina. "Fly this thing!"

Sarina and Katrina quickly strapped in. As they flew, they tried to get a good look at their pilot's face, but the helmet and tinted visor she wore kept her appearance masked.

Sarina leaned over to talk into Katrina's ear and asked, "Have you ever heard of her before?"

"No," replied Katrina. "She has black hair, though. I can see it below her helmet."

Dee glanced up at the helicopter's "cargo check" rearview mirror, noting Sarina and Katrina's questioning looks. She retrieved a flight helmet from the net bag beside her seat.

"Here," she called out, "we can talk better with these. They are wired for inflight communications."

Dee passed the helmet back and then a second one. Sarina and Katrina slipped them on and adjusted them.

"Now you may ask your questions," Dee said over the earpieces in the helmets. She glanced at the avionics in front of her. "Good," she said, "so far, so good."

"Where are the Wright cousins?" asked Sarina.

"They have been transported to the valley of their plane crash," replied Dee. "They—just a minute—yes, okay, ETA twenty-two minutes. I have extracted S2 and S3. Tell them to prepare. No, you will have to take care of that. Roger. Over."

Dee was silent for a moment and then said, "Princesses, the Wrights are in terrible danger. We have no time. We are going to have to go in to extract them. There is equipment in the two smaller duffle bags behind your seats. I must instruct you in their use as we travel. First, get into the snow clothes you will find in the blue duffle bag—."

The pilot glanced back down at her control panel and saw a red warning light flashing. "Change of plans. We're going to have to take evasive action. Hold on, this might get crazy!"

Dee nosed the helicopter downward and they rapidly lost altitude. She leveled off just above the trees, popped over a ridge, and swooped down into the next valley. Glancing back through a side rear window, Sarina and Katrina could see an ominous dark shape following them.

"It appears to be a large drone," said Dee, focusing on her flying as the object mimicked their flight pattern. "We've been located."

"Who's doing it?" asked Sarina.

"Slagg and Kreppen, your father's enemies," Dee replied. She tapped a button on her flight controller. A heads-up display appeared, bracketing the drone following them and scanning it.

"No humans aboard" appeared on the display. "Take jamming action?" asked an electronic voice.

"Yes," Dee spoke into her helmet's microphone.

A small, black disk pivoted above the helicopter's rotors, tracking the drone. Energy impulses streamed from it, causing the drone's operators to lose control. The drone's momentum carried it forward, tracing out an arc as it plummeted toward the ground. But it leveled off and started following the helicopter again.

"Oh, they want to play that game, do they?" said Dee, pushing another button. "Well, we shall see about that."

The drone suddenly burst into flames and fell rapidly toward earth.

"They've been tracking us," said Dee over her headset.

Katrina was about to speak when Dee spoke up again, talking to someone over the radio.

"Yes, the drone is no longer following us," said Dee. "Okay. We will extract the Wrights. Get us some cover...will do. Roger. Over."

The Straunsee girls heard a crackle in their earphones. "Princesses, you'd better get into that snow gear," said Dee. "We're running short on time."

"Right," said Sarina, retrieving the blue bag and opening it. Inside were white snow clothes and boots. Sarina pulled them out and handed a set to Katrina. Both girls started slipping them on over their regular clothes. To get the coveralls past their waists, both girls had to unlatch their seat harnesses. The helicopter suddenly pitched and the girls were thrown from their seats, tumbling forward. Katrina's left knee slammed into the back of the pilot's seat. The nose of the helicopter suddenly rose, sending the girls rolling backwards toward their seats.

"Sorry about that," said Dee. "I wasn't expecting turbulence in this zone." She checked their position.

The helicopter continued to pitch and sway as they gained elevation, finally smoothing up in its flight. Seizing the opportunity, the twin princesses hurriedly got their coveralls up over their shoulders, zipped up the fronts, and strapped themselves into their seats. Katrina felt a sharp pain in her left leg as she put on her snow boots.

"Hang on," said Dee. "We're going in!"

CHAPTER 13

Stairs

The Wright cousins pulled open the trapdoor to the well stairway. Switching on their lights, they rushed down the stairs. Robert was the last to go. He rigged the hatch so that when they closed it, the old canvas tarp and paper would fall over on top of the trapdoor to hide it. That done, he closed the door above him and quickly joined the others.

When the cousins got to the underground well room, they found the pipe still in place, going down the round shaft, but there was no water in the hole. The cousins got down on their hands and knees and carefully looked down the shaft.

"I don't think the plane is down there. I think it got blown to bits like those soldiers said," said Kimberly as they shined their lights down the hole.

"There's only one way to find out," said Jonathan. "We'll climb down and see. We brought some rope."

"But what if we get stuck down there," said Kimberly.

"There's no water here. That probably means the lava tube is open on the downhill end," Jonathan replied.

Kimberly was about to protest but Jonathan held up his hand. "Kimberly, we told Mr. Gervar we'd help the Straunsees find the plane. There are a whole bunch of Slagg's soldiers out there. Remember, he's the creep that tried to wipe us out in space. There's no way we can let him get that technology.

Besides, this looks like our only chance to beat them to the plane. If we do have to come back out this way, we'll leave our rope tied in place, okay?"

"Tim and I should wait here," Kimberly said flatly. "It's not safe down there."

"Lava tubes are usually large and relatively smooth," said Lindy.

"And don't forget Slagg's soldiers are coming," Robert added. "That helicopter certainly saw us come into this building and radioed the troops."

"Yeah," said Tim. "And besides, we've got to help the Straunsees. They need us, Kimbo, and I've never been down in a lava tube before and this is a cool adventure!"

Just then, a gust of warm air shot up the well. "A warm, cool adventure," added Tim.

Hesitating, Kimberly glanced up the stairs and then back down the well.

"It looks like this shaft is about twenty-five feet deep," said Robert. "Jonathan and I can just go."

"I'm coming, too," said Lindy. "If we find the plane, you'll need my help digging it out."

"Me too," said Tim. "You'll need my pepper."

Jonathan grabbed hold of the metal pipe going down the shaft and shook it. It felt strong enough, so he and Robert got rope out of their back packs and started tying it onto the pipe, beginning with a clove hitch.

Once the rope was secured, the cousins all put on gloves and got ready to rappel down. Jonathan attached a small flashlight to the brim of his hat and was the first to go. He disappeared down the hole and a few seconds later there was a loud *THUNK* when he landed on the solid rock below.

"What do you see?" Robert called down from the top of the

well.

"It opens up wide down here," Jonathan's muted voice replied. "It looks like a lava tube, all right. The tunnel is roundish and must be twenty feet wide or more. It goes off in both directions. I can't see the ends."

Lindy rappelled down next, followed by Tim and Robert. Kimberly hesitated. Then she heard muffled talking and footsteps coming from the direction of the stairway. She gripped the rope firmly and started down. The noise from the stairway was growing louder.

Kimberly landed hard on the solid rock ground below. Her knees buckled and she collapsed on the ground.

"Are you okay?" asked Jonathan, helping her up.

"Yes," Kimberly replied. "I lost my grip. Jonathan, it sounds like there's a bunch of soldiers at the top of the stairs."

"Then we'd better hurry," said Jonathan quietly, glancing down the lava tube in each direction. "Which way is east? Kimberly, do you still have your compass?"

"Sure, I've got one on my key chain," Kimberly replied. She reached into her pocket but didn't find it. "I'm sure I had it. Where did it go?"

"Here it is," said Tim, picking an item up from the ground and handing it to her. "It must have fallen out when you landed."

"Thanks," said Kimberly, reaching for the compass.

"You're welcome," said Tim.

Kimberly quickly glanced down at her compass, waiting for it to stabilize. "That way," she said, pointing toward the passage to their right. "That way is east."

"Okay, let's get going," said Jonathan, leading out at a fast pace. "The sooner we find that plane, the sooner we can get out of here."

Hiking at a fast clip in the lava tube was a new adventure for the cousins. It was totally devoid of light except for the light put off by their flashlights. The solid rock walls were sparkling with moisture. The air was so humid and warm that the cousins had to unzip their heavy coats.

At first, the floor of the lava tube was smooth but after travelling about two hundred feet, they started encountering sand and rocks spread across the floor. It made for slower going.

"It's getting hotter down here, Kimberly," said Tim. "Do you think we'll run into hot lava?"

CHAPTER 14

Underground

"No," said Kimberly. "It's all extinct. You heard the helicopter pilot; they haven't had any active volcanoes around here since 1965."

"There's always hot lava under the ground," Tim said. "Did you see the smoke coming off the top of that cone-shaped mountain."

"Those were just clouds," Kimberly replied.

"I'm not so sure," said Tim.

"What are you guys talking about back there?" Robert asked.

"Hot lava," said Tim between breaths. "Do you think we could outrun it if it started chasing us?"

"Good question," Robert replied.

The cousins came to a wide puddle of steaming water and had to walk around it.

"Hot lava can move pretty fast," said Robert.

"I think we could outrun it if we ran our fastest," Tim said.

"Maybe you guys could run fast," said Kimberly, "but I've got these big, heavy hiking boots on. There's no way I could beat hot lava. I hope we don't find any."

"Kimberly, did the map say how long this lava tube is?" asked Tim.

"I didn't see the scale on the map," Kimberly replied.

"I'll ask Lindy," said Robert. He caught up with her and soon came back. "Lindy says she doesn't know about this one, but the longest lava tube ever found is over 40 miles long."

"40 miles?" said Tim, suddenly feeling very tired. "If we run into hot lava, I can't run that far. Maybe we could make a raft or something."

"Hey, maybe that's what the aluminum boat is for," said Robert. "Wait, no, it would just melt to pieces."

"Um, guys, can we change the subject, please," said Kimberly.

The cousins were now traveling through a rockier zone. The lava tube was partially plugged with sand, silt, and assorted sizes of rocks and boulders. Tim glanced back into the darkness behind them. It was pitch black at first but then he thought he saw a faint light. "Hey guys," he said, "I think there might be somebody–." Tim peered into the blackness a moment longer. "No, I guess not."

Tim turned to look for the other cousins and saw their lights moving amongst the boulders farther ahead. "Hey, you guys, wait for me!" he called out, scrambling to catch up with them.

The air was still growing moister. As the cousins climbed over a jumble of rocks the height of their shoulders, they found the passage blocked by more rocks, sand, silt, and even larger boulders. Near the ceiling of the lava tube, twenty feet above them, they could see the trunk of a tree wedged amongst the rocks; its roots dangling in the air and dripping with water.

"Wow," said Jonathan, looking at the huge mess. "This must be where the ceiling collapsed."

"What are we going to do?" asked Kimberly. "It looks like the whole lava tube is blocked. It would be too dangerous to try to dig it out."

The cousins shined their lights at the massive pile of debris before them. Noting a three-foot-wide waterfall cascading down from the ceiling on the left side, Jonathan said, "That water's not backing up into our side of the tube. Let's find out where it's going."

The cousins followed the water's route but found their way blocked by large rocks. The water could get through; the cousins could not.

After five minutes of trying, Jonathan suggested they spread out to look for another way through. They probed the nooks and crannies amongst the pile as quickly as possible.

"This may be something," Lindy called out from the right side of the tunnel near the ceiling. The cousins scrambled over to where she was shining her light. In between two boulders, there was a gap the cousins could squeeze through. Lindy went in first to explore. She came back a moment later and said, "Follow me."

One by one, the cousins slipped into the passage. It wound around several boulders. At one point, there was a small waterfall pouring from the ceiling. The water was bitterly cold. Finding no way around it, the cousins had to crawl through the falls as fast as they could to get to the other side. They shrieked despite themselves. Kimberly shrieked the loudest, Tim's was the shrillest.

Dripping wet, the cousins emerged from the boulders at the other side of the cave-in. There was rubble strewn about but the rocks no longer went clear to the ceiling. A stream of water was flowing from the base of the rock pile. The air was noticeably colder here. Rising to their feet, the cousins shined their lights around the lava tube. It was several feet larger than the previous side.

"The lake water must have gouged it out," said Lindy. "Look over there."

Lindy was pointing to the left side of the tube where a huge room had been made. As the cousins shined their lights into it, a silver glint caught their eyes.

"The plane!" said Robert excitedly.

The cousins scrambled down from the rock pile and raced for the airplane. It was jammed in tight by several large boulders and smaller rubble. When they reached it, both wings and most of the tail appeared to be missing. The body of the plane, or fuselage, though heavily dented and scraped, appeared to be mostly intact. There was a large boulder resting against the passenger door. Kimberly took several photos of the damaged airplane.

"It looks like we'll have to go in through the cockpit," said Jonathan. "Okay, Lindy, tell us what we're looking for again."

Lindy closed her eyes to picture Robert's note from Dantzel and said, "Retrieve black box, green plane data drum, Pallin computer backup. Glasses Xlcr, Dantz."

"Black box, green data drum, computer backup from Pallin, glasses," said Jonathan. "Let's get to work."

The cousins started pulling rocks away from the plane so they could get into the plane's fuselage. The airplane's windshield was totally gone. The cockpit was partially filled with sand and gravel. They dug as fast as they could, throwing out handful after handful of rubble.

"We're supposed to find the black box," Tim said to Robert. "Does that mean the flight recorder?"

"Yes, but they're not black anymore," Robert replied, throwing a large rock out of the cockpit, "they're orange."

"An orange, black box?" said Tim.

"Yes," said Lindy, who was digging nearby. "Flight Data and Cockpit Voice Recorders are orange so they can be found more easily. They're usually in the plane's tail so they'll survive better.

They're made to withstand temperatures over 1800 degrees Fahrenheit and huge impacts. Aircraft safety standards, page 25."

"How hot does hot lava get?" asked Tim.

"Up to 2200 degrees Fahrenheit," Lindy replied.

"Then we'd better get that box out of here before the hot lava comes," said Tim. "By the way, was that an orange, black box or a black, orange box we're looking for?"

"Just dig," said Kimberly, "and hurry. I want to get out of here."

The youths had to force open the cabin door. To their happy surprise, the passenger cabin beyond was not totally filled with debris. Shining their lights around the cabin, they found that several of the seats had been broken off their bases.

The cousins fanned out to search the passenger cabin. Jonathan and Kimberly headed toward the tail of the plane to find the "black box" while Robert, Lindy, and Tim started searching for the computer drive and the green plane data drum.

Robert spied the overhead locker where he had stowed the Pallin computer drive. When he got there, he found the locker door was missing. Shining his light inside he saw the compartment was empty!

CHAPTER 15

Searching

"Where is it?" said Robert, frustrated with himself for having left the important computer drive there during their crash evacuation.

"What did it look like?" asked Lindy from behind him.

"A small, boxy thing in an olive drab duffle bag," Robert replied as he, Lindy, and Tim searched the passenger compartment. "From what I remember, I put it in one of these overhead compartments."

"Just tennis shoes in this one," announced Tim, peering in a cabinet. "They aren't mine, though, because these shoelaces are still tied."

They opened more of the overhead luggage cabinets.

"Is this it?" said Lindy, retrieving a small duffle bag from a compartment and handing it to Robert.

Robert quickly opened the soaking wet bag and peered inside. "More tennis shoes?" he said, pulling one out and looking it over. "Wrong bag."

Robert, Lindy, and Tim searched all the overhead storage but found no other duffle bags.

"I must have put it somewhere else," said Robert, trying to remember.

The three youths turned their attention to the small lockers near the plane's cockpit.

"Nothing here," said Lindy.

"Nothing here either," said Tim. "Not any duffle bag or green drums. Are you sure the note said drums?"

"Yes," Lindy replied, "keep looking."

"Robert, have you got your multitool on you?" called out Jonathan from the back of the plane.

"Yes," said Robert.

"Good," said Jonathan, "we're going to have to unscrew this panel. I think the black box is behind it."

"I'll take it to him," said Lindy, retrieving the multitool from Robert. "You keep looking."

Lindy made her way to the back of the cabin and handed the multitool to Jonathan. On her return, she stubbed her toe on a dark object. "Here's something," she called out, reaching over for a dark bag behind a bent passenger seat. Retrieving it, she found it to be a small duffle bag. It was dripping wet and covered in sand. She quickly rushed forward and handed it to Robert, who opened it.

"This is it," Robert said excitedly. "Good job, twin sister."

"Now for the green drums," said Lindy with a determined smile.

Jonathan was just removing the last screw from the panel when Kimberly spoke up. "Jonathan, what's that?" she asked, pointing out one of the plane's broken windows.

"What?" said Jonathan.

"Those lights shining on the lava tube wall over there," Kimberly replied.

Jonathan stood up. As he did, he glanced at all the cousins' lights to see where they were pointing. One look out the window confirmed his fears. "Somebody else is out there."

Jonathan glanced toward the caved zone and saw light

coming from behind a boulder. He hushed his voice and said, "Everybody, get your gear. We've got to get out of here. Kimberly, keep an eye on those lights. I'm going to try to get the black box before we go."

Jonathan knelt down, pulled the panel off, and looked inside. "The black box," he said, greatly relieved. It was indeed orange in color. A few hard kicks with his right foot broke its holding bracket off the rest of the way. The box tumbled to the floor. Reaching in, he retrieved it and loaded it into his backpack. "How are you guys doing on finding those drums?" he called forward quietly.

"No drums yet," Lindy replied.

"Not even a drumstick," said Tim. "Why are we looking for drums anyways. We don't have time to play any music."

"Drum is the shape," said Robert.

"Oh, well why didn't you tell me?" said Tim. "I thought we were looking for instruments. There are a bunch of cans in that front cabinet thing over there."

Without saying another word, Lindy and Robert rushed over to the cabinet Tim was pointing to. They threw open the door and discovered six plastic, olive drab drums inside.

"Let's get them stowed in our backpacks," directed Robert.

"What about the wires attached to them?" said Lindy.

"We'll just have to pull them off," said Robert, yanking one of the drums free. The drum was about four inches in diameter and five inches tall. He handed the drums to Lindy who in turn handed them out to the other cousins to load into their backpacks.

The cousins had found the flight recorder, computer backup, and, they thought, the green drums.

"Time to go," said Jonathan.

"What about the glasses Xlcr?" said Lindy, thinking of the

last items on the note

"I don't know what that is," said Robert. "But I do know we've got to get out of here now before whoever it is that's out there finds us." Lindy nodded in agreement.

The cousins quickly climbed out of the stricken plane. Tim was the last to leave. He had positioned something on the top of the cabin door.

There was more intense light now shining around in the lava tube. The cousins could hear muffled voices above the sound of the waterfalls. For a second, they saw a man in a white snowtrooper uniform. It looked like the soldiers had just discovered a different passage through the rocks.

Kimberly froze. Lindy grabbed her arm and whispered, "Come on, Kimberly, we've got to keep up with Jonathan."

The cousins dimmed their flashlights as they headed further down the old lava tube. For now, it was their only route of escape and hopefully the end of the lava tube, wherever it was, was still open.

Rocks and rubble, strewn about the floor of the lava tube, made the going more difficult. A light shined from behind them and the cousins immediately had to drop to the ground.

"Oomph," said Robert as Tim landed on him.

"Quiet!" whispered Lindy. "Don't move."

A bright light shined in the direction of the cousins, highlighting the boulders around them. It moved to the left, and then to the right, and then stopped directly on Tim's brown backpack. A second light was moving along the side of the tunnel.

"What's that?" called out a voice.

The cousins froze, daring not to even breathe.

"Hey, look over there," said another voice. "That looks like part of a plane. I told you it would be down here. Now we'll get the bounty for sure."

From where Jonathan was laying, he could see at least eight soldiers. Each carried a menacing submachine gun.

"Don't move until they get to the plane," Jonathan whispered to the other cousins.

The soldiers quickly made their way over to the airplane. When they disappeared from view, Jonathan whispered, "Okay, get up quietly and let's get out of here."

Drawing from their many childhood games of "hide and seek", the cousins noiselessly rose to their hands and knees and then to their feet. Shielding their lights until they could barely make out the terrain, they slipped away. They were almost clear when Tim tripped on an unseen rock and fell with a loud *CRUNCH!*

"What was that?" called out a voice from back near the plane.

CHAPTER 16

Chase

The cousins dropped to the ground again. In the dim light, they could see a soldier looking their way, shining his light. "Sir, I think I heard someone," said the man. He was soon joined by a second soldier with a flashlight. Together, they shined their lights in the cousins' direction.

"I don't see anything, corporal," said the second man. "But keep your eyes looking, those kids could be somewhere around here. We can't let anybody beat us to the data."

"Yes sir," replied the corporal.

The cousins waited until the corporal was looking at the water flowing from the large cave-in zone before they moved again.

"Sorry guys," whispered Tim. "I didn't see the rock."

"Just be more careful," Kimberly whispered back.

"Let's get moving," Jonathan whispered.

The cousins quietly rose to their feet and started on their way again. They were relieved when they turned a bend in the lava tube one hundred feet further on and could no longer see any light from the soldiers.

"Okay," whispered Jonathan, "let's pick up the pace. I don't want to be around when those guys find out that we've got what they're looking for."

"Sir, somebody's been here recently," called out one of the soldiers back at the airplane. "Here are some footprints!"

The cousins didn't wait to hear any more. They shined their lights more brightly on the ground in front of them and took off running as fast as they could. They rounded another bend and found more rubble. Carefully but quickly, they picked their way through the rubble and ran on. Their packs were feeling heavier.

As they rounded another bend, the cousins could hear behind them the clang of metal being pounded. *Clang! Bang!* came the sound, echoing down the large lava tube. Then suddenly, there were a bunch of *Achoo—achoo—ACHOOs!*

"What was that?" asked Kimberly.

"My pepper for the Sneezy Monster," Tim replied.

"Good job, Tim," said Robert as they ran.

Breathing heavily, the cousins rounded another curve and then another. The lava tube was getting larger in diameter. The tube forked. The cousins paused for a second to get their bearings.

"Let's take the right fork," said Jonathan. "It looks like the bigger one and it's going downhill."

The cousins headed down the right fork; after 300 feet, it dead-ended at a large pool of water and a cave-in.

"Back to the other tunnel," said Robert.

The cousins turned around and raced back to the fork. When they arrived, they could see faint light coming down the tunnel from the direction of the plane.

"This way," called out Jonathan as he headed down the left fork. The rest of the cousins followed him. Robert paused long enough to make more footprints in a patch of sand heading into the right-hand tunnel. He erased their tracks going to the left fork and then dashed to catch up with the other cousins.

"Good going, brother," said Lindy with a smile as they ran. "I can always count on you to cover our backs."

"You mean 'tracks'," Robert replied with a grin.

After running several minutes more, the cousins had to stop to catch their breath. They found a large boulder against the left side of the tunnel and hid behind it. Jonathan and Kimberly kept a lookout while they rested.

Then they set out again, jogging this time. They were about to round another bend when a beam of light shone directly on them.

"There they are," shouted a voice. "Get them!"

The cousins didn't wait to see how many soldiers there were. They just bolted down the large, dark, dripping tunnel with their lights fully on.

"Halt!" called out one of the soldiers, his voice echoing up and down the lava tube.

"There's no way we're doing that!" said Jonathan, running briskly. "If any of you get too tired, give me your backpack so we can keep going."

The lava tube went straight for another 250 feet and then swept to the right. Rounding the bend, the cousins hit a slippery zone of smooth, water-polished rock and went sliding into the base of a small waterfall. To their surprise, the water was warm.

Soaking wet, the five cousins clambered to their feet and raced onward. They didn't care anymore whether they were making noise or not. Their race for life was on!

The cousins rounded another bend. There was an eerie glow up ahead. Was the lava tube on fire?

"Better not be hot lava," said Tim. "I'm running out of new tennis shoes."

The cousins spied some bent-up pieces of their airplane's wings but kept on running. The light in the lava tube was getting even brighter now, blindingly bright.

They shut off their flashlights and kept running toward the light, hoping beyond hope it might be the end of the tunnel. They could hear shouting behind them.

There was a roaring sound ahead. Water, it sounded like water. The floor was getting slippery again. Rounding another bend, the cousins' feet went out from under them and they all plunged into a large, earth-warmed flowing river. They found themselves being swept rapidly down the lava tube in a three-foot-deep torrent. The water raced faster and faster. The tube grew steeper. There was no way they could stop; the floor of the tube was too smooth and they were gaining too much momentum. One bend, two bends, three. They could see brighter light up ahead, it looked like sky light. A fourth turn and they found themselves speeding toward the end of the lava tube.

The sky outside was filled with falling snow. The cousins screamed in fright as they shot over the top of a tall waterfall and plummeted thirty feet to the deep, clear blue pool of water below.

Splash, splash-splash! They plunged into the water fifteen feet deep or more. Their feet finally touched and they sprang off the smooth rock bottom. There was steam rising from the water in the frosty, cold air as Jonathan, Lindy, Kimberly, Tim, and finally Robert popped up to the surface, gasping for breath. Struggling under the weight of their packs, the cousins made their way for the shore. They knew the soldiers could arrive at any moment.

Above the roar of the waterfall, the cousins could hear the ominous sound of a large helicopter approaching. Things had just gone from bad to worse!

CHAPTER 17

Pursuit

Dee swung the helicopter over a snow-covered ridge and into a narrow ravine. "Let me know when you see the Wright cousins," she directed.

Far below, Sarina and Katrina Straunsee could see a large, steaming waterfall cascading into a bubbling blue pool. Five heads bobbed up.

"There they are," said Sarina excitedly. "I see Jonathan!"

"And there's Robert," said Katrina. "They're all there. They're swimming for the shore."

Dee brought the helicopter down and landed it on a flat space seventy-five feet from the water's edge. She turned to tell the girls to go help but she was too late: the two Straunsee girls, polarized snow goggles and all, had bolted and were already halfway to the cousins.

Nearing the steep rocky shore, Sarina and Katrina quickly but carefully made their way down to help pull the exhausted cousins from the water.

"Sarina, what would I do without you!" Jonathan said. "Enemy soldiers are chasing us."

"I'm so glad you're okay," Sarina replied with a grin, reaching for his hand, and pulling him up the slippery bank. "We've got a helicopter."

Jonathan and Sarina worked together to pull Lindy and then Kimberly from the water while Katrina helped Tim.

Katrina next went to help Robert. She was reaching for his arm when her feet slipped out from under her. As she fell, her left snow boot flew off and hit Robert in the chest. Robert caught it by reflex and dropped to his knees to regain his balance.

Without delay, Robert loosened the boot's Velcro, slipped it back onto Katrina's stocking foot, and tightened the straps. Robert noted the surprised look on Katrina's face. "I used to work in a shoe store," Robert explained with a grin.

"Thank you," said Katrina, blushing slightly. "And *I* was supposed to be helping *you*."

"Everybody to the helicopter!" said Jonathan.

Robert helped Katrina to her feet and all the youths scrambled to the helicopter and climbed aboard.

"Hurry and get seated," called out Dee as the youths closed the door behind them. "Enemy soldiers just came over the waterfall."

The rotor blades pounded hard as Dee revved the helicopter and lifted off. The soldiers were swimming now, trying to reach the shore. Dee turned the helicopter and headed over the nearest ridge. The snowfall was increasing.

Seeing their prey getting away, one of the soldiers retrieved a waterproof radio from a parka pocket and fumbled to click it on. "Delta One, this is Delta Two. The birds have flown the roost. They must have the tech in their packs. Repeat. They must have the tech in their packs. They are in a white helicopter. Pursue at all costs."

Dee flew low and fast. She knew it was only a matter of time before they were located again by the enemy.

Katrina, Sarina, and Jonathan were in the forward seats.

Kimberly, Tim, Lindy, and Robert were in the back. Their helicopter cleared a second ridge and dropped into the valley beyond. They were flying over a snow-covered forest.

"Where are we going?" called out Jonathan.

"Base," said Dee. "Everybody hang on, this may get interesting."

The trees cleared as they crossed over another ridge and a frozen lake. It was the same lake where the cousins had crash-landed. The cousins could see through the falling snow many alarmed soldiers far below, preparing to shoot at them. A helicopter was just taking off from among them.

The cousins could now see the stone buildings they had visited earlier that day. There were several snowcats and snowmobiles parked near them.

A cone-shaped mountain loomed ahead. Dee flew to the south of it. A wide valley spread out below them. Steam was rising from several points in the valley.

A warning buzzer sounded. "Brace yourselves," called out Dee over the intercom. "We've got company."

"Who is it?" asked Jonathan.

"One of Slagg's helicopter gunships," said Dee.

"Can we outrun it?" asked Jonathan.

"We're going to try," Dee replied. "We should be okay as long as they don't have any friends ahead of us."

The warning buzzer sounded again.

"Never mind," said Dee. "They've got friends."

Full throttle, Dee took the helicopter down to the "deck", which meant flying as low as she could without hitting anything. Trees swished by just below them, the helicopter's turbulence knocking snow off their tops.

Jonathan saw the trees and looked at Sarina in alarm.

"Don't worry," Sarina replied, white knuckled, with a grin,

"she's a good pilot."

The cousins looked out a rear window. In the distance, they could barely see a sleek helicopter giving chase. It had a menacing chin cannon.

Dee flew around a mountain ahead and dropped into a new canyon veering to the right. The helicopter gunship was still following them. Dee's instruments were tracing the movements of the threats pursuing her: three helicopter gunships, and they were closing in for the kill. She tapped a button on her controller. A heads-up display appeared, bracketing the white copter pursuing them and two additional helicopters waiting in ambush just over the next mountain.

"Scan," directed Dee.

"Chain guns: 30mm type. Air-to-air missiles: 2 pods, 152 kg.," replied an electronic voice.

"Electronics?" said Dee.

"C93-2 control module, Rev-3," answered the electronic voice.

The two menacing helicopter gunships suddenly appeared over the mountains ahead. "Gütenberg helicopter LAND NOW!" commanded a voice over the radio. "LAND NOW OR WE WILL SHOOT YOU DOWN!"

Dee tapped a red button. "Software: Rev-3," appeared on her Heads-Up Display. "Critical update Rev-4 not installed."

"Good for them," said Dee. "Interrupt C93-2. Download DECOM file to 3 aircraft. Disable weapons. Vector three helicopters to nearest clearing."

"File sent," replied the computer.

"Take them out," commanded a stern voice over the radio.

Guns aimed, the two helicopter pilots squeezed their cannon triggers but nothing happened. Their joysticks suddenly stiffened and their helicopters started to turn. Dee quickly flew between the two enemy helicopters, waving as she went by.

On the verge of total victory, Slagg's forward two helicopters were giving their pilots fits as they would not respond to their controls. The helicopters flew straight upward and then headed to a wide, snow-filled meadow. Once there, the pilots discovered the third helicopter joining them from the east. The helicopters—locked into an unbreakable autopilot mode—landed in the deep snow and shut down. As their rotors wound down, three angry pilots and their copilots climbed out to find out what in the world had gone wrong with their gunships.

CHAPTER 18

Challenge

Sarina, Katrina, and the Wright cousins continued to look out the windows into the snowstorm. They got a jolt when they saw a fighter jet streak by.

"Don't worry, it's one of ours," said Dee. "They've been flying with us for a while now. They're escorting us to the base."

"What do you mean *they?*" asked Katrina.

"There's six of them," said Dee. "When your father found out what was going on, he scrambled a flight of planes to meet us."

The rest of the journey went without incident. Dee landed the helicopter at Kleinstattz Air Force Base, the base the Wright cousins had been at only the day before.

While the Straunsee girls stayed aboard the helicopter to speak with Dee for a moment, the Wright cousins climbed down onto the slushy, snow-covered tarmac to stretch their tired legs and then walked over to look at a nearby airplane tug. It was softly snowing.

"It sure feels good to be back on solid ground," said Lindy as they strode along.

"You can say that again," Kimberly said, stretching her legs. "It's nice to be out of that lava tube."

"I thought it was kind of cool," said Lindy. "My mom would

love to see that one."

"Yeah, maybe," said Kimberly. "But I sure don't miss those soldiers chasing us."

"Ditto," Lindy said with a grin.

"Speaking of soldiers," said Jonathan just after they had reached the tug, "it looks like we're going to have some company."

Two jeeps rapidly pulled up near the Wright cousins and stopped. Kleinstattz Air Force Base commander, Commander Trelland, and a squad of armed soldiers climbed out of them.

"Hello, Commander Trelland, sir," said Jonathan as he and the other cousins turned to talk with them.

Commander Trelland eyed the cousins in their damp, disheveled clothing. "Quite the outfits," he said, half grinning. "My aide said you were back. Looks like you guys had a rough trip."

"Yessir," spoke up Kimberly. "But this time we've got the evidence for you about our crashed plane, sir, and we need to get our passports back from you, please, sir."

"You found the plane?" Commander Trelland said with an incredulous smile.

"Of course," said Kimberly. "I've got the pictures on my phone."

"And we got the flight recorder and the Straunsee Aerospace data, too," added Tim.

"Good job," said the commander, "I've had my soldiers searching for those items for days. Tell you what, let me take those off your hands for safe keeping and then we'll go get your passports."

"I'll get my phone," said Kimberly, anxious to be done with the whole matter.

The Wright cousins led Commander Trelland quickly over

to the helicopter.

"So, where did you find the plane?" asked Commander Trelland as they walked.

"In a big lava tube way under the ground," said Tim. "It was all scrunched up."

"I'm surprised none of my soldiers ran into you," said the commander.

Arriving at the helicopter, Jonathan opened one of its doors and Kimberly climbed in. "Where's my phone?" she said in dismay. "I had it in my pack. Where are the backpacks and where are Dee and the girls?"

"I thought so," Commander Trelland replied, his smile fading, "what kind of prank are you kids trying to put over on me this time? Let me tell you this: if you do not produce the recorder and the Straunsee Aerospace Works computer data, I will have no choice but to have my soldiers put you in the guardhouse. Now, what will it be?"

"Okay," Tim whispered to Robert, "this *is* awkward. I think I'm going to just sit in the back of the helicopter while you guys get this thing figured out." He turned to climb in but there was a soldier barring his way.

"Sergeant," Commander Trelland said, "I want that Straunsee data found. These kids say the information is here. Turn this helicopter upside-down if you have to, but I want it found."

"Yes sir," saluted the sergeant. He commanded two soldiers to begin the search.

Commander Trelland turned back to face the cousins and lined them up against the side of the helicopter. "I have been told from the field that you guys have taken top secret military information from a classified plane."

"We had it but it's gone, sir," Jonathan replied. "Somebody

cleaned our gear out of the helicopter."

"And you expect me to believe that?" said the commander, eyeing the five cousins. "Sergeant, take these youths to the guardhouse. I want a full interrogation of them. That was vital military information and I will not let them get away with this!"

"Really, Commander Trelland," called out a voice from behind the commander. "Picking on teenagers?"

Commander Trelland turned around to face the speaker. When he saw who it was, his manner changed drastically. "King...Straunsee...I...your majesty, I was just following your orders."

King Straunsee, standing in the newly falling snow, was flanked by two squads of soldiers. Beside him were his two daughters, Katrina, and Sarina. Dee was nowhere to be seen.

"Trelland, *come here!*" bellowed the king.

"Yes sir," said the commander, walking swiftly toward the king. They talked briefly. When Trelland returned to the cousins, his eyes were wide.

"The king said you indeed found the items needed and he has secured them," Commander Trelland said. "Also, that I am to apologize for my treatment of you Wright cousins. I...am...you see, it was like...I apologize."

"And commander," said the king, "*you are to treat the Wright cousins as if they are part of the royal family.* Let that be understood by everyone here!"

"Yes sir, Your Majesty," everybody replied.

Surprised, Sarina and Jonathan glanced at each other, grinning widely.

"And if I *ever* hear of you treating them otherwise," continued King Straunsee, "you will have to reckon with me. Do you understand me, Commander Trelland? You are an exceptionally good military strategist but you really need to work on your interpersonal communication skills."

"Yes sir, your majesty, sir," replied the commander.

"Commander, there's also the matter of their passports," said Sarina.

"Yes, your highness, princess," nodded the commander, "I shall get them back to them shortly."

"On second thought, maybe you should burn them," said Sarina straight-faced.

"Princess?" said Commander Trelland.

"No, you'd best return them," Sarina said, glancing again at Jonathan with a smile.

Commander Trelland ushered the royal family and the Wrights to his headquarters building where he promptly returned the Wright's passports. Before leaving the base, the Straunsee princesses and the Wright cousins met with officers Stedt and Velasco for debriefing. Officer Velasco did most of the questioning. He explained that the Gütenberg military needed to know what the youths had seen and heard, the approximate number of soldiers Slagg had sent in, and how they were equipped. Lindy's photographic memory proved to be a great boon.

The door to the debriefing room swung open and in stepped the helicopter pilot that had taken the cousins out to the valley of the airplane crash. He saluted the two officers and got permission to talk with the youths.

"I just wanted to make sure you guys were okay," the pilot said.

"But we thought you were one of the bad guys," said Tim.

The pilot looked surprised and said, "I got word that you were on snowmobiles. When I finally located you, you were just getting to the stone buildings by the lake. I landed to try to extract you from the battlefield, but you had disappeared."

"That was you?" said Lindy.

"Yes, didn't you recognize my helicopter?" the pilot replied.

"Her goggles must have been foggy or something," said Robert, "and we were in a big hurry to find the plane and get out of there."

"Several of Slagg's troops approached on snowmobiles and started shooting at me, so I had to take off again and call in our ground troops."

The cousins chatted a moment more with the pilot and thanked him for his help. The pilot then excused himself and turned to leave.

"Wait a minute," said Tim, "aren't you supposed to be grilled, I mean, interrogated, too?"

"I'm a civilian," said the pilot.

"Yeah, but we're civilians, too," Tim replied. "Wait a minute, you just saluted these officers when you came in."

The pilot grinned and opened the door.

"Wait, Mr. Pilot sir, you can't get out of it that easy," whispered Tim.

The pilot grinned, pretended to tip an invisible hat at Tim, and then stepped through the doorway. The door closed after him.

"I guess he can," said Tim in surprise.

"Mr. Velasco, sir?" asked Jonathan, "we were asked to retrieve several things from the plane. "The black box—."

"It's really orange," said Tim, and then glancing at Kimberly, said, "Well, they need to know."

"Thanks, Tim, I think they already know," Kimberly replied.

The officers nodded affirmatively.

"There was also the Straunsee Aerospace data," said Robert. "We know what that is. But what were the green drums?"

The senior officer nodded to the other and said, "They flew

the plane, they know how it was militarily equipped."

"The plane you flew in," began the second officer, Mr. Stedt, "was a surveillance plane. It has side-looking radar and—let us just say—many other capabilities. We have been recording incursions made by our neighboring country infringing on our sovereignty. It is evidence that we have been under attack. We need that evidence to show to the world we are not the aggressors."

"The side-looking radar," said Katrina, "was that SLAR or SAR?"

"What?" said Tim.

"Side looking real-aperture or synthetic aperture," Katrina replied.

"Good question, Katrina," said Robert.

CHAPTER 19

Family Legend

"I'm just glad I'm on your side," Tim said to Robert and Katrina.

King Straunsee checked on the status of the royal retreat, Alpenhaus. When he found it to be secure, he arranged for one of their family helicopters to take they and the Wright cousins there. A nice sit-down, relaxed dinner was planned for that evening. Emotions were ranging all over the place, for it was also going to be the Wright cousins' last night in Gütenberg. They were leaving for America in the morning.

During the flight to Alpenhaus, the youths had a chance to finally rest and talk. It was an extremely comfortable helicopter with very plush furnishings. King Straunsee spent most of the flight speaking with his advisors and military leaders by secure communications. Slagg's forces had to be removed from their invading locations and punished for their attempts to overthrow the government and put Kreppen on the throne.

As the group walked in the front door of Alpenhaus mansion, they were greeted by a new staff and butler. The previous butler and staff were now in prison for their traitorous behavior, awaiting trial. The six security team soldiers Dee had taken there by helicopter had turned the tide and made Alpenhaus safe for the royal family once again. Security measures had been updated.

"There's Mr. Gervar, the octogenarian," whispered Tim as he elbowed Kimberly.

"Greetings," said Mr. Gervar, "I am glad to see you are all well. I am sorry I could not greet you before your helicopter flight this morning. I was called out of town."

The Straunsees, the Wright cousins, and Mr. Gervar all sat down to a wonderful meal together, "American Fare with Traditional Gütenberg Dishes": ribeye steak, delicious hamburgers for the non-steak eaters, salad, tasty onion rings, Gütenberg blackberry pie served with ice cream, and milk or water to drink.

Midway through the meal, Tim asked Kimberly a question he had been wondering about, "Kimberly, do you think the Straunsees are related to Cinderella?"

"*Cinderella* is just a pretend story," said Kimberly.

"Oh, I know all the mice and the pumpkin carriage are just made up, I think," Tim said, "but something happened today to make me think that Katrina *has to be* related to Cinderella."

"What's that?" said Kimberly.

"Well, for one thing," said Tim, "when Sarina and Katrina were helping us out of the water, Katrina's boot flew off her foot. Robert knelt down and put it back on her foot. It was totally the *Cinderella* thing."

"Are you sure?" asked Kimberly.

"It looked like it to me," said Tim. "With all my cooties experience, I'm totally a pro at noticing that type of thing. Yep, it was the Cinderella thing all right."

"Well, Tim," said Kimberly matter-of-factly, "if Robert wants to do the Cinderella thing, it's okay by me."

"Me too," agreed Lindy, who overheard their whisperings. "Robert, you did good with the boot."

Jonathan, Sarina, and Katrina were now listening in.

"Now hold on you guys," said Robert. "All I did was put her shoe back on. You wouldn't want her to have to walk around barefoot in the snow, would you? Besides, she was helping us."

"Did you kneel down when you did it?" asked Tim.

"Well, I had to so I wouldn't slip and fall down like Katrina had," said Robert.

"*Totally* Cinderella," said Tim.

Sarina grinned and Katrina started blushing.

"He was just being kind," Katrina explained. "And no, Sarina, don't you even think about that. It does *not* count toward our old family legend. He just did it once. And besides, he was just being nice."

"Sure," said Sarina with a teasing grin. "*Real* nice."

"What's this about a family legend?" asked Jonathan.

"Well," Sarina began with a smile, "legend has it that a Straunsee princess—."

"Sarina, don't you dare!" said Katrina, blushing really good now. Katrina glanced quickly at Robert and then back to Sarina. "We needn't bother the Wright cousins with that old family tale."

"It might be important to them someday," Sarina replied with a grin.

"I will tell him—them—another time," said Katrina with an embarrassed grin. She turned to Robert and said, "So, Robert, how did you like the lava tube today?"

"Lava tube?" said Robert, looking at her curiously. "Okay, yes, well, it was pretty amazing, and when we went over the waterfall, now that was *totally* fun."

"Wait a minute," said Tim. "But what about the family legend? Katrina just totally changed the subject."

"Princess privilege," said Kimberly, smiling back at him.

"Besides, she's a girl."

"*Girls!*" mumbled Tim.

That night, the cousins stayed in the guest wing at Alpenhaus. The next morning dawned bright and clear. After breakfast, the Wright cousins started loading their things into the Straunsee limousine to be taken to the airport. Sarina and Katrina were helping them.

"So, Kimberly," asked Tim, "why doesn't writing paper move?"

"Why doesn't writing paper move?" said Kimberly. "Ooo, you know, I've always wondered about that."

"Really?" said Tim. "Wow, I didn't know that. It's a good thing I asked you so you could know, too."

"Tim, the paper?" said Kimberly.

"Oh, yeah," Tim replied, "writing paper doesn't move because it's *stationery*."

"Ha!" said Kimberly.

"What was that?" asked Tim, chuckling.

"Half a ha-ha," Kimberly replied. "Personally, I use a computer."

Once everything was loaded, the time to say good-bye arrived. Sarina and Katrina stepped inside Alpenhaus for a moment to fix their hair. Sarina was already getting teary-eyed. "Katrina, why must we always say good-bye? Why can't we say 'Hi, it's so wonderful to see you!' Greetings are so much better."

"I'm beginning to see what you mean," said Katrina, wiping some moisture from her eyes as well. "That Robert, he's a good guy."

"Not you too," chuckled Sarina, wiping tears from both her eyes. "Ah, my eyes are getting all red. I'm going to be such a mess!"

"The Wrights are good people," said Katrina. "Come on, sis,

let's go say good-bye to our dear friends."

There were many tears all around.

"You're a good guy, Robert Wright," said Katrina Straunsee with a sweet smile as she shook Robert's hand.

"So are you," Robert replied with a grin. "I mean, well, not the guy part. You're a pretty amazing girl. And thank you for letting me help you with your snow boot."

"Anytime," said Katrina, her eyes starting to tear up again. Katrina gave him a quick hug and said good-bye.

Jonathan and Sarina, now that was a different story. Both were doomed from the start. They did not even try to shake hands, they just hugged. Hugged and bawled their eyes out.

"I'll see you again soon," Jonathan whispered in Sarina's ear. "We are sweet friends, you and I. I feel like we have known each other forever. Keep preparing for a good future...my special friend."

"I will," Sarina whispered in reply with warm tears rolling down her face. "Take good care, my special friend, and God be with you."

"That's what *good-bye* really means," said Jonathan. "God be with you."

"Smoosh and mushies!" said Tim. "Come on, Jonathan, we'd better get going or we'll miss the plane."

"Thank you so much for everything," called out the Wright cousins. They climbed into the Straunsee limousine, waved good-bye, and were on their way, on their way to America. The last memory, etched in Jonathan's mind as they drove away, was of Sarina and her sisters, Katrina, and Maria, waving good-bye from the porte cochère at the front of Alpenhaus. He had no idea how that would all soon change.

CHAPTER 20

The Airport

"WELCOME TO EXCELSIOR AIRPORT," said a large sign over the roadway.

"And not a moment too soon," said Kimberly. "We've got to hurry and get our luggage checked in."

Security was heavy as the cousins entered the large airport. It seemed that every space and every seat was taken.

"Why is it so busy today?" Jonathan asked one of the airline personnel.

"Haven't you heard?" said the woman. "We're on the verge of an all-out war with Slugdovia. Their country has already attacked one of the eastern sectors of Gütenberg. Most of the foreign countries have told their citizens to leave our country. All non-essential embassy personnel and families are being evacuated on specially chartered planes."

Jonathan glanced at Kimberly. "Sarina didn't say anything about that. We've got to go back and help them."

"Mom and Dad have told us to come home," Kimberly said. "You remember that phone call last night."

"Yes, but it didn't sound this serious," Jonathan said.

"Well, evidently it is," said Kimberly. "King Straunsee and his daughters will be okay."

The lines were getting thicker as the cousins waited to board their airplane. Planes were so filled to capacity that some of the passengers' luggage would have to be flown out in the following days.

"Now I know how our ancestors must have felt at Ellis Island," said Kimberly.

"Yeah," said Tim, "but at least they had the Statue of Liberty."

"Yes," Lindy said, "but the Statue of Liberty was on a different island, Liberty Island."

The news being presented on the overhead video screens was not looking good. Reporters were showing national guard troops being called up. Military bases were on high alert and all leaves had been cancelled. The stakes were high. Gütenberg had to show that it would maintain its sovereignty. Slugdovia had to learn that it could not, with impunity, take over its neighboring country's territory.

"Oh hi, Robert," said a young woman wearing cute glasses, walking in the bustling crowd near Robert and Tim. "Imagine running in to you clear over here in Gütenberg. Have you had a nice stay?"

The girl with the shoulder-length black hair looked very familiar, but Robert could not place where he had seen her before. It seemed like they had been away from America for a long time and the girl's friendly, familiar manner kind of threw him off-balance. Was the girl on the yearbook staff in his high school back home?

"It's been fun," said Robert. "How about you?"

"Totally fun," said the girl, "Gütenberg skiing is awesome."

"Do you think there will be a war?" asked Robert, noticing the television again.

"It doesn't look good, does it," the girl replied. "I hope war can be averted. It's funny I should run in to you like this. My mom just asked me this morning how you guys were doing."

"Wow, well, tell her 'hi' for me," Robert said.

"You can tell her yourself at the family get together next week," said the young woman, smiling. "But I'll tell her for you, too."

"I think we might be in the wrong line," said Tim, tugging on Robert's elbow.

"Hi Timothy," said the young lady, reaching out to shake his hand. "It's nice to see you, too."

Tim shook her hand quickly and said, "Sorry, we have to say good-bye now. They've already opened the boarding gates and if Robert and I don't get there soon, we'll have to swim to America."

"Then you'd better be on your way," agreed the girl. "That ocean water is very cold."

"That's what I've been telling Robert," said Tim. "Come on, Robert, our line is over there."

"Hey, well, we'll see you next week, then, at the family thing," Robert said to the girl.

"See you then and have a safe flight, and don't forget your glasses," the girl replied. She disappeared into the thronging crowd.

Robert caught sight of the TV screen again. "XLCR" it said in the corner. "The note. That's what it meant," said Robert. "Glasses Xlcr—Glasses at *Excelsior*. The glasses. That was Dantzel!"

Robert stood on his tiptoes to look for her. "Tim," he said, "that was Dantzel. Why didn't you tell me? There's so much I want to ask her."

"Girls," said Tim, pushing Robert toward the loading ramp. "How many times do I have to tell you? You've got to watch out for them. And besides, you heard what that girl said: that ocean water is *really* cold."

Once on the plane, the cousins found their seat numbers, stashed their carry-on luggage in the overhead cabinets, and sat down. Tim was sitting next to Kimberly and Lindy. Robert and Jonathan were sitting in the row across the aisle.

Tim started playing with the lights and air vents, so Kimberly suggested he should instead put on his seatbelt and get ready for takeoff.

"Kimberly, how come I always have to sit beside you on these plane rides?" asked Tim.

"Because somebody's got to make sure you survive until your twenty-first birthday."

"But I like sitting next to Robert and Jonathan better. You always turn green when we're taking off. And, well, I didn't bring a plastic bag for you this time."

"I did," said Kimberly.

"Wow, those self-reliance classes really do help. Hey, look over there," said Tim with a plotting grin, pointing across the aisle, "there are still two empty seats over by Robert and Jonathan. I'm going to go sit by them. You or Lindy can have my seat."

"You'll do no such thing, Timothy Wright," Kimberly replied. "We've had a hard-enough time getting our passports back and getting onto this flight. We might get into trouble if you're not in your assigned seat."

A noise at the front passenger door of the plane signaled several last-minute arrivals. They quickly headed down the aisle toward their seats. Two of them, young women with long, dark brown hair stopped at Jonathan and Robert's row and slipped into the seats beside them. A third late arrival slid into the empty seat next to Tim. She, too, had dark brown hair. She was close to Tim's age and was wearing sunglasses. Her brown hair hung down, covering much of her face.

Tim squirmed, leaned over toward Kimberly and whispered, "Please trade seats with me. She has cooties."

"Timothy Wright, she does not," Kimberly scolded him. "Besides, the seat numbers, remember?"

Tim grimaced, but as he did so, he felt a light tap on his left shoulder. He turned to see the new passenger looking at him. She brushed her long brown bangs out of her face and whispered, "Hi, brother dear, how do you like our wigs? Father says it's too dangerous here in Gütenberg and that we girls have to go to America."

"Cooties," Tim whispered back. "Wait, Maria, is that really you?"

Maria scrunched her nose at him. "I've got 24-hour cartoons," she said, holding up her phone.

"You do?" said Tim. "Are you sure?"

"Yes. Now what about the cooties?"

Tim looked torn. "I guess cooties...can wait until we get to America," he finally said. Then he grinned. "So, which cartoons do you want to watch first?"

Mr. and Mrs. Olsen, the Straunsee's chaperones, were seated in the row behind the youths. Three rows behind the Olsens was a young woman with long black hair and wearing cute glasses. She was nonchalantly reading a book about U.S. geography. Her name was Dee: *Dee* for Dantzel.

GREGORY O. SMITH

Please Write a Review
Authors love hearing from their readers!

Please let Greg Smith know what you thought about this book by leaving a short review on Amazon (scroll down on the book's page to where it says "Write a customer review" near the bottom of the page) or your other preferred online store. If you are under age 13, please ask an adult to help you. Your review will help other people find this fun and exciting adventure series!

Thank you!

Top tip: be sure not to give away any of the story's secrets!

About the Author

Greg exploring the bottom of the mine shaft seen in the book video trailer for *The Treasure of the Lost Mine*. You can watch the book video trailers at the author's website, GregoryOSmith.com.

Gregory O. Smith loves life! All of Greg's books are family friendly. He grew up in a family of four boys that rode horses, explored Old West gold mining ghost towns, and got to help drive an army tank across the Southern California desert in search of a crashed airplane!

Hamburgers are his all-time favorite food! (Hold the tomatoes and pickles, please.) Boysenberry pie topped with homemade vanilla ice cream is a close second. His current hobby is detective-like family history research.

Greg and his wife have raised five children and he now enjoys playing with his wonderful grandkids. He has been a Junior High School teacher and lived to tell about it. He has also been a water well driller, game and toy manufacturer, army mule mechanic, gold miner, railroad engineer, and living history adventure tour guide. (Think: dressing up as a Pilgrim, General George Washington, a wily Redcoat, or a California Gold Rush miner. Way too much fun!)

Greg's design and engineering background enables him to build things people can enjoy such as obstacle courses, waterwheels and ride-on railroads. His books are also fun filled, technically accurate, and STEM—Science, Technology, Engineering, and Math–supportive.

To see the fun video trailers for the books and learn about the latest Wright cousin adventures, please visit **GregoryOSmith.com** today!

GREGORY O. SMITH

**Enjoy every fun and exciting book by award-winning author
Gregory O. Smith**

The Wright Cousin Adventures
The Treasure of the Lost Mine
Desert Jeepers
The Secret of the Lost City
The Case of the Missing Princess
Secret Agents Don't Like Broccoli
The Great Submarine Adventure
Take to the Skies
The Wright Cousins Fly Again!
Reach for the Stars
The Sword of Sutherlee
The Secret of Trifid Castle
The Clue in the Missing Plane
The Wright Disguise
The Mystery of Treasure Bay
The Secret of the Sunken Ship
Wright Cousin Adventures Trilogy Sets 1-5

The Wright Cousin Adventures Cookbooks
#1 Fun Cookbook: Sweet Desserts that Bring a Smile!

Additional Books
Rheebakken 2: Last Stand for Freedom
Strength of the Mountains: A Wilderness Survival Adventure
The Hat, George Washington, and Me!

To be kept informed of my new releases, please sign up for my mailing list at www.gregoryosmith.com. At my website, you'll also find an array of free extra content, including video trailers for many of the books.

Please tell your family and friends about these fun and exciting new adventures so they can enjoy them too! Help spread the word!